THE room was lighted by some candles. The wall alongside the bed had been paneled with squares of mirrored glass. On the opposite wall was a poster-sized rendition of a girl's torso. The head was a photo of Allison herself. The rest was a very lifelike painting. The figure wore an unbuttoned shirt. One hand held back a flap of the shirt revealing a round, golden breast. I tried to whistle, but my lips went dry on me.

"I'd like to meet your model sometime," I said to Allison.

"You already have. I never found a body better than my own for that sort of thing. . . . Let's dance, mister."

I put down my glass and she moved in close, locking her hands behind my neck. I held her lightly. After a while I held her closer. We drifted for a few miles, and when I kissed her she responded as if she'd been waiting for me to do it.

"I think we should go to bed," she said frankly.

Books in Fawcett Gold Medal's Bragg Series
by Jack Lynch:

☐ BRAGG'S HUNCH   14449 $2.25

☐ THE MISSING AND THE DEAD   14462 $2.50

THE
MISSING
AND
THE
DEAD

Jack Lynch

FAWCETT GOLD MEDAL • NEW YORK

THE MISSING AND THE DEAD

Copyright © 1982 by John T. Lynch

Published by Fawcett Gold Medal Books, CBS Educational and Professional Publishing, a division of CBS Inc.

ISBN: 0-449-14462-3

Printed in the United States of America

First Fawcett Gold Medal printing: April 1982

10 9 8 7 6 5 4 3 2 1

For the first time in his life he had to figure out what he was going to do with a body. He didn't have much time for it, either. And it had to be very nearly foolproof if he wanted to preserve his identity and, perhaps, his wife's sanity. She had said that to him the last time they'd had to pack up and dash off, leaving no trace, assuming new roles.

"One more time and I'll lose my mind."

No hysterics. His wife wasn't that way. In fact, she had been the one to hold him together during the rockier times of his long career. She was firm and strong. She understated things. If she told him she was afraid of going to pieces, so be it. And it had been their last slapdash move. Into retirement for John Roper—his most recent identity—and the Hobo, the name by which he was known in certain police and prison circles. Retirement also for the reclusive painter, Pavel, who conjured portraits of his victims to curb the blinding headaches. Good-bye, all. Retirement time. Ta-ta. They traveled abroad for the better part of a year. In style and comfort. God knows he'd earned it over the years, along with enough money to do it.

He opened the hood to his Land Rover and stood staring bleakly at the engine. His mind was on other things. Nearly thirty years. God Almighty, that was a long time to have gotten away with it all. Not a serious miscue, either. Not one mistaken victim. Never an arrest. Probably stalked at one time or another by more lawmen than in the history of crime and punishment. His wife, poor girl, who could blame her? Moving here and there and then off someplace else. The new identities. A career of role-playing, that's what it had been, long before the term had become jargon. The ever more clever and involved arrangements for solicitation and payoff, all those codes and maps, the letter drops and midnight phone calls . . .

It was intricate mental work. He felt sure that was what led to the headaches. Anybody burns out after a while. An outsider, he knew, would suspect some form of guilt or remorse for his victims, but such was not the case. He and his wife used to talk those things through, long into the night. His work was no more demeaning than that of the heroic young warrior. And certainly more noble than that of the vivisectionist with his tortured animals. He never consciously hurt anybody. Something quick and sure, for the most part, a rap on the head followed by a needleful of arsenic. Quick and very nearly painless.

And there were, he knew with utter certainty, a lot of miserable bastards out there who he'd gotten rid of. Not that he ever let such judgments influence his work. But it was a fact and he knew it, and knew as well that many of the police who pursued him would equally have clapped him on the back for having helped purge some of the world's scum.

But back then, as the Hobo, he hadn't thought about such things. And as the name suggested, he was a moral tramp in those matters. If the price was right, if he could set it up to guarantee execution and escape, he would do it, be the victim saint or scamp. He couldn't let those things gnaw at him.

There, of course, had been those who paid society's price for the work that the Hobo did. Among the hundreds who had hired him over the years, there had been plenty whose boasting, stupidity, drunkenness or conscience had led to their own arrest or confession. But none of them ever knew enough about the Hobo to identify or describe him, which was only fitting. The Hobo was but a smoking gun. Let the twisted or jealous or hate-filled or greedy minds that conceived the act in the first place pay the price of it.

Pavel, a different, creative side of his nature, had emerged late in his career, after the onset of the crippling headaches. One of his victims, a young man in Oklahoma, had realized at the last moment what was about to befall him, and had exhibited a stark, terror-filled expression. It had been unsettling, to say the least. Back home, he told his wife about it. And in one of those quantum leaps the mind is capable of, she had urged him to try to capture the expression on canvas. He'd been doubtful at first. He'd never been more

6

than a half-hearted painter at best. It was a challenging discipline and he'd seldom used it for anything else, working his mind the same way he worked his muscles, in order to meet the demands of his profession.

But he'd tried it. He'd painted the young man's face, as best he could recall it, and the headaches had receded to little more than an annoyance.

He had thought about that some in the years since. Wondering if somehow that portrait business was what had very nearly unraveled his identity and led to his capture in Southern California. But he couldn't think of how it might have, any more than had a dozen other facets of the aging process. His work, though, had taken a ragged turn there. He knew that, now. He should have stuck with sap and needle, rather than get into the decapitation business. It was messy and awful, and dangerous. But to curb the headaches, he'd found it was very nearly the only manner of impending death that could evoke the stark fear he could later reconstruct on canvas, and through whatever chemical workings of the brain, banish the headaches. He didn't even like to think about that late period.

He liked to dwell more in the present. He and his wife had talked and thought about the roles they would assume in retirement. They had decided to return to California. It was a large enough place so there could be little fear of having events in one end of the state connected with those in the other. And his wife always had wanted a garden. To watch the growing cycle through the seasons. That pleased her, and they'd never been able to do that before. He, on the other hand, was able just to kick around and feel the soil and tramp the hills and read voraciously and putter at the palette, as his wife put it.

He might have known it was too good to last. In recent days there had been a disturbing sequence of events. Call it chance or whimsy or whatever, Fate was showing him her heels. First had been that surprising showcase of the Pavel portraits in San Francisco. He'd had to take quick steps there.

And now, there was the detective. The very man who down south years before, had tripped him up, forcing his retirement. And just minutes ago he had been in the heart of town, asking his questions. He was the man who had made the connection between John Roper and the Hobo and

Pavel. What in God's name could have brought him to Barracks Cove?

No matter. He was there, that was the thing to be addressed. Fortunately his wife had recognized him and helped steer the man out to their home. He would be arriving soon, and he would have to be killed. No question about that. That's why the Land Rover's hood was raised and he pretended to be fussing with the engine. At his side, on the fender, was a dirty rag. The detective would drive up, get out of his car and address him. He in turn would look up, turn, and take up the dirty rag to wipe his hands and to grasp the pistol concealed within it and then blow out the man's brains, just like that. No time for nonsense. Not even a hello. No, sir.

Then there would be the body. He'd never had to conceal a body during his years in the business. But he had to this time and he had to be very good about it. His wife had told him. She couldn't move again. She just couldn't bring herself to do that again.

He had a half-baked plan. That was his strong suit, of course, the mental work of planning these things. It had pulled him through time and again. It was the surprises he hated.

And then, just as he heard the sound of a car's engine approaching the old road leading to their home, another, absolutely sickening thought occurred to him. He was a sitting duck, now. He still had enough confidence in his nerves and skills to kill, but this time he couldn't fade away after.

And suppose, just suppose, there was another. Oh, God, what if there were somebody else who could make the same connections the approaching detective had? What might he look like? Who would he be? Dear God. Who?

8

Chapter 1

I agreed to look for a young man named Jerry Lind only
because I owed a couple of favors to Don Ballard, who runs
the publicity department for one of the local television stations. Ballard had asked me to speak with the missing
man's sister and to do what I could to help her. The sister
was a station personality of the sort that made me feel radio
is going to make a big comeback some day. Her name was
Janet Lind. She was one of the new breed of "happy talk"
deliverers of the day's events, a member of the station's Now
News Team. She had developed a flair for it, along with a
repertoire of about thirty posturings, and she managed to
trot out each of them at least once while we chatted in a
small inverview room in the bowels of the station out on
Van Ness Avenue.

She was a tall woman in her late twenties wearing a trim
pantsuit the color of weak, red wine. She talked about her
brother as if he were one of her feature stories. If she wasn't
flashing a smile she was giving a wink, heaving a sigh,
snapping her fingers, fluffing her hair or arching an eyebrow. It took a while to be able to ignore the nonsense and
concentrate on her story. That, at least, stirred my interest.

Her brother Jerry was twenty-six and married to a young
woman his sister didn't approve of. The couple had no children. Lind lived north of the Golden Gate Bridge in Marin
County, but he worked in San Francisco for Coast West
Insurance Co. He had dropped out of sight nearly two weeks
earlier, on a Sunday. Lind had told his wife he had some
things to clear up at the office, and after that he'd probably
leave on an out-of-town assignment. His wife had gone to a
movie with a girlfriend and when she got home later that

9

evening some of Lind's clothing and toilet articles were gone, so she had assumed he'd left town.

So far as Janet Lind knew that was the last anyone had seen of her brother. Lind's wife, when she hadn't heard from him for two days, telephoned her husband's office, but nobody there knew where he might have gone. Lind's wife called Janet to see if she knew his whereabouts, then called the police and reported her husband missing. According to Miss Lind's story and my pocket calendar, Lind had dropped out of sight on a Sunday, June 8. This was Friday, June 20.

"I kept hoping he would turn up," said Janet Lind, showing me the palm of her hand. "Now I've decided I'd better get somebody working on it."

"How come his wife hasn't hired somebody to look for him? Or has she?"

"She says not. In my opinion, Mr. Bragg, she is not terribly mature. She did say that in addition to the police, she spoke to Jerry's boss about it, urging him to look into the matter."

"Have you spoken to Jerry's boss?"

"Yes, but he wasn't too helpful. He did suggest we meet for cocktails some evening and talk about it if I wanted. I haven't wanted. His name is Stoval."

I made a note of it. "What does your brother do for them, sell policies?"

"I don't know."

"Are you serious?"

"It never came up in any of our conversations." She blinked her eyes and stared at something over my head.

"How old is your brother's wife?"

"Marcie? Twenty-two or three, I think."

"Did they seem to get along all right?"

"I couldn't tell you. I can't stand his wife."

"Why not?"

"She's a cheap little sexpot."

"That's blunt enough."

"So I avoid her. Jerry and I meet for lunch once or twice each month. He never indicated that anything was wrong between them. We seldom spoke about her."

"What did you speak about?"

"My work, mostly. Jerry found it nearly as fascinating as I do."

"Did he seem to like his own job, whatever it was?"

"He seemed content."

10

"What did he do before he worked for Coast West?"

"He was in the Army. Before that he was going to school in Santa Barbara. That's where he met Marcie."

"At school?"

"Hardly. She's more the sort you would meet at juvenile hall."

"Then it could be possible your brother is missing on purpose. And if he is, he could be hard to find."

"I don't believe he's missing on purpose, Mr. Bragg. He might drop out of the lives of other people, but not mine."

"That sounds as if you haven't told me everything."

"It's nothing mysterious. Jerry and I have been orphans since we were very young. Our parents died in an automobile accident. After that we were raised by our father's brother and his wife. Uncle Milton had land holdings in Southern California. Aunt Grace died five years ago. Poor Uncle Milton had a stroke and died last week. They had no children of their own. The estate is valued at well over one million dollars."

"And you and your brother are the beneficiaries?"

"For the most part, yes. That's why . . ."

She dropped her stagy shenanigans for a change and leaned forward. "Please don't get me wrong, Mr. Bragg. I hope that nothing has happened to my brother. I love him as much as any sister could love her brother. We were through some pretty grim times, emotionally, right after our parents died. We didn't accept our aunt and uncle at the start. For a time we had only each other to cling to.

"However," she continued, sitting straighter, "if the very worst should have happened—if Jerry is dead, I would want to know if he died before or after our Uncle Milton died."

"If your brother died first, you get the whole million dollars plus."

"Yes."

"But if he died after your uncle did, half of the estate would go to Jerry, and in the event of his subsequent death, to his wife, who you can't stand."

"Now you know all there is to know, Mr. Bragg. Jerry is as aware of the estate as I. Uncle Milton was eighty-seven. He was an old and feeble man. Jerry and I—we discussed it the last time we had lunch together. Neither of us expected him to live out the year. So while Jerry might disappear from his wife . . ."

11

"You have a convincing argument, Miss Lind. When did your uncle die?"

"Monday morning, the ninth."

"Just a day after your brother disappeared."

"Yes."

"When was the last time you spoke to Jerry?"

"We chatted on the phone along about the middle of the week before he disappeared."

"Did he seem in normal spirits?"

"Yes."

"What did you talk about?"

"I had phoned to tell him about an exhibit of new paintings at the Legion Palace Museum. They were modern works, quite unusual for the most part. I had helped do a feature report on them for the news shot. Jerry is a weekend painter himself. I urged him to see the exhibit."

"Does your brother have many close friends in the area?"

"Not that I'm aware of. He mentioned people at work occasionally, but nobody outside of that."

"Is he a gambler?"

"I doubt it, Mr. Bragg. He's a cautious man with a dollar."

"Does he drink much, snort coke or things of that nature?"

"He drinks a little. That's all I know about."

"Did he run around with a lot of girls before he got married?"

"I really don't know," she said with the first blank expression of the day. "I was away at school by the time he would have been doing that sort of thing."

"Okay, Miss Lind. Give me your brother's address and I'll get started on it."

"You're going to see his wife?"

"Of course. What's wrong with that?"

"I just don't want to pay for any time you might spend— making friends with her."

"Don't worry about it. Why, do you figure she might cheat on your brother?"

"I believe she might do anything. Even murder."

It wasn't the best interview I'd ever conducted, but I doubted if there was much else she could have told me about her brother. Up to now Janet Lind had been mostly interested in her own career, not her brother's. Now it was Uncle Milton's money at the head of the parade. I couldn't blame her for it. It just made my job a little tougher, but she would pay for that.

After she wrote me out a check and gave me the unlisted telephone number at her apartment in a highrise building overlooking the Golden Gate, I went upstairs to a public telephone booth in the station lobby. My first call was to the Hall of Justice on Bryant Street. I knew several San Francisco police officers on a nodding basis, but only a couple of them well enough to ask favors of. One was John Foley, an inspector on the homicide detail. It was the romantic branch of the force, but not one especially helpful to most of the jobs I had. On the other hand, the police don't maintain an information bureau for private cops, and a friend is a friend. Foley was in, listened to my story and said he'd check it out with Missing Persons when he had the time.

Then I phoned Carol Jean Mackey, the receptionist-secretary I share with a couple of attorneys named Sloe and Morrisey in offices on Market Street. I asked Ceejay to make some calls to postpone some things, then I looked up the number of Coast West Insurance. The main office was over on California Street, just above the financial district. I dialed the number and asked if there were a Mr. Stoval working there. I was put through to a secretary.

"Mr. Stoval's office . . ."

"Hi, my name's Peter Bragg. I'm a private investigator working on something I think your Mr. Stoval might be able to help me with. It's pretty important, Miss . . ."

"Benson."

"Miss Benson. I'd like to see him for a few minutes, before he goes to lunch, if possible. I could be over there in about ten minutes."

"Ummmm. He is one busy man today, Mr. Bragg. Maybe if you could give me some hint as to what it's about . . ."

"The missing Jerry Lind."

"I see. Please hold the line."

It took a couple of minutes.

"Mr. Bragg? It's all set. He can see you at twenty to twelve."

"Thank you very much. Was he on another phone or did you have to talk him into it?"

"I had to do some talking. We're on the fourth floor."

"I'm in your debt, Miss Benson. By the way, what end of the operation is Mr. Stoval concerned with?"

"The same as you, Mr. Bragg. Investigations."

13

Chapter 2

Jerry Lind worked out of a wide, carpeted office with desks on the left for girls and desks on the right for the fellows. At the deep end of the room, denoting where the power was on the fourth floor, were glass-enclosed individual offices over-looking California Street. The receptionist summoned Stoval's secretary. Miss Benson turned out to be a woman about Janet Lind's age. She had longish legs and a pleasant face, but her hair was done up in a severe bun and she wore eyeglasses with sensible frames.

"I'm Miss Benson. Will you follow me, please?"

"Sure. And thanks again for the help earlier."

She gave me a little smile over her shoulder. Miss Benson was dressed conservatively, in a dark blue skirt and a loose-fitting, high-necked blouse. But she had a pretty smile and a lilting swing to her walk.

About a third of the men's desks and all of the women's were occupied. Some of the fellows were on the phone, others riffling through folders. An older guy with gray-streaked hair and a tube of stomach hanging over his belt stood to stretch. He sat back down and stared at his desk top with faint distaste.

"Here we are, Mr. Bragg." She ushered me into one of the glass cubicles and quietly closed the door behind me. The man behind the desk half rose and extended his hand.

"Bragg? I'm Stoval." The sign on his desk said his first name was Emil. He didn't look like an Emil. He looked younger than Miss Benson. He had a strong grip and a round face with an alert expression. Some of his hair was missing.

"Nice of you to see me, Mr. Stoval. I've been hired by Jerry Lind's sister to find him. She said he's missing."

"Either that or he's being damn secretive about his work. I haven't heard from him in nearly two weeks."

"Has he ever done anything like this before?"

"Certainly not."

"What's his job?"

"Standard insurance investigation. We review death policies, run checks on bonding applicants, look into theft, fire and auto accident claims."

"Did Lind have a background for it?"

"Not really. He spent some time with Army intelligence, but that was mostly code work. This isn't a top-dollar job. We can take any reasonably bright young man and train him ourselves. People with too much experience, ex-cops say, don't always project the image the company tries to maintain."

"Do you think he could have been on company business when he disappeared?"

"Why should I think that?"

"I understand he said something to his wife about leaving town on business."

"A man tells his wife many things, Bragg."

"When you smile like that, Mr. Stoval, are you implying there's a reason to believe Jerry wasn't telling the truth?"

The smile went away and Stoval leaned forward. "I'm not implying anything. All I know is that the man's AWOL. He has been for two weeks. When he shows up he might have a perfectly good explanation for staying out of the office. Until I hear from him I'm not judging one way or the other."

"Has he gone out of town on business in the past?"

"Certainly."

"When he did, would he phone in from time to time?"

"Up until now he did." -

"Have you tried tracing his movements?"

"I've phoned his wife a few times asking about him."

"That's all?"

"Listen, Bragg, you seem very determined to place the company and myself in some position of responsibility in this matter."

"It might work out that way."

"But Lind's job is a standard nine-to-five, five-day-a-week job. He dropped out of sight over the weekend. Until somebody proves differently, I have to assume it's a personal matter."

"Does the company carry a policy on him?"

"Yes. The same as it does for all the employees."

"What sort of salary does he make?"

"That we keep confidential."

"What are you doing about his pay, since he's not here to pick up his check?"

"We mail it to his wife."

"How long will that go on, provided he stays missing?"

"That's not for me to decide."

I shook my head with a smile. "You're sure as hell casual about it."

"What do you mean?"

"I mean one of your men is missing. A man in one of the occupations allied to cops and robbers. He's not a peddler or a tuba player, Mr. Stoval, but an investigator. Now if I were in your place and one of my men dropped out of sight for even two days, let alone two weeks, I'd be off and looking for him."

"Very heroic, Bragg, but I think it's nonsense. As I said, there's nothing to link his disappearance to his job. Therefore, under company policy, my hands are tied."

"Maybe so, during working hours."

"That's not fair. Besides, Lind wouldn't get himself into anything of a dangerous nature. This is an old and conservative company. Our men have orders to avoid anything that even smells of danger. If they have any suspicion of illegal activity they report back here and we bring in the police. And believe me, we impress our people with the firmness of that policy. There's no reason to think young Lind would have ignored it."

"What sort of man is he?"

Stoval shrugged. "Pleasant enough. He dressed well, spoke well. Was a team player. That's another thing. Jerry wasn't too adventuresome. If anything, he was a bit more conservative than most men his age today. I don't think he'd take any gambles in his work."

"I hope you're right. Can you tell me what he was working on two weeks ago?"

Stoval looked at his watch. "I'll just have time to show you before my luncheon appointment."

"It would be kind of you."

The insurance man rummaged through a lower drawer of his desk and brought out a slender folder. He lifted out three forms. I thought I saw a fourth that he left in the folder.

16

"It was a light caseload at the time," Stoval said. "These are all minor matters."

"Mind telling me about them?"

Stoval went through the three sheets. "One was an auto theft out in the Sunset. Victim's name is Jonathan Thorpe. Twenty-nine twenty Klondike. The car was a new Mercedes. It was reported missing three weeks ago."

I made notes.

"Then there was a small painting stolen from a traveling exhibit at the Legion Palace Museum. Owner of the painting is a man living in Santa Barbara, but the policy is carried by the museum people."

"How much was it insured for?"

Stoval tilted his head and pinched one lip. "We're out a thousand if it isn't recovered. The work itself isn't appraised that highly." He studied the third sheet with a frown. "This is a home fire claim, but hell, I think I had one of the other men handle it." He went back into his file drawer and extracted another folder. He took a sheet from it and clipped it to the one from Lind's folder.

"Yes, that's closed. So there's really only the two." He looked at his watch again. "Afraid now I must leave, Bragg. Nice to have met you."

We touched palms and I left the glass box. I looked around for Miss Benson, but the floor was deserted except for a different receptionist up front. It was two minutes past noon. I took an elevator back to the street floor. The sidewalks were crowded with furloughed office workers. I trotted across California Street in front of a dinging cable car and was about to go into the parking garage where I'd left my car when I saw the older gentleman from Coast West with the gray-streaked hair and paunch. He was standing between Banyon's Cafe and a bar called the Silver Lode. He made a couple of false starts toward each, looked up the street with a frown and finally went into the bar. I followed. The bartender was just putting a drink down in front of him when I squeezed in beside him.

"Can I pay for that?" I put some money on the bar.

"Why should you?"

"I can use some help. You just saw me up talking to Stoval. The name's Bragg."

The man introduced himself as Wallace and lifted his glass with a shrug. I ordered a beer.

17

"I'm trying to get a lead on what might have happened to Jerry Lind. Stoval wasn't much help."

"What's supposed to have happened to Jerry Lind?" He spoke with an accent that sounded lonely for New York.

"Nobody seems to know, but he hasn't been seen or heard from for a couple of weeks. Didn't you notice?"

"Not especially. He spends a lot of time out of the office."

"Don't all of you?"

"Not as much as him."

"You an investigator too?"

"That's right."

"How long have you been with the firm?"

"Fifteen hilarious years."

"That's a long time. Still like the job?"

"Not all that much. But fifteen years is quite an investment. They have a nice retirement plan."

"Is it a good outfit to work for?"

"So-so."

"Do you have a family?"

"I thought you wanted to ask about Jerry Lind."

"I do. But I don't know anything about him. I figured if I could find out a little bit about his job—same as yours—I could learn something about him."

"It wouldn't help that much," Wallace said. "We're a varied bunch."

"So, okay, what can you tell me about Jerry?"

"Not a whole lot. I feel he's sort of a lightweight, myself. Personable, but not too bright. But the company doesn't seem to care. Rather, Stoval doesn't."

"About the jobs you do?"

"It's not the same with all of us."

"You mean there was something special about the relationship between Lind and Stoval?"

"That's not exactly what I said. But I don't think I want to pursue that."

"Have a heart, Wallace. If you didn't have anything personal against Lind yourself, why not help out? I think the kid's in trouble."

Wallace turned to study me. "What makes you say that?"

"Things I turned up so far indicate he had good reason not to drop out of sight. I don't think he would have done so voluntarily. I haven't the vaguest idea what might have happened to him, but I think he needs help. I'd like to give it to him."

"You a friend of the family, or what?"

"Sorry. Private cop. Should have told you before."

I opened my wallet and he studied the photostat. "Peter Bragg, huh? I have a friend in robbery over at the hall. Name's Mueller. Know him?"

"Not personally. Might have met him some time or other. Why?"

"We got into a discussion about private cops one time. Your name came up."

He turned back to the bar. There wasn't much left in his glass to swirl around the ice. I signaled for the bartender to bring him another.

"I can't help you much, except for one thing," Wallace said. "And that's just speculation. I wouldn't want anyone else to know I even had such a rotten thought."

"Done."

"The job used to be a little better than it is now. One of the reasons was the outside work was spread a little more evenly among the staff. It's a pleasant break, you know, leaving the filing cabinets and telephones for a while."

"Sure."

"Then about eighteen months ago the department head retired and they brought up this guy Stoval, from L.A. One of the first things he did was throw a little party for the staff and our spouses, to blow off about what a swell working family we all were going to be.

"Not long after that a funny thing started happening. There seemed to be a trend of giving most of the outside work—things that would take you out of town for a few days—to a small group of the younger guys. Somebody mentioned it in a kidding way one time when Stoval could overhear it. He said something about us senior guys being more valuable for our brains than our feet. Curiously, a couple of us older hands noted one day over a drink after work that the guys who got most of the out-of-town assignments had the best-looking wives sitting at home, pining away the lonely hours. Or whatever."

"Did you ever notice anything concrete in that way? Whatever it was you old hands might have suspected?"

"Just once. There was one young fellow, a go-getter named Harry Sund. His was a nice looking woman. Real nice. After one of Sund's out-of-town jobs he came steaming into the office and flat out quit. None too gently. He marched into Stoval's office and hung over the boss's desk. There were

19

rumors from the people nearest the office at the time that Sund threatened to stuff the out-of-town folders up Mr. Stoval's ass. Then Sund turned and marched out of the office, never to be seen again, with Mr. Stoval sitting there with his face about the shade of a fresh Bloody Mary."

"Tell me something about Mrs. Lind. Is she an attractive woman?"

Wallace looked up at me with heavy brows over the rim of his drink. "Let me put it this way, Bragg. I had occasion to dance a slow number with her at the company party I mentioned. It gave me the first erection I'd had in a month." He stood a little straighter, thinking about it.

"But as for anything more definite," he continued, raising his fresh drink in toast, "like I said. It would be but the wildest speculation on my part."

Chapter 3

I went over to my own office to make more phone calls, ask more questions and wait for answers. Back when I worked for the *San Francisco Chronicle*, the paper kept a back file of several other newspapers, including the *Los Angeles Times*. It turned out they still did, and a friend called back later to tell me he'd found Milton Lind's obituary in the *Times* of June 10. He'd been a minor league land speculator. His only survivors were the niece and nephew in Northern California. Another call to a credit rating outfit I subscribe to brought the news that Jerry Lind had a normal load of debts which he handled with no difficulty.

I didn't have much luck trying to reach the fellow who ran the Legion Palace Museum, a man named Bancroft. He either was on another phone or too busy to talk the several times I called. The last time, I was told he was gone for the day but that he'd be in for a half day on Saturday.

I also tried to reach a man in Southern California who was an executive officer with Coast West Insurance Co. I hadn't seen the need to tell Emil Stoval about it, but I knew a little bit about the company's operations myself. Stoval had been wrong when he said the company always went to the police when something tricky came up. Sometimes they went to private investigators to do jobs they didn't want their own men to handle, or for matters involving internal operations. I had done such a job for them two years earlier. I'd gotten all the breaks and the company had liked the way I handled it. I hoped the executive I'd dealt with then would still be grateful and willing to give me a little information about Stoval. As it turned out, the man I wanted had already left the office for the weekend. So much for trying to do a job on a Friday afternoon.

It was after three when I drove north to Marin County and the town of Larkspur. It was a warm day, steaming out things that had been drenched in a surprise rainstorm the night before. Lind's address was on a street off Madrone. I knew the area. Madrone wound up a wooded canyon climbing toward Mt. Tamalpais. There were a lot of older homes in the area, some of them ramshackle enough to offer lower rents. They attracted kids with misplaced minds who strummed guitars and didn't worry about tomorrow. It wasn't really an area where you'd expect to find a man who worked for an old line, conservative insurance company. But then it wasn't easy to find reasonable rents in Marin County any longer, either. Every time they put up another office building in downtown San Francisco, rents rose thirty miles away.

The Lind home was up at the end of an asphalt street with the closest neighbors fifty yards below. The house was a newer structure, a one-story frame building perched on stilts punched into the hillside. I parked out front behind a blue Karmann Ghia, climbed up a lot of stairs and rang the bell. I stood there a while waiting for somebody to answer, but it was worth the wait. The girl who opened the door was small, part Oriental and very cute. She wore her glistening black hair in a long ponytail. She had a saucy face with bright, alert eyes and a full mouth that looked ready to surprise you. I couldn't tell about her body. She wore a loosely belted, white terrycloth robe.

"Mrs. Lind?"

"Yes?"

"My name's Bragg. I'm a private investigator." I held out the wallet. "I've been hired to look for Jerry."

She stared at me for a moment. "All right," she said at last. "Come along out back if you want."

She unlocked the screen door and turned to lead me through the house. "Excuse the mess. I had a little birthday party for a girlfriend last night. Haven't had a chance to clean up."

The front room was a mess. There were overflowing ashtrays, glasses with liquid residue, chip dip gone bad and the aroma of stale good times. A couple of unmatching shoes were near the sofa and a pair of woman's underpants in a chair nearby.

"Looks as if everyone had a pretty good time." I followed her through a devastated kitchen and out onto a stone patio.

"Christ, they should have with all the booze I bought," she replied. "I don't know how it all ended. I passed out at two this morning." She sat in a canvas recliner and lit a cigarette, motioning me to a nearby chair in the shade of a Japanese plum tree. Before sitting down I gave her one of my business cards.

"You're not from the regular police, then?"

"No."

"Those bastards. I never heard back from them." She blew a sharp spike of smoke through her nostrils, made a face and glared at the tip of her cigarette. "Goddamnit, these things taste awful today." She looked about her, then got up again. "I have to get something to drink."

She was wearing high clogs and they were a little clumsy for her. She reminded me of a kid playing grownup as she stumped across to the kitchen doorway. I listened to her clinking ice and pouring things. She seemed to be bearing up well. She clumped back outside and sat down with a tall, clear drink.

"Why is it the regular police don't help?"

"They have a fairly hard-nosed approach to cases involving a missing husband or wife, if there's no history of mental illness involved. A lot of married people get fed up with their lives and decide to do something about it. They don't always want to go through the hassle of divorce or the big scenes at home so they just up and take a hike. The cops know all this so after some routine steps don't turn up anything, they're not apt to spend much more time on it. They have a lot to do."

"Do you think that's how it is with Jerry?"

"I don't know, I just started working. What do you think might have happened, Mrs. Lind?"

She gave her mane of hair a backward toss. "I don't know. I've been through a lot of heavy trips thinking about it. Worrying. Imagining things. It didn't really start to hit me for two or three days. I thought he'd left town on business. He does that sometimes on Sundays, to get a start on a case the first thing Monday."

"Doesn't he phone you when he's out of town?"

"Not always. It's how he does his job. He takes it very seriously. I guess he likes to drop out of sight when he's working on something." She shrugged and made a little face, then took another drag of her cigarette. "You know, I don't like to mention all this, but if you're trying to help—see, I don't know what's reality and what's fantasy when Jerry's on a case. He used to talk sometimes about trying to get into the CIA or something. I think lots of times he pretends things are more important, or at least something different, from whatever it really is he might be doing. Does that make any sense?"

"Sure it does. But it's more the sort of assessment I'd expect from an older woman. Mind telling me how old you are?"

She gave a wave of her hand. "I'm twenty-three, but don't give me any of that flattery bullshit. You can't live with a guy without figuring out some things about him."

"This fantasy element, does it extend to other parts of his life, or just to his job?"

"I don't know. But then he's really into his job. He spends a lot of time at it. I can't figure it, to tell you the truth. He doesn't get paid any overtime, just some travel expenses. But he's always working. I mean, a lot more than other young people I know."

"Could you tell me his salary?"

"Three hundred a week. That really isn't very much money any more. I used to ask him what the job was going to lead to. How much more he could expect to make if he stayed with the company. But he doesn't like me nagging him like that. He says it's a perfectly fine job. Not the CIA, but he's satisfied."

She flicked ash off the cigarette. "Big deal. I should let him do the grocery shopping some time."

"Maybe he figures he'll come into half a million bucks some day."

The girl snorted. "He never told me about it if that's what he thinks."

"But all in all, Mrs. Lind, would you say that yours is a reasonably successful marriage?"

She waved her hand again. "Oh, you know . . ." She stopped speaking and stared at me as if I'd just thrown a handful of dice that rolled funny.

"You know, there's something very important I forgot to find out. Who hired you?"

"Jerry's sister."

"Jesus," she cried, getting out of the recliner. "I might have known. Well, you can just go and dig up your dirt somewhere else."

"Hey, wait a minute, Mrs. Lind. Why can't you be as shrewd about this as you are about the way your husband does his job?"

"What do you mean?"

"I'm not trying to dig up any dirt. Only to find Jerry. It would seem to me you'd want to do the same. My job will be easier if you can figure I'm doing it for you, only his sister is the one paying for it."

"She's paying you to snoop into our private lives."

"She's paying me to find Jerry, but to do that I need to know everything you can tell me about him. The bad along with the good. I don't even have a jumping off place on this one yet."

She took a little breath and ground out her cigarette. "All right. So Jerry and I don't get along like love birds all the time. So what? A lot of young couples have trouble adjusting. You married?"

"Used to be. I know what you're talking about."

She liked that and gave me a small smile. We were friends, or at least fellow veterans of the same old campaigns.

"But we don't fight all the time, either," she continued. "His job is the biggest pain in the ass. For me, at least. I'm a little jealous of it. We don't go out enough. I mean, I know who and what I am. Men have been watching me since I was twelve years old. I've been dating since I was fourteen. You'd think Jerry would want to show me off a little or something. I like to get out and have a little fun sometimes. But it gets so I might as well be living with a sailor who's shipping out all the time. And for a lousy three hundred a week."

"Could he be seeing other women?"

"Are you kidding?" She stood and opened the terry cloth robe. Beneath it she had on a string bikini. She tossed the robe aside and posed with her hands on her hips. I had to work some to keep from swallowing my tongue. She was, as they used to say in the movies, quite a dish.

24

"Tell me," she said, "would you be out chasing other girls if you had this waiting at home for you?"

"No, Mrs. Lind, I don't guess I would. But then a lot of guys are funny that way. They can't seem to settle down in their heads with any one mate."

"Hey, I like the way you put that. One mate." She sat back on the recliner and ignored the robe. "Okay with you if I sit here like this?"

"Sure, just so long as you don't expect me to be staring you straight in the eye all the time."

She giggled. "No, that's okay. I like to turn men on. What's the sense of having a nice body if you can't show it off a little?" She grinned at me. "I feel like a peacock."

"Does it ever go beyond showing it off?"

She took away the grin. "If it did I wouldn't tell you. Unless I decided I wanted you. Let's change the subject."

"Okay, Mrs. Lind."

"Call me Marcie. All my friends do. What's your name?" She looked at the card again. "I'll call you Pete, okay?"

"Sure. How come you don't like Jerry's sister?"

"That snob bitch? She's full of phony bullshit airs, that's why. Like she was last season's Miss Bryn Mawr. And she thinks I'm common. Not good enough for her fucking brother. Of course I don't think of Jerry that way."

"How do you think of him?"

"Lots of ways. As my husband, mostly." She tucked her feet up on the recliner. "But that sister of his is too much. I never finished high school. I got into some trouble down in Santa Barbara. I was holding a guy's stash when the cops stopped us one night. It was no big thing, but I had to drop out of school, and by the time I got that hassle straightened out I decided why bother?

"Well, Miss Bitch holds that against me. And she doesn't like some of the language I use, but I figure fuck her, it's the best way I express myself. And of course she's jealous of my looks and how I like to show them off."

"How did you and Jerry meet?"

"I met him on the beach at Santa Barbara. We both like to surf. And we just sort of felt mutually attracted. He was going to school at Isla Vista. He was a little more straight and clean-cut than most of the boys there then. I mean, I guess it's part of my vanity. I've got a good, healthy body and I didn't want to sleep around with guys who had crabs or were all strung out on speed or something. We lived together the last six months of his schooling, then he went into the Army for two years. We wrote regularly and saw each other when he came home on furlough. And during that time I didn't meet anybody I liked better. So we just started going together again when he got out of the Army. When he got the job with Coast West we got married. He went through a training program, then he was assigned to the office in San Francisco. And here we are."

She lapsed into thought, and it lasted for a while.

"What is it, Marcie?"

"I was thinking about what you asked. If he could be chasing around with other girls. He's gentle and shy, most of the time. Oh, he can lose his temper when he's at home here, but I don't think he'd have the guts to cheat on me. He might, once, if he was drunk or something, and things just happened that way. But he'd blurt it out to me in a day or two."

She thought about it some more. I don't think she was quite as sure of all that as she used to be.

"But what if it turned out that he was seeing somebody?"

She reached for her cigarettes and gave me a weak grin. "I don't think we should pursue that." She made a little gesture of apology and lit her cigarette. "It's just that I got some pretty strong passions. I get emotional about things sometimes. Since I don't have any reason to think that Jerry's playing around, why think about it and have a nervous breakdown in front of you?"

"Right. That wouldn't help find him. You've lived here about two years?"

"Yes."

"Has anything out of the ordinary happened to either one of you in the past year or so?"

"What sort of thing?"

"Lawsuit, accident, a spat with your neighbors. Anything like that."

She thought carefully before replying. I wished all the people I talked to were like that. Once you got used to her cuss words she was a pleasure.

"The only thing different was that Jerry was in the hospital for about a week, in December. He'd strained his back playing handball in the Army. It never seemed to bother him until just before Christmas. Something went wrong and he was put in traction."

"Does he get disability pay from the government?"

"No. He said he'd look into it if this becomes a regular

26

thing. But he doesn't like the hassle of that. Forms to fill out and all."

"Are your parents living, Marcie?"

"Sure. Down in Santa Barbara. My dad's a retired postman. We write once in a while, but we're not really close."

"Who are Jerry's close friends?"

She frowned as she considered it. "He really doesn't have any, around here. There was a crowd he used to run with down south, before we started living together. But he's never met anybody up here he wanted to spend much time with. Outside of work."

"How does he spend his spare time?"

"We go out to the beach some. Surfing's pretty good out at Bolinas. And he likes to paint. He got into the art thing while he was going to school. He's happy to pack up his shit and spend a day sitting and painting a bunch of boats rotting away down in Sausalito."

"Does he gamble? Hang out in bars much?"

"No, none of those things."

"Do you know his boss, Emil Stoval?"

"I've met him."

"How do you get along?"

"You mean how do he and Jerry get along? Okay, I guess. I haven't heard anything different."

"Do you have much occasion to see Stoval?"

"No."

She got up and walked out into the center of the patio to stare at the sky. "We get shadows back here pretty soon. I'd like to get a little sun first. Without my clothes on, you know? Is this going to take much longer?"

"It doesn't have to. I would like a recent photo of Jerry, if you have one."

"Sure. Come on in, I'll get you one."

I followed her back into the house. She pointed across the living room debris. "There's a picture of us together on the wall. I'll get you a smaller one you can take with you."

I crossed to look at it. It was a photo taken of them at some beach. He was a tall, spare-looking youngster with an open face and moderately long blond hair. It must have been taken before he went into the Army. He looked a lot younger than twenty-six.

The girl returned with a pair of snapshots. One showed Lind leaning against an automobile. The other was a mug shot.

27

"Will these do?"

"They're fine. Is this the car he's driving?"

"Yes, a Ford Mustang."

"Do you know where he keeps the title to it? Maybe the same place he keeps the insurance policy on it."

"I'll see."

She clumped back down the hallway. I wandered over to a bookcase running the length of one wall. It had some Book-of-the-Month Club selections and a broad collection of paperbacks. They ranged from high-class soap opera with lurid covers to *Walden,* Hemingway and Ayn Rand. There were any number of one-volume surveys—world religions, Roman history and the occult included. Marcie returned with the title to the Mustang and I wrote down some numbers.

"I see Jerry's quite a reader."

"Are you kidding? He doesn't read the morning newspaper half the time. He's—you know, arty. More visually attuned. He'd rather sit and watch the color TV with the sound off, just to enjoy the images."

"Those books are all yours?"

"I bought and read them, if that's what you mean. Just because I'm a dropout doesn't mean I'm illiterate. That's what Jerry's sister can never understand. My folks turned me on to reading a long time ago."

"My apologies. I appreciate the help you've been."

"It's nothing. I'm going to feel better knowing somebody's looking for Jerry."

She followed me out onto the front porch.

"If you think of anything else that might help, I'd like you to call the number on the card I gave you. If it's after office hours an answering service will take the call. I check in with them regularly."

"I'll remember. And I'm sorry I yelled at you earlier."

"That's okay. I've had lots worse."

I went on down the stairs and climbed into my car. Just before driving off I glanced back up at the house. Marcie was still out on the porch, watching me. She saw me looking and gave me a funny little wave, as if she were throwing me a lucky wish.

Chapter 4

I headed back for San Francisco. The Marin-bound commuters were leaving town in a tide of iron. Bridge traffic going in my direction was pinched down to two lanes, leaving four lanes open to outbound traffic. It was a minor annoyance. The same as what I'd learned so far about Jerry Lind was a minor annoyance. He didn't seem to behave right, all things considered. Maybe deep down he was as wacky as his sister seemed to be.

I avoided the clogged downtown area, driving down Bay Street and along the Embarcadero to Howard, then shot on up to the parking garage across from the Chronicle, left my car and walked over to the office on Market.

Carol Jean Mackey was just leaving when I arrived. She's a tall, practical girl from Minneapolis with a long face that she used like a jujitsu throw, reminding me of a horse with the capacity for social commentary. California, even Northern California these days, gave her a lot of opportunity to show her stuff.

"Able to get everything postponed, Ceejay?"

"Yes. What's the big new job?"

"I'm working for Janet Lind, the TV newswoman. Her brother's missing."

"You mean you actually talked to her?"

"Yes, why?"

"I can't believe her act, that's all. From what I've seen of her while dashing across the room to change the channel, I've decided she's just a big version of those dolls with a string coming out the back. Pull the string and they talk."

"You might be right, but she's got a long string."

"And lots of money, I hope. You'll be last to leave today. The counselors are banging away over at the tennis club."

29

"Did a police detective named Foley call?"

"No."

"Okay, thanks. Have a good weekend, Ceejay."

I went on into my office and dialed the Hall of Justice. Foley was out working and they didn't know when he'd return. I sat thinking about things for a while then looked up the number of Coast West Insurance again. There had to be somebody around who could give me a better idea of what went on inside young Jerry Lind's head. I got through to Stoval's secretary.

"Hi, Peter Bragg again, Miss Benson. Sorry I missed you to say good-bye."

"You nearly missed me now. I'm just leaving. Mr. Stoval's already gone for the day."

"That's okay, it was you I wanted to talk to. I'm spinning my wheels over Jerry Lind. I had the impression when I first called that you were concerned about him."

"Of course I am. He's a nice boy."

"How long have you known him?"

"For as long as he's worked here. Nearly two years."

"Were you familiar with his work?"

"Somewhat. I'm not exclusively Mr. Stoval's helper."

"That's interesting. Maybe we could meet for a drink somewhere and talk about Jerry."

"I'd be happy to help, Mr. Bragg, but I can't right now. I'm meeting an old school chum who's passing through town."

"I see. Well, I know how that's apt to go. Tomorrow, maybe?"

"I'll tell you what. How about later this evening?"

"Fine, if you're sure you won't still be with your friend."

"No, as a matter of fact you'd be doing me a little favor. My chum might think we're still as close as we once were, and he knows I'm not married any more. He is. I'd like to have the appointment with you as an excuse to break away. I'm just not a very good liar."

"Okay. Want to meet somewhere in town here?"

"Not especially. I live in Sausalito and I'm meeting my friend there, at the Trident."

"That'll be handy. I live in Sausalito myself."

"Fine. Then why don't you come up to my place later. Any time after nine."

"Okay. What's the address?"

She gave me a number on Spencer Avenue, up in the hills, and told me how to find my way back around to her basement apartment. A few minutes after she hung up I had a call from Foley.

"Hello, Peter, I got pulled out of the office."

"So I heard. Anything special?"

"Not really. I'm calling from a dead whore's apartment on Eddy. She and her boyfriend had a beef. Listen, I just phoned in to see what we and the Marin sheriff have on Lind. It isn't much. Sacramento doesn't have anything unusual on his car. He doesn't have a local police record and because of his job a run was made on his prints in Washington. It only showed he had an okay Army record. So unless his car or a body turns up there's not much more to be done."

"Okay, John, I appreciate the help. You might ask the guys to flag his file. Tell them you have a half-assed friend who's interested if anything develops. I'm beginning to worry about the guy."

"Why's that?"

"I can't find anywhere he would have gone off to, or a reason to go. And he knew he'd be coming into a bucket full of money if he stayed put."

"Any idea it could be a San Francisco matter?"

"Not yet. He worked here, lived in Marin and traveled. If I see where it might be I'll let you know."

"Do that, Peter. Gotta go now."

I went back to the phone book and found the listing for a J. Thorpe, on Klondike. The male voice that answered had a curiously breathless quality to it.

"Yes, hello?"

"Mr. Jonathan Thorpe?"

The voice took a turn. "Who is calling?"

"The name is Bragg. Mr. Thorpe doesn't know me, but it's about a matter of some importance."

"This is Thorpe."

There were other voices, all male and gentle in the background. Laughter. The sound of glass meeting glass.

"I'm a private investigator, Mr. Thorpe. You might be able to help me with a case I'm on. If you'd be good enough to spare me a few minutes."

"When?" The voice was guarded.

"As soon as possible. I could drive out there right now."

"That's impossible. I'm in the middle of a cocktail party."

"I'm sorry, Mr. Thorpe. But this could turn into a police matter at any moment. I was just speaking to Inspector Foley of the homicide detail. Maybe if you could talk to me for a few minutes it won't be necessary for you to talk to him."

"Just a moment."

The receiver at the other end was put down and I heard the riffling of pages.

"Bragg, you said your name was?"

"That's right."

"Are you calling from your office?"

"Right again."

"Hang up, please. I'll call you back."

I hung up, to let him prove it for himself. I couldn't really blame Thorpe, if he and his friends were part of San Francisco's populous homosexual community. Things were better for them in San Francisco than in a lot of places, and even better than they used to be in San Francisco a few years earlier, but it still wasn't an easy life. And even private cops who professed to be ethical didn't hesitate to bring a little pressure to bear when they needed help. The phone rang.

"Bragg here."

"All right, Mr. Bragg. I suppose I'll have to see you. Do you have the address?"

"If it's the one in the phone book."

"It is. We're in a two-story flat on the corner. We're in the upper."

I drove on out. Thorpe lived in a quiet neighborhood of stucco and stone. I pushed the button under his mail slot. When the buzzer sounded, unlocking the front door, I stepped inside and climbed some stairs. They led to a hallway running the length of the flat. There were a lot of people and smoke in the place. Jonathan Thorpe came out to greet me. He was a tall, cadaverous-looking gentleman in his late thirties with thinning hair and eyes that didn't look as if they'd been getting much sleep. He wore dark slacks and a turtleneck sweater beneath a white sports jacket.

"You're Mr. Bragg?"

"That's right."

"Come along and have a drink."

"That won't be necessary. If we could just find a corner where we could talk for a few minutes . . ."

"No, Mr. Bragg," Thorpe said with a vengeful smile. "You insisted on barging in here. Now you'll just have to let me exhibit you." He paused at the doorway to a large living room at the rear of the building. "You aren't gay, are you?"

"Not beyond a friendly handshake."

32

"I thought not. As you might have surmised, everybody else here is. With the exception of one or two who might be closet straights gathering material for a book. At any rate, when I announced that a real private detective was on his way over, they thought it was just a scream, and insisted that I bring you in so they could size you up, so to speak. This way, please."

I sighed and followed the fellow into the crowded room. It wasn't the first occasion I'd had to mingle with groups of homosexuals. This was a pretty refined bunch. They dressed well and could easily have been taken for any stag bunch of men. If some of them seemed to hold their cocktail glasses kind of funny, or to posture a bit more than seemed normal, I figured it was just because I was looking for it. But they had a way of making you pay. When a solitary straight guy entered their midst, they could remind him he was in lonely country. As Thorpe and I worked our way through the crowd I tried to ignore the quiet comments usually made somewhere just behind me.

". . . some muscle . . ."

"Not a youth, by any means . . ."

"If I had his body I'd make you *all* behave . . ."

Thorpe led me to a bar setup. "What will it be, Mr. Bragg?"

"Bourbon and water will be fine."

"James, a bourbon and water for Mr. Bragg here."

James was the bartender. James was slender and graceful. Almost willowy, you could call him, and not a day over 18. James was not overdressed. He wore a pair of men's yellow bikini swim trunks and a knowing smile. He gave me my drink and Thorpe led me over to a corner window with a fine view of the sloping rows of homes marching toward the sea.

"Now, Mr. Bragg. What is this about homicide?"

"We don't know for sure that's what it is. If we did, you'd be speaking to somebody on the municipal force. But let's start with your car."

"My what?"

"Automobile. A blue Mercedes, this year's model. License number Four-Zero-One-Bee . . ."

"Yes, that's my automobile, what about it?"

"You don't know where it is, right?"

"I certainly do. It's in the garage downstairs."

"You have it?"

33

"Of course I have it. Would you like me to go back it out a few times for you?"

"You reported it stolen to the Coast West Insurance Company."

Thorpe raised one hand to the side of his long face. "Oh my dear God, I certainly did. And when I got it back I telephoned the police and told them, but I forgot to notify the insurance people."

"Mind telling me about it?"

"You want to hear about the Mercedes?"

"If you don't mind."

Thorpe turned to search the crowded room, then called out. "Ted? Oh, Teddy, over here, please."

A round-faced man with a deep tan crossed the room toward us. He was a few years younger than Thorpe. He wore casual sports clothes, a white shirt and cherry-colored ascot. He joined us with a tentative smile and arched eyebrow.

"Teddy, this is Mr. Bragg, the detective I announced was coming."

Teddy's eyebrow straightened.

"Mr. Bragg wants to know about the Mercedes, Teddy."

Teddy's smile went the way of his arched eyebrow. When he spoke it was to Thorpe, as if I'd wandered off over a hill.

"I borrowed it."

"For an entire week," Thorpe declared.

"That's right, I drove up to Lake Tahoe and stayed there an entire week because I had time on my hands and I didn't think you'd be going out anywhere for some while."

"And you didn't tell me you were taking it, did you, Teddy?"

"You *knew* I had a set of keys to it."

"I *did* not."

Teddy turned in my direction now, his face getting a little flushed beneath the tan.

"Do you know anything about . . ." Teddy's eyes quickly encompassed the room. ". . . us, Mr. Bragg?"

"Sure."

"Well, Jonathan and I were—close friends . . ."

Now it was Thorpe's turn to be nettled. "Teddy . . ." he warned, his voice rising.

"Don't 'Teddy' me, Jonathan," Teddy snapped. "You wanted me to tell this gentleman about the Mercedes and I'm going to tell him about the Mercedes . . ."

34

Thorpe shot a glance toward the ceiling. "Oh, for God's sake." He turned and hiked over to the bar for another drink.

"Well?" I asked.

"Jonathan and I were thinking of sharing this place," Teddy continued. "I had made arrangements to take a week's leave from my job to make the big move, when on Friday night I dropped in to find him with a boy he'd picked up over at the Lance—that's a bar—and I had thought we had all that straightened out. His promiscuousness, I mean. But it turned out that we hadn't. Well, I was just plain mad. And here I was with a week to do nothing in, and I wasn't even going to speak to Jonathan again. But he had given me a set of keys to his car, so I just took it. And he knew it, because it was parked right in front and I drove off in it right after catching him and that child right in this very room. And that's the entire story."

"Okay. Thanks for the help."

I went back over to the bar where Thorpe stood talking to the skinny kid in the bikini.

"That's an interesting yarn your friend just told me, Thorpe."

"Mr. Bragg, why don't we go out into the hall, where it's a little quieter."

"No, Thorpe, you wanted it in here, and in here is where it will be."

The voices of nearby guests dropped to a murmur.

"The story your friend Teddy tells could leave you open to some criminal charges."

"Such as?"

Our end of the room was dead silence now. "Falsely reporting a criminal felony to the police. Attempt to defraud the insurance company. There are a lot of ways to stub your toe when you report a crime out of spite, Mr. Thorpe."

"But how was I to know he didn't plan to keep it? It wasn't a false report to me. And I'm sorry I forgot to tell the insurance people that I had it back. It was an honest mistake."

"All right, Thorpe, so it was a mistake. But in the course of the time your car was gone, you probably were interviewed by an investigator from the insurance company."

"Yes, I was."

I showed him the mug shot of Jerry Lind. "This the man?"

"Yes. I don't recall his name."

"It's Jerry Lind. What did you talk about?"

"The car, naturally."

"Nothing else?"

"No."

"Okay. What did you tell him about the car?"

"That it was stolen from the street out front. I didn't tell him the story Teddy told you, if that's what you mean."

"That's what I mean. Then so far as Lind was concerned, the car was just gone when you woke up the next morning, and you didn't have any idea who took it."

Thorpe lowered his eyes. "Is this going to get me into trouble with the police? I didn't tell them any more than that, either."

"It won't so far as I'm concerned, so long as you're telling the truth now. How long a talk did you have with Lind?"

"Not long. Ten minutes at the most."

"Where did you talk?"

"In the downstairs landing. My mother was visiting that day. I didn't want to disturb her."

"Do you remember what day it was?"

"On Tuesday, following the theft."

"Theft, my eye," said Teddy from across the quiet room.

"Okay, Thorpe, so you had a brief talk about the car. Now this, I want a frank answer to. Jerry Lind is a young fellow. A pretty handsome young fellow. Did you make any sort of advance toward him—however vague?"

"I don't quite know what . . ."

"Yes you do, Mr. Thorpe. We both know what I mean."

Somebody in the crowd snickered. I turned toward it and a hush settled.

Thorpe made a gesture with one hand. "Oh, I don't know, I might have said something. But he didn't respond to it."

"You're sure about that?"

He raised his head and spoke in a firm voice. "Yes. Quite sure."

I turned to the others gathered around. "Gentlemen, maybe one of you can help me. I'm questioning Mr. Thorpe about a young man who is missing. I'm personally beginning to fear for his safety. He might already be dead."

A couple of them cleared their throats.

"Now, while I'm not a part of the gay community, my work has brought me into contact with people who are. I know it is not an easy life. I also know a man can be happily married to a woman and have children and still have urges in other directions. I hold no moral judgment on any of this,

"The man I'm looking for is Jerry Lind. He's an investigator for Coast West Insurance. I have a photo of him here that I'd like you all to look at. If any of you recognize him, I'd like to hear about it. Nothing I'm told will be passed along to his family or anyone else. I just need your help."

I made a slow circuit of the room, holding up the snapshot. The speech seemed to have worked. There was no longer any snide hostility. They were a group of concerned citizens. I hoped. But nobody responded. There was a lot of shaking of heads and murmured no's. I worked my way back to the bar and showed the photo to the boy in the swimsuit. He shook his head.

"Okay, Mr. Thorpe, I'll tell the insurance company that it was just a mixup. That you've got your car back. Here's my card. If you remember anything else about Lind, I'd like to hear from you."

Thorpe nodded. "I'll do that. Let me see you to the door."

I followed him down the hallway. Just before I started down the stairs, Teddy hailed us.

"Just a moment, Mr. Bragg." He hurried up to us, glanced once at Thorpe and fidgeted with the glass in his hand. "I just wanted to say, Mr. Bragg, that what Jonathan told you is the truth. About the missing man, I mean. Jonathan told me about it when I got back. He mentioned—as you observed—that this Lind is a pleasant-looking chap. Jonathan told me he'd dropped his hanky a time or two in the course of their conversation, but that the young man ignored it. Jonathan might be an old goat, but—well, I just wanted you to know."

"All right, Teddy, thanks."

"Yes," said Thorpe. "Thank you, Teddy."

I left them at the top of the stairs looking at each other as if they were seeing a sunset together. Or maybe a sunrise. What the hell. It wasn't any of my business.

Chapter 5

I drove back downtown and had dinner at Polo's, on Mason Street. I ordered their special, a platter of ground beef with an egg and some spinach stirred in, and washed it all down with a couple glasses of the house red. I also did some more thinking about the missing Jerry Lind. I still hadn't pinned him down. An Army veteran in his middle twenties, but from the sound of things he still was a half-formed personality, full of romantic notions about his job. He wasn't particularly good at his job, either. It wasn't just the way his co-worker, Wallace, had assessed him. The boy hadn't pursued the matter of Jonathan Thorpe's missing Mercedes with nearly the wit or energy he could have. Properly handled, he should have gotten the real story soon after his original interview with Thorpe. As for home life, he was married to a girl with a sensational body and questing mind who was crying for a bit of attention. Lind didn't seem to know what to do about it. Lind also seemed to be a loner, but his solitary nature didn't translate into a particularly thoughtful individual. Maybe he was a whiz of a painter. But I still didn't know what sort of things went on inside his head. I could only hope that Miss Benson might be able to give me an idea.

I got to her house a little after ten and made my way down to her apartment. Her door had an upper pane of glass covered with some sort of graph paper. I squinted at it, light filtering through from inside. It was an old actuary graph showing at what age people in various occupations tended to die. It didn't carry a rating on law enforcement people. Of course cops started the dying process inside, where the insurance statisticians couldn't see. I rang the bell, and after a moment a different-looking Miss Benson opened the door.

"Hi," she said, gesturing me inward with a swing of her head. Her hair wasn't in a bun any longer. It fell below her shoulders. She'd taken off her glasses and changed into a taut white sweater and low-belted pair of gray slacks that were made out of a material that gave a little, emphasizing the slight pouch of her stomach and her upswept buttocks.

"Can I fix you a drink?"

"Sure."

"What would you like?"

"Anything handy. Bourbon, Scotch . . ."

"Good. I have bourbon."

"If you have some water to go with it I'll be a happy man."

She crossed to a sink, stove and refrigerator beyond a small dining table to my right. The place was really just a large, one-room apartment. There was one other door next to the kitchen that probably led to the bathroom. The opposite side was mostly glass, looking out over a wooden deck and offering a view of the water below. The room was divided by a sofa and chair, and there was a queen-size bed beyond that. When she carried a couple of drinks over to the sofa, she walked in a manner that indicated she was a little drunk.

"Have a good time with the old school chum?"

She groaned and settled on the sofa with a slope-mouthed face. Women who did that made me uncomfortable. I'd known two of them who used the expression regularly. They both were acute neurotics. Maybe Miss Benson only did it when she drank. I sat a ways down from her on the sofa.

"It went about the way I expected. He didn't want to buy me anything to eat down at the Trident, but suggested we pick up a couple of steaks and come up to my place, et cetera, et cetera. So I just drank with him until almost nine, then told him I had to come home for a very important appointment. He wanted to come along anyway, so I told him about you. We argued in the parking lot for so long I barely had time to get home and shower before you got here."

"If you haven't eaten, why don't you fix yourself a sandwich or something? I can wait."

"No, that's okay." She had an open can of mixed nuts on a stand beside her that she dug into. "Want some?"

"No thanks."

"They're good." She was looking at me alternately with

39

one eye then the other. Miss Benson, it seemed, was more than a little drunk.

"What's it like?" she asked.

"What's what like?"

"Being a detective. I have a whole shelf over there filled with detective stories." She waved her hand in the direction of a low bookcase. It was the hand holding her drink, and some of the amber liquid slopped down across her taut, white sweater. "Is it exciting the way they write about it?"

"No. It's mostly a lot of very dull phoning and walking around talking to people and researching land deeds and going through court records. The only time it gets a little exciting is when somebody resents one of the questions you ask and takes a smack at you."

She leaned some in my direction. "Do you carry a gun?"

"Sometimes."

"Do you have one on you now?"

"Nope."

She leaned back with another twist of her mouth. "Is there much sex?"

"While working?"

"Yes."

"No."

"Oh." She took a drink from the glass. "Not ever?"

"Hardly ever. Look, Miss Benson . . ."

"Laurel."

"Okay, Laurel. Like a lot of other jobs it can be about what you want to make of it. If you're in a business where you come into contact with a lot of people of the opposite sex you're obviously going to meet a certain number who have whatever chemistry attracts the two of you to each other. Or else people who are lonely, oversexed, inebriated or any combination of those. If you're the sort of person who needs that all the time then you take advantage of it. If not, you go on about your job."

"What do you do?"

"Since I didn't just enter puberty the day before yesterday I usually go on about my job. But that isn't what I came up here to talk about." I was getting a dry throat from all that talking and had some of the bourbon.

"I guess you think I'm terribly nosy."

"I hope you are. You'll be able to tell me more about Jerry Lind that way."

40

"You might be a little disappointed. I don't know him all that well. He's a likeable boy. That's all."

"How was he at his job?"

"All right, I guess. He went out and came back and made his reports."

"Were his reports like all the other reports?"

"Pretty much. They weren't as terse as some of the others, but the boss seemed satisfied."

"That's something else. What sort of fellow is Stoval?"

"Easy to work for. A little stuck on himself, maybe. But then it's a pretty responsible job for somebody his age."

"I understand there used to be a fellow named Harry Sund who worked there."

She took a sip of her drink and stared at me. "I thought you wanted to talk about Jerry."

"We are talking about Jerry, and the people in his life. I understand Sund quit. There was some sort of scene. Can you tell me about it?"

She giggled. "I was home sick that day. The other girls said Harry threatened to punch out Mr. Stoval. Harry was ranting something about his wife. I could hardly believe it when they told me. I still can't, really."

"Why not?"

"I just don't think Mr. Stoval is that way. He's never made the slightest pass at any of the girls working there."

"Are you sure of that, Laurel? It could be important."

"Yes. I'm sure. We're a gossipy bunch. He really hasn't. That's why we feel Harry Sund must have made some sort of mistake. Maybe his wife told him a story. Because there are some girls in the office who are—let's say available, and they sort of let fellows know about it. In a nice way, of course."

"Sure."

"But Mr. Stoval never makes a move. So why would he try anything funny with the wife of somebody who works for him? Besides, he's got his hands full with his own wife. She's a beautiful girl. She does a lot of modeling in the city under the name Faye Ashton. I see her in Macy's ads all the time."

"Was it like Jerry to leave town on a job without telling you or somebody else at the office where he was going?"

"No, but he did a lot of outside work. If he decided over the weekend to go somewhere, he might just get an early start without coming in or phoning first."

41

"Did Jerry ever joke around with the available girls in the office?"

"I like the way you put that, joke around."

"Did he?"

"No. Jerry was sort of a pet. I mean he was a little clumsy and things. He's the sort of boy that arouses a girl's mother instinct. I think he did that everywhere he went."

"How do you mean, Laurel?"

"Oh, you know, he was just that sort." She lifted her glass again. There was nothing left but ice. She got up and went back across to the kitchen. I followed her.

"You said this afternoon you were married once."

"Yes. Johnny was a big goof," she said, tilting the bourbon bottle. "In fact Jerry reminded me of him in ways. He was older, but he had the same apparent helplessness in lots of things."

"Apparent?"

"Uh huh. After a while I finally doped out that there was a lot of laziness beneath it all. But we don't have to talk about that, do we? I've been trying to forget that part of my life."

"I'd be interested only to the extent his behavior coincided with Jerry Lind's, and you figured they might have acted or reacted the same way about things. Do you think Jerry is basically lazy?"

She leaned against the sink, sipping the drink. "I don't know if lazy would be quite the word. He was a little self-centered, I think. A little selfish, maybe. I can't really put my finger on it. He's very boyish and charming, like I said. But there's a funny little undercurrent to him. I know that sounds crazy, but it is the woman's appraisal you're after, isn't it?"

"Sure, and you're doing great. Did you ever meet his wife?"

"I think so, at a company party one time. But I can't remember who she was."

"She's Eurasian. Short, well-built, uses some street talk."

"Oh, I remember her now. But we didn't really have a conversation."

"Did Jerry talk about her around the office?"

"No. Come to think of it, that was kind of funny, I guess. I've known people having domestic problems. Heading for a breakup of their marriage. They never talked about their

42

home life, either. Hmmm. I'll have to think about that some."

"There's something else I'd like to go back to for a minute. I had the feeling there might have been something more you could tell me, only you decided it wasn't important enough or something."

"What was that?"

"About the mother instinct you said he brings out. Everywhere he went. Did you ever see it outside of the office?"

She lowered her eyes and thought about it. She was either making up her mind or falling alseep.

"Who hired you?" she asked, looking up.

"His sister, Janet Lind. Know her?"

"Yes, the newsgirl. She came up to the office one day. Well, she made a wise choice. You're quite good."

"I've had a lot of practice. Want to tell me about it?"

"I suppose I should. Frankly I'd forgotten about it until you brought it up just a moment ago. I saw Jerry one evening here in Sausalito, by accident. Do you know the No Name bar in town here?"

"I ought to. Even worked there one time when I was at loose ends with myself."

"Well, about a month ago a girlfriend and I were having a drink there one evening. We were off in a corner, where people going in and out aren't apt to notice you unless they're looking for someone. And I saw Jerry come in from the back patio with a girl. They left together and didn't notice me. I recognized her, too. Jerry had a back injury, around last Christmas. He spent a week or so in the hospital. Some of us went up to visit him a couple times. The girl I saw with him at the No Name was a nurse I'd seen at the hospital."

"Do you know her name?"

"No. I was never introduced."

"What hospital was it?"

"Horace Day, on Masonic."

"Do you remember the room number or floor that he was on?"

"It was the third floor, near the south end of the building."

"Was the No Name the only place you saw the two of them outside of the hospital?"

"Yes. Just that one time."

"Did they seem to be on friendly terms when you visited Jerry at the hospital?"

43

"I never noticed. But she had that maternal quality about her. She was a small girl, but very brisk and efficient."

"What else can you remember about her appearance?"

"She's younger than I am. Probably twenty-five or six. She has rather sharp features. Small, dark eyes. And good teeth. Very white."

"You have a good memory."

"I saw her both times I visited the hospital, then in town here. She's quite attractive really. I think I remembered her because of that, and the take-charge quality I mentioned."

I finished my drink and my mind began edging toward the door.

"Let me fix you another."

"No thanks. I've got some work to do, and you look as if you could do with some rest."

She formed another sloped smile. "Yes, I sort of overdid it before you got here. I'm sorry. I guess I was thinking some funny things." She followed me to the door, her arms hugging herself. "I guess I practically came right out and asked if we could get something started between us."

"I'm flattered. Under the right circumstances you wouldn't have to practically come right out and ask. You're nice looking."

"Come on . . ."

"Seriously. I watched your legs and bottom all the way into Stoval's office today."

"That's something, at least. My number's in the phone book if the circumstances ever get better."

"I'll remember that. Oh, I almost forgot something else."

"What's that?"

"I asked Stoval for a rundown on the cases Jerry was working on when he dropped out of sight. Stoval mentioned a fire report that later was given to somebody else."

"Yes. Howie Brewster looked into it. Very routine. Cigarette meets mattress."

"Then he mentioned a couple of thefts. A painting from the Legion Palace Museum and a Mercedes out in the Sunset district."

"That's right."

"How about another?"

"What?"

"I think your boss was holding out on me. There was another case sheet in Jerry's file that he didn't tell me about. I'd like to know what it was."

44

"That's supposed to be confidential, you know."

"I suppose it is. But if Stoval's holding something back, I have to wonder why."

"All right. I'll find out Monday for you."

"Thanks. Incidentally, the company can quit worrying about having to pay for the missing Mercedes. It belongs to a man named Thorpe. He got into a lover's quarrel with his boyfriend and the boyfriend took the car. Thorpe finally got the car back, but I'm not sure about the boyfriend. He's having a tough time."

Laurel Benson opened the door and gave me a frank stare. "At least he has somebody to quarrel with."

I got on out of there. At the top of Spencer there's a fire station with a parking area and outside phone booth. I drove up to it and dialed directory assistance to get the number of the Horace Day Hospital in San Francisco. Then I called the hospital and asked to be put through to the nurse's station at the south end of the third floor, or the nearest thing to it. A woman who identified herself as Mrs. Burke answered. I told Mrs. Burke that I was Dr. Frank Thatcher and that I was trying to locate a nurse who had been working in that area of the hospital in December, tending one of my patients. I repeated Laurel Benson's description of the woman she'd seen with Jerry Lind.

"Oh yes, Doctor, that would be Donna Westover. She's not on right now, and I know for a fact she isn't at home, either. We tried to get her earlier, to work a shift for one of the other girls."

"Can you tell me when she's due back?"

"Just a minute, please."

The phone booth I was in was about fifty yards from where Highway 101 crests Wolfback Ridge. I could hear traffic buzzing home from the city. A light blue patrol car of the Sausalito police pulled into the lot from the frontage road that parallels the highway. The lone patrolman dimmed his lights and stared in my direction. A moment later another powder blue car came up Spencer and drove in alongside the first car. The two officers talked. I'd noticed over the years that the Sausalito cops did a lot of that sort of thing, as if the two-way radio hadn't been invented yet.

Nurse Burke came back on the line. "Dr. Thatcher? Miss Westover is due in tomorrow at noon."

"Thank you very much."

I had seemed to run out of things to do for the night. While trying to decide whether to go down into town for a drink or to go home for a drink I called in to my answering service. They gave me something more to do. They'd had a call thirty minutes earlier from Marcie Lind. She needed help.

Chapter 6

I turned off Madrone and drove up the road toward the Lind home, dimming my lights. I wasn't sure what to expect, but when I pulled up below the house at the end of the road things seemed calm enough. There were lights on inside, nobody was screaming and there weren't any police cars or ambulances around. I hustled up the stairs and rang the bell. The door was opened by a tall, slender black woman with snapping eyes. She was wearing a long, striped gown.

"I'm Peter Bragg. I received a message that Mrs. Lind wanted to see me."

"I'm Xumbra," she said simply, swinging open the door.

Marcie came up behind her. "Oh, Pete, thank God. Come in." She turned to the black girl. "Thanks so much, Mary. It'll be all right now."

Xumbra–Mary gave me a sharp appraisal. "You sure about that, baby?"

"Yes. I'm sure."

The black woman went out past me as if she harbored strong doubts.

"I'll phone you in the morning," Marcie called after her. She closed the door and leaned back against it. She was wearing light blue denim pants and a white shirt with the tail hanging out. They both looked as if they'd been to war, but Marcie Lind still managed to look sensational.

Xumbra?" I asked.

"Oh," said Marcie with a wave of her hand. "She tries to lay down that back-to-Africa crap on people she doesn't know, but it's all bullshit, because she never signed any enlistment papers or changed her religion or whatever. So far as I'm concerned she's still Mary Becker who lives down the road and is a good friend. Can I get you a drink?"

"No, thanks. What's the trouble?"

Marcie crossed the room and sat on the edge of the sofa. She'd cleaned up the place some.

"Mr. Stoval was here."

"What did he want?"

"I'm not so sure now. I thought I did at first." She lifted her hands over her eyes, as if she were trying to remember something. But then her shoulders began to tremble and I could see she was crying. She looked up, angry with herself, and sniffed back tears. "Mr. Stoval said I'd better get used to the idea that Jerry is dead. Or might be dead. Or something like that." She blew her nose and got better control of herself. "I guess I'd never really considered that."

"When was he here, Marcie?"

"He left about twenty minutes ago. Thank God for Mary. She'd been to a movie and just stopped in to say hello. Between the two of us we got him out of here. Mary can come on pretty strong."

"I noticed. How long had he been here?"

"Almost an hour. It was okay at first. He was very business-like. Then he asked the way to the john. I got a whiff of his breath and could smell booze on it. I gave him directions and he was in there for quite a while. I finally went and listened outside the door. He was poking through the medicine cabinet. It spooked me. That's when I called your number."

"Don't you suppose he might have been trying to make a play for you?"

"Well yes, finally," she said, getting to her feet and pacing briefly around the room. "You'd think I was still fourteen, I acted so dumb. I really fell for it, you know? He hit me with this very heavy trip to do with Jerry, and how decisions would have to be made in the office about how long to leave him on the payroll—meaning my getting a weekly check—and that they have to be business-like about things. Then I realized he'd been ogling my fucking chest, like if I unbuttoned my shirt, there's next week's paycheck. Shit!"

She sat back down on the sofa. "But the things he said,

Pete, about Jerry's disappearance being so strange. About something maybe happening to him. It's true, and it really shook me."

"Marcie, he's just trying to psych you. It isn't the first time he's made a play for somebody else's wife. He knows I've been hired to find Jerry, and he knows it isn't going to take me until the Fourth of July to do it. You're a sexy broad, Marcie, and he's probably wanted to take a shot at you for a long time. He figures the best time to try it is while Jerry's away."

"But Pete, the things he said. They're still true, even if he does have a hard-on for me."

"The things he said are a tub of baloney. Any number of things could explain Jerry's absence. He might have found himself in a situation too embarrassing to explain right now. He might have gotten walloped on the head and temporarily lost his memory. He might be trying to pull off some convoluted entrapment. You told me yourself that he gets a little fanciful at times."

"But not tell his own wife?"

"You might unwittingly be involved, by knowing somebody who's a part of the intrigue."

"Such as?"

"Maybe Stoval, even. I'm not saying that's the way it is, but it could be. And you've got to keep control of yourself, Marcie. Since I've seen you I've come up with a couple of leads. It's too late tonight to check them out, but I'll be back working on it the first thing in the morning."

"What did you find out?"

"Like I said, I have to check them out. Now why don't you just fix yourself a stiff drink and go to bed?"

She smiled bleakly. "Yeah. Maybe I will."

I went on down to the car. Near the bottom of the road I saw lights on in a small frame bungalow. More interesting was the glow of a cigarette being passed from one person to another on the front porch of the place. I stopped the car and got out. The people on the porch quieted as I crossed over to them.

"Xumbra?"

"What is it?"

"It's Peter Bragg. The guy who was just up talking to Marcie Lind."

"So?"

"I've been hired to find Jerry. By his sister. But Marcie

48

seems pretty anxious to have him back too, so I figure I'm trying to do her a favor at the same time. Marcie said you're a pretty good friend. I'd like to talk to you."

"All right," she said after a minute's reflection. "Sam, honey, how about waiting inside?"

Sam, honey, was the white dude with long hair sitting beside her with his cowboy boots up on the porch railing. He exhaled a lungful of smoke and got to his feet haltingly.

"Leave the joint, please," she told Sam firmly. Sam handed it to her with a grunt and went on inside.

"One thing you might as well know right now," she told me. "I don't much like white people. Sam there's a cool dude who goes back a long way in my life and mind. But as for all you others . . ."

"Yeah, I know, it's a bitch," I agreed, climbing up the stairs and resting on the railing. "I didn't used to think that way. Thought it would happen sooner. But I figure now it'll take at least another generation to make us comfortable with one another. Cal Gentle is a little more pessimistic. He figures closer to half a century. But I told him I thought . . ."

"Cal Gentle?"

"Yeah."

"The Oakland Panther?"

"Ex-Panther. He's trying some other things these days."

"How come you know Cal?"

"I testified at a trial. About a cop he was supposed to have roughed up."

"Sheeeit! You're the one who got old Cal off."

"I might have helped. At least it got that particular cop off the Oakland force, where he had no business being."

"What's your name again?"

"Peter Bragg."

"Well, Pete, you just lost some of your paleness," she said, holding out her funny smelling cigarette. "Want a toke?"

"Not now, thanks."

"I went to school with Cal. How did you get to know him?"

"We ran into each other a couple months after the trial. Took time out for a talk. A pretty long one. Since then we've done some things together."

"Work or play?"

"Both."

"Huh. What do you know. Marcie still calls me Mary. She just laughs at Xumbra. How about you?"

49

"I'll call you Mother Superior with a straight face if you want, so long as you'll talk to me."

She made a cackle and put aside the dope to light a legal cigarette. "Call me Zoom, then. I really like that. I'll bet you're a mean dude, too, huh Pete?"

"I can be brought to that point."

"Extra-ordinary. I could see it in your face up at Marcie's. You came in looking ready to beat up on people."

"How long have you known her, Zoom?"

"As long as she's lived here. A couple years. We hit it right off."

"How about Jerry?"

"Oh, you know, he's her husband. We say hello."

"But the two of you don't really hit it off."

"Neither of us goes out of the way."

"How come?"

"I don't know. I guess I might have intimidated him some. Not meaning to, but some things are my nature. And I think he puts on some. If not Marcie and the rest of us, maybe himself."

I waited in the stillness. "I was hoping you'd go on to give an example."

"I'm trying to think of one. Bear in mind, Marcie and I have a tight time together. We would even if she was married to the neighborhood zero. So I haven't spent all that much time trying to figure out Mr. Jerry Lind. But he's a strange dude. A couple of things do come to mind. Some days around here in the summer it gets wickedly hot, and I sort of drift around without my clothes on. Marcie was here visiting on one of those days, and Jerry came down to fetch her for some reason or other. So he comes on in and gets a little peek of my fine black skin. And whoooeee! He gets all stammery and red in the face . . ."

"That's usually just upbringing, Zoom. Doesn't mean much."

"Now you hear me out, Peter Bragg. I don't care what sort of hangups he has, he just isn't consistent that way. Another time they were both down here at a party I threw one night. I had just a whole lot of people in. Some a little spaced out. Some from here, some from there. Even had some gay lib types I'd met in the city. They didn't come on hard about it, more funny and arty. Anyhow, there was a little black girl tagging along with them. Called herself Moxie or Foxie or something."

"Did she go the gay route?"

50

"I think she went whichever way the boat was going. Anyway, Jerry Lind picked up on that chick the minute she came through the door. She was a little girl with a big grin for everyone, wearing a sloppy pullover and a pair of cut off jeans that just barely covered her tight little ass. Jerry was pretty cool about it, but I saw him watching her. Then, I guess after he'd had enough to drink inside himself, he made his little move. I was hustling ice or something out in the kitchen when I saw them through the screen door over in a corner of the back yard necking up a storm. I didn't have time just then to worry about it. That sort of thing happens at parties. But a few minutes later I was out getting something else from the refrigerator and I heard them coming back toward the house. They seemed to be having some sort of argument. I heard her tell him, 'Not now. Call me in the city some time.' Mind now, Pete, I haven't even told Marcie about this, but later on in the night, before little steamy buns left, I cornered her in an out-of-the-way place and sort of interrogated her to find out what Jerry was after. I suspected sex, but I wanted to confirm."

"And what did you find out?"

"He wanted her to go down on him out in my back garden there. Sheeeit, the boldness of some of you crackers."

"I'd like to talk to this Moxie or Foxie. Know where I can get in touch with her? Or the friends she came with?"

"Unnecessary. She was just playing him for laughs. I heard her telling somebody later. Besides, she didn't live where she told him. She was just passing through the area from L.A. She was on her way to visit people in Tacoma, then she was going back to New York. I just wanted you to realize why I figure there was a little put-on involved when he made such a to-do over seeing my own backside. I guess you'd have to say he's a man of many parts, and I never bothered trying to sort them through. My friendship is with Marcie."

"Does she talk about Jerry much?"

"Not in depth. She'll mention funny little things that happen, but not much more than that. And I don't pry."

"One last tough one, Zoom. I have to ask them where they might help."

"I know."

"How about Marcie? She's a very pretty girl. She could have guys stumbling all over themselves to spend time with her. Do you think she ever does?"

51

"No, I don't. She likes to be seen. Likes to be admired. But the times I've seen anyone try to come on a little bit, and there have been some really pretty fellows, too, she just lets them know it's a nice compliment, but no thanks. She seems to be a definite one-man woman."

Zoom put aside the regular cigarette and relit the other. She inhaled deeply and held it for the better part of a minute before exhaling.

"And that," she said, "leaves me with a chill when I think about what went on out in the garden that night."

Chapter 7

The next morning I phoned the Legion Palace Museum and made an appointment to see Dean Bancroft, who ran the place. The museum was in a magnificent setting up behind the cliffs on the south side of the Golden Gate, just seaward of the bridge itself. I arrived a little before eleven and was sent down a long marble corridor to Bancroft's office. The museum director turned out to be a wiry, middle-aged man with his sleeves rolled up and a cigarette between his lips. He rose from behind a cluttered desk and extended one hand.

"Bragg, what can I do for you?" he asked, waving me to a chair.

"I'm doing some work involving Coast West Insurance. I understand they had a policy on a painting that was stolen here last month."

"Right. I talked to another Coast West man about it."

"The painting hasn't been recovered?"

"No. The exhibit itself is up in Portland now. The missing painting was just a minor piece of the whole traveling show. It was called New Directions. Frankly, it's the sort of stuff I call woodshed modern. Real out of the mainstream pieces.

52

To tell you the truth, I wouldn't have given you a thousand bucks for the lot. And that's what we'll get for just the one piece. Or rather the owner will."

"How come you even had the exhibit if you didn't like it?"

Bancroft coughed a couple times and ground out his cigarette, then groped through things on his desk until he found the rest of the pack. "I'm just one of the voices around here. That damn collection was like a Herb Caen column. Most everybody found one or two things in it they liked. So we brought it in. Besides, it was put together by a friend of mine, Sy Norman at the L.A. Museum of Modern Art. I figured if he liked the thing, there must have been some merit in it somewhere, although I'll tell you, bud, it wasn't apparent to this tired old gent."

"You sound kind of hostile."

"Well I feel hostile about a lot of that stuff. To my mind it's worthless. A lot of these people will put in a few years trying to learn the craft and some of them do a good job of it, but a lot of them don't, and they don't have anything in their heads or their hearts to say in the first place, or a sense of humor or eye for design or anything else. So they're apt to fluke around until they stumble on some gimmick and exploit it as if they'd started a whole new movement. Now in its own way that's fine, if they want to show it along with a lot of other third-rate stuff at a supermarket parking lot art festival. And I guess it's all right if the solid Americans from the suburbs want to be taken in by it all and pay cash money to own a piece of it. But I don't think it's all right to put a collection of that stuff inside the same walls that exhibit Rodin or Matisse or Degas."

Bancroft blew a stream of smoke toward the ceiling. "Jesus Christ, what set that off? If I were a girl I'd suspect I was getting my period."

"Did you feel the stolen painting was as bad as the rest?"

"I knew I'd be wide open after that outburst," he said with a wan smile. "Actually, no. It was a repelling piece, but fascinating at the same time. One of four works in the exhibit done by somebody who worked under the name Pavel. I don't know if that was his real name. They were life-like and showed some unusual techniques, but the most startling thing about them was that they all portrayed individuals looking out at you with expressions of startlement bordering on terror. It was as if they had stumbled onto something catastrophic. They were scary numbers. One actually raised the down on the back of my neck. But who the hell could live with something like that staring out at you? They looked like the product of a crafts wing in the nut house."

"Do you know anything more about the painter?"

"Heard he lived in Southern California someplace. Want the name of the guy who owns them?"

"Sure, it might help."

Bancroft picked through stuff on his desk, then went into a desk drawer and finally pulled out a black binder. He paged through it. "Here it is, a guy named Bo Smythe, in Santa Barbara."

"Bo?"

Bancroft nodded. "That's it. Sounds like the sort of bird who'd buy paintings in a supermarket parking lot, doesn't it?"

"Do you have a copy of the missing piece?"

"No," said Bancroft, going through the desk drawer again. "But here's a brochure we had on the show. It has a reproduction of one of the other Pavel works that was in the exhibit."

He gave me a pamphlet on brown, grainy stock. The reproduction wasn't large, but it effectively showed a man's face looking out at you as if he'd just had the biggest scare of his life.

"Can I keep this?"

"Be my guest."

"Was the man from Coast West that you spoke to named Jerry Lind?"

"Something like that. He came around a few days after it happened. Couldn't tell him much more than I'm telling you. The snatch was on a Wednesday evening, when we're open till nine. One of the guards just noticed on his rounds that somebody had cut the thing right out of its frame. It was simple enough to do. The painting was on treated canvas."

"How big was it?"

"It was a little larger than the other Pavel pieces. About twenty by thirty inches. Showed a woman looking over a porch railing as if she'd just seen her little boy swallowed up by a hay baling machine."

The Horace Day Hospital was two blocks from the Sears store on Geary. At a little before noon I was lounging around the third floor corridor. I was in time to see the girl Laurel

54

Benson had described coming into work. She bordered on the petite, but had a brisk manner.

"Miss Westover?"

"Yes?"

I opened my wallet. "My name's Peter Bragg. Jerry Lind's secretary over at Coast West said you might be able to help me on a matter."

The small girl in white glanced around, looked in the doorway of a nearby room and motioned me in. It was unoccupied. Donna Westover closed the door and turned like a young lynx.

"What is this? Are you working for his wife?"

"No, his sister. Did you know that he's missing?"

It surprised her. "No, I didn't."

"When was the last time you saw him?"

"He was in the hospital last December."

"That isn't what I asked."

"What you asked isn't really anybody's business, is it?"

"Suppose he's lying dead somewhere, Miss Westover? Then the last few months of his life would be police business. Maybe I can keep it from going that far if people cooperate. So maybe I've learned Jerry was seeing other women. It doesn't exactly scandalize me. All I want to do is find him. Honest."

Her mouth softened a little. "What is it you want to know?"

"When was the last time you saw him?"

"Three or four weeks ago."

"Can you pin it down any closer?"

She took a wallet out of her purse and looked at a calendar. "Friday, three weeks ago."

That had been a week before Lind dropped out of sight. "What did you do?"

"We had dinner together."

"That's all?"

"That's all you're going to hear about. I'll admit that I saw him from time to time. I thought he was cute. But I don't intend to tell you anything more than that. I don't know where he is, and I don't know what happened to him."

"I'll accept that. But I'd like to know if you went to bed with him."

"You're out of your mind."

"It would help if I could learn he was apt to do that."

"You can believe he was apt to do that, or at least to try.

55

Whether or not he did with me I won't tell you. It doesn't matter now anyway."

"What makes you say that?"

"Anything we might have had between us is finished."

"You quarreled?"

"No, we didn't quarrel. He just phoned one night to tell me it was all over. He said he'd been chatting with an old art school pal about his life, and had decided to give another try to being an honest husband. That's how he put it. As if I had tainted him somehow."

"Don't let it bother you, if it still does. From what I've learned about Jerry, and what I've seen of you, I think you could do a whole lot better."

"Thanks so much. Anything else?"

"Yes. When did he phone to tell you this?"

"That one's easy. It was a Monday evening, a week after our last date."

"You're sure of that?"

"Yes. Unlike most people I try not to repress the bad in my life. I had to work the entire following week after the dinner we had together. Two other girls on the floor were out sick. Jerry and I had a dinner date for the next Tuesday evening. I was looking forward to it. But he phoned just the night before. It was the shining end to a wonderful work week."

"Did he call from in town here?"

"I wish he had. He called collect. I accepted because I figured he was stuck somewhere without change. And of course I didn't know then he was about to call off the Whole Big Thing."

"Where did he call from?"

"A town up north on the coast. A place called Barracks Cove."

From a downstairs telephone booth I made calls to Janet Lind and Marcie. So far as either of them knew, Jerry didn't know anybody living in Barracks Cove. They both wanted to ask questions of their own, but I stalled and said I'd get back to them later. I left the hospital, drove over to Park Presidio and turned north toward the bridge. It was beginning to shape up into a nice day. Donna Westover seemed pretty sure of her dates; she had good reason to be. And if she were right, she had spoken to Jerry Lind more than twenty-four hours after he'd dropped out of everybody else's life.

Fifteen minutes later I was in my Sausalito apartment, packing. It didn't take long. I figured all I needed was enough for a day or two of motel living. In the event of emergencies, I always have junk in my car trunk for living off the land. Just before snapping shut the suitcase I went to the locked desk in a work alcove off the front room and took out a couple of holstered handguns and some ammunition. There was no indication I'd need them, but if it should turn out that I did, I wanted them in my suitcase rather than in my Sausalito apartment.

There were two ways to drive to Barracks Cove. One was up the winding coast highway, and the other was to take Highway 101 north for about 150 miles, then turn onto the slow, loopy road over the coast range to the ocean. It was about a five to six hour drive either way, but I went up Highway 101 because during the early part of the journey it gave the impression you were making good time. Of course I paid for that heavily on the loopy road part of the trip. I had forgotten that there was some serious logging going on east of Barracks Cove. The government was about to take possession of several thousand more acres of prime timber land to add to a national park. The lumbering people were working day and night and weekends to harvest as many redwoods as possible before the deadline and its ensuing cutting restrictions. As a youth driving roads on the Olympic Peninsula up in the state of Washington I had learned that there are few things as humbling as seeing 80,000 pounds of truck and timber in your rear-view mirror roaring up behind you and whipping past. Those people should have their own roads. But they don't, and several of the rigs made me hunch my shoulders on my way over to Barracks Cove, just like in the old days.

It was early evening when I got there. I bought a tankful of gas and consulted a local phone directory. There was only one art supply store listed. It was called the Frame Up, and a small advertisement in the Yellow Pages said it was "On the Square." The Square turned out to be a great plot of lawn and trees in the center of town. It probably had been a parade ground back in the town's Army days. The town hall and police headquarters were at one end, and the rest was given over to a playground, picnic benches and a small rose garden. Across the surrounding streets on all four sides were the shops, restaurants and stores that marked it the hub of Barracks Cove. By now the sun had dipped behind an offshore fog bank, and a sharp breeze was blowing in from the sea. People were deserting the park as if a quiet warning had been passed. Most of the shops already were closed.

The Frame Up was on the south side of the Square. A big, plate glass window provided a nice display area to pull in passing foot traffic. It now featured a huge mural filled with caricatures of local people and places. It was a busy piece of work, almost disjointed, with funny juxtapositions and oddly shaped forms in a variety of styles. It showed the Town Square, including the Frame Up, the ocean and state park up north, skinny dippers, service stations, firemen, sexy drive-in waitresses, humorless cops, dairy farms, bars, a chugging train, souped-up cars and enough other people and things to make a person dizzy.

I went inside, tinkling an overhead bell. The shop was narrow, cramped and seemingly deserted. Things elbowed one another for space. Paintings covered the walls, hung from the ceiling and stood propped on the floor. Glass display cabinets stored charcoal, oils, pencils and blades. The propped and hanging work showed a multiplicity of styles, from delicate still life to portraits to exploding heavens. Something clattered behind a curtained doorway in the rear and a man's voice cursed.

"Hello!" it cried out. "Is there anybody out there?"

"That's right."

"Well come on back here and give me a hand, will you?"

I went back through the curtain to a disordered storage area more crammed with things than the front shop. Racks suspended from the ceiling held empty frames and wooden boards and slats. A long, sinewy fellow in his fifties wearing a smock was atop a stepladder. He leaned at a precarious angle with a large, ornate frame in one hand.

"Take this for a minute, will you? And be careful of that one on the floor beside the ladder. I just dropped the damn thing."

I took the ornate frame and retrieved the fallen one. The man on the ladder did some more business with the rack until he pulled out yet another frame. "Now, if you'll be kind enough to take this one for me."

I took it and put it aside.

"Then hand back those others."

When we were all through he climbed down and wiped his hands on his smock. "Much obliged, mister. Something's got

58

to give, there's just no more room. Either I gotta expand or else touch off the whole shebang with a match."

"You're not serious?"

"I am mightily torn," said the older fellow, carrying the frame into the front of the shop. "What with all the different media and material the art gang wants—always something different. I swear to God I spend half my time on the ladder in back and the other half on the telephone to San Francisco ordering things. My name's Wiley Huggins, by the way. Owner and proprietor."

He offered a narrow hand that had a strong grip. "Peter Bragg," I told him. "Saw in the phone book you seem to be the only art supply place around."

"That is correct. Wish to hell I had some competition. But you have to know your business, same as with anything else. Plus not have any big dream to become a millionaire. That seems to be a hard combination to find any more."

"At least it should make my job easier. I'm looking for a young fellow from San Francisco. I was hoping to find him through a friend he went to school with, living up here now. Probably an artist."

"Well there are plenty of them around. Some real, some pretending and a whole slough in between. The one who might be an artist you say, is it a man or a woman?"

"I don't know that. Here's a picture of the man I'm looking for. His name is Jerry Lind. He was supposed to have been around town here a couple of weeks ago. Maybe he came in here with his friend."

Huggins adjusted his glasses and squinted at the photo. "No, I've never seen this man."

"You're sure?"

"Yup. He bears a strong resemblance to a nephew of mine. They both have weak chins."

"His friend would probably be about the same age. Middle or late twenties. Went to school down in Southern California."

"Oh, God," said Huggins, dusting off the frame. "I don't know where they all come from, or where they're going. Half of them don't know themselves. They're a little crazy, you know, artists. And some of them, the long-haired and the unwashed, are apt to shamble around town with glazed eyes not knowing where they are right at the present."

"Is there a drug problem in town?"

"I wouldn't say that. It's mostly people passing through. There was one of those commune things a few miles back in the hills one time, but they've pretty well moved on. Still, you see somebody from time to time who looks as if that's where they'd be headed."

"Do the serious artists around town have a special gathering place?"

"They have several of them. Any bar in town. Of course you're a lucky fellow, coming through this particular night."

"Why is that?"

"There's a big bash going on out at Big Mike Parsons' place. Barbecue, picnic and drinking contest. He throws one every year. Half the town attends, though it's supposed to be mostly for the arty types. That's why my part-time help, Big Mike's wife Minnie, isn't here to help me shift things around."

"How come you're not out there?"

"I went last year. Made the mistake of overindulging. My wife wouldn't let me back in the house for two days."

"Can you give me directions?"

"Sure, I can," he said, looking about him with the frame still clenched in his hands. "But wouldn't you like to buy something first? There's no goddamn room left where I can put this sucker down."

Chapter 8

Parsons lived northeast of town in rolling, wooded country. It was a fairly remote location, back a quarter of a mile from the main road. A dirt drive climbed up and finally emptied out into a large clearing. The house behind it was a big old place with a pair of cupolas at either end and a large, stone chimney. There were more than twenty cars parked in the clearing. I pulled in beside a VW bug with one rear fender missing. The front of the house was dark, but there were crowd noises from around back. They sounded as if they'd been drinking for a couple of days. A lighted path went along one side of the place, but I was intrigued by the house itself. I went up the stairs and rang a cowbell hanging beside the door.

It took a while, but the porch light finally went on overhead. The woman who opened the door looked like the classic farmer's wife. She was a small, straight person wearing bib overalls, a plaid shirt and straw hat. Her hair was tucked up under the hat and her age was indeterminable. She had a rubber glove on one hand and squinted out at me.

"Yes? Do I know you?"

"No, Ma'am. My name is Bragg. I'm from San Francisco. Are you Mrs. Parsons?"

"Yes . . ."

She was a little wary, as if she didn't like to have strangers at the door. "I was sent out by Mr. Huggins at the art shop in town. I'm trying to find somebody living in this area. Probably a painter. He said you were having a party this evening and that I might find the person I'm looking for out here."

"You might at that. Come along in. I was just trying to straighten out some of the mess in the kitchen."

I stepped into a high-ceilinged room with sparse furnishings and a mammoth fireplace to one side. When she closed the front door the sound echoed off bare walls and something like a sigh came from the fireplace. Mrs. Parsons noticed my curiosity.

"This is a funny old house. We don't use this room much. Too damp and gusty."

I followed her into a room that looked a little more lived-in and on out into the kitchen. "Who is it you're trying to find?"

"I don't have a name. I don't even know if it's a man or a woman."

She laughed and crossed to the sink to begin rinsing off plates. "You do have yourself a problem, don't you?"

"I'm afraid so." She was a bright-eyed woman who attacked her chores with considerable energy. Her skin was browned by the sun. Her cheekbones and chin were prominent. She'd probably be fit and and doing her own housework when she was a hundred.

"Why is it you're looking for him or her?" she asked, glancing up to peer through an open window at the milling throng of people.

"It's an estate matter. If I find who I want, and they can help me in turn, it might make somebody pretty rich."

"That's nice to hear. There's so much terrible news all the time, it gives a person heart to think there's going to be some happiness." She wiped her hands on a towel and crossed to the back door. "Let's see if we can find Father for you now."

I followed her outside. We went down some stairs and onto an expanse of lawn nearly the size of the parking area in front. There were picnic tables and lawn furniture scattered here and there and burning lamps on poles stabbed into the ground. Off to one side was a large barbecue grill over a bed of charcoal, and near that a plank table being used as a bar. People were standing around talking and drinking and singing and engaging in horseplay. On a slope above, half a dozen persons were sailing Frisbees. She led me across to a cluster of older people and touched the arm of a large man with deep-set eyes and a dark beard flecked with gray. He was dressed similarly to his wife in a plaid shirt and bib overalls.

"Father, this man would like to talk to you. He came up all the way from San Francisco."

The man turned and extended a large hand. His other dwarfed a can of beer. "Howdy, I'm Mike Parsons. Big Mike, they call me." He honked a short laugh.

"Nice to meet you. My name's Peter Bragg."

"Did Minnie offer you a drink?"

"Oh goodness, Father, I didn't have time. I still have chores to do back in the kitchen."

"What'll you have?" Parsons asked, leading me over to the drinking table.

"I'll have a beer."

"How about something to eat? We got some real man-sized steaks."

"Thanks, but I had a sandwich on the road."

"Too bad. You'd have done us a favor getting outside some of the grub. These people here don't know how to eat. God a'mighty, back in Nebraska, Iowa—back there you sit down to a noon meal and can watch those old boys stoke in more than these folks eat all week."

"You're from the Midwest, Big Mike?"

"That's right, and damn glad to have it behind me, too. Help yourself in the tub there."

Beside the table was a washtub filled with water, ice and

cans of beer. I popped open one as a yell came from the direction of the Frisbee players and one of the discs plopped to the ground nearby. Parsons picked it up and with a little flick of his hand sent it sailing back to the players.

"God damndest toys—never even seen one 'til I moved to California. What was it you wanted to see me about?"

"I'm looking for a man who's been left some money, and I'm having a hard time finding him. I learned he has a friend he went to school with in Santa Barbara, probably an artist, living up here now. I don't know if it's a man or a woman, but he or she is probably in their middle twenties. I spoke to Huggins at the art store in town, and he sent me out here."

"We do have a lot of people around here in that age group. Where they come from, though, I couldn't tell you. I try not to pry, myself. Artists are a funny bunch, you know? They got all this stuff inside their heads." He made a little churning motion in the air. "Makes for some pretty creative stuff, but it can mess up their personal lives something awful. They seem determined, a lot of them, to kill themselves or get hooked up with the wrong mate or messed up with booze. I've seen it happen so often it makes me sick to heart. That's why I try to help out some, with the serious ones, you know. It's one of the reasons we ask all these folks out for a big party every now and then."

"Do you paint, Mr. Parsons?"

"Naw, hell, not really. The talent I got you could stick in your belly button. But I've always been interested in art. I've. . . ." He made another swipe at the air, as if it might help unblock the words. "I admire the people who can do that sort of thing, and I know what's going on inside them. When I see paint on canvas, even some of this modernistic stuff that don't make sense to lots of folks, well, I can see where it come from and what it is they're trying to do. God, I get the biggest kick out of it." He looked around until he found a trash carton, tossed his empty beer can in it and went to the tub for another.

"It excites me, I guess that's what I'm trying to say."

"Too bad you don't work at it yourself, feeling the way you do."

"Who knows, maybe I'll get back to it one day. Used to some when I was a kid, but then I had my own business for years, back in Omaha. It didn't leave me time for doin' much besides working my tail off from sunup to midnight or after. Come on along. I'll try to get the gang's attention for you."

He led me to the center of the yard and shouted to get the crowd quieted. When he did I told my little story, saying I was looking for a person who had gone to UC Santa Barbara four or five years earlier.

"If you're the person I'm looking for, you've got a friend who's coming into a lot of money. You'd be doing him a big favor by identifying yourself."

There was a lot of head turning, but nobody volunteered anything.

"I went to UCLA," said a young fellow in a T-shirt and Levi pants. "And I could sure use a rich friend."

"I'm pretty certain the person I'm looking for went to Santa Barbara," I called out. "Let me tell you the name of the lucky young man getting the money. He was supposed to have been in the area a couple of weeks ago. Maybe his friend introduced him to one of you. He's Jerry Lind."

Still nothing from the crowd. I turned back to Parsons. "I guess I should have known it wouldn't be this easy."

The boy from UCLA joined us, searching the crowd. "How about Allison?" he asked of nobody in particular. "She's from Southern California."

"Did she go to school in Santa Barbara?"

"I'm not sure. But I saw her around just a bit ago."

An older man nearby removed a pipe from his mouth. "I saw her and Joe Dodge talking earlier. They might have wandered off together someplace."

I looked around the edges of the crowd but didn't see any strolling couples. "Maybe I'll get lucky after all," I told Parsons. "Mind if I hang around until they return?"

"Heck, no. And help yourself to whatever you'd like. I'm going in to give Minnie a hand."

He turned and ambled back toward the house. I went over to the boy from UCLA. "Who's Allison?"

"Oh, probably about the best-looking girl in Mendocino County, is all. At least that's what most of us fellows in Mendocino County think."

"Your girl?"

"No, she doesn't go out much with guys. She's pretty dedicated. Probably turns out and sells more work than anyone else around."

"She isn't married, then."

"No, so there's always hope, we like to think, on full moon

nights and other odd moments. But now you can see for yourself. That's her and Joe coming now."

The couple approached along a path from the wooded slopes above. They were carrying on an animated conversation.

"She and Joe Dodge pretty good friends?"

"Yeah," said the boy. "Sort of like brother and sister. Or father and daughter." He pursed his lips. "And sometimes like mother and son." He shrugged. "They seem to have known each other for a couple of lifetimes."

As the two of them drew nearer, I could appreciate how the fellows in Mendocino County felt. She was a tall girl, five feet eight or nine inches, with a pretty face, full lips and a mane of blonde hair that tumbled halfway down her back. She was wearing brown Levis, but the way she carried herself made me suspect she had grand looking legs. She also wore a tan jacket hanging open over a T-shirt with the legend "Lodi Buckeyes" printed across its front. She was taller than her friend. He was an intense, narrow-featured man smoking a cigarette who walked with his eyes to the ground. His face was worn down some from living. They were within hearing distance when Joe Dodge's mouth sliced sideways in a loose smile at something the girl had said.

"I'll try," he told her, raising one hand. "But now I need a drink."

The girl slowed and watched her friend cross to the makeshift bar. She didn't seem very happy about what she saw, or maybe what she remembered.

"Allison?" called the young man from UCLA.

"Yes, Benny."

"This gent here's from San Francisco. You might be the one he's looking for. Can't say's I blame him."

The girl gave him a smile that brought up the temperature of the night air. Benny threw her a kiss and trotted up to the Frisbee toss.

"I'm Peter Bragg, Miss . . ."

"France. Allison France." She offered her hand for a firm clasp. It matched the pleasant, warm tones of her voice.

"I think Benny's in love with you, Miss France. He says you cast the same spell over most of the male population hereabouts."

"It's not really love, Mr. Bragg. It has to do with the face and the body I happened to be born with. I try not to let it interfere with my life."

65

What she said might have been true, but I could tell she spent a little time on upkeep as well.

"Benny said you wanted to see me?"

"Maybe. He said you're from Southern California."

"That's right."

"Did you go to school in Santa Barbara?"

"Yes, half-a-dozen years ago."

"And did you know a young man there named Jerry Lind?"

She hesitated, then replied calmly, "Yes."

"Did you see him here in Barracks Cove two weeks ago?"

She took a breath deep enough to bring the Lodi Buckeyes to life. "I'm afraid, Mr. Bragg, I now am going to have to fall back on that tired old phrase and ask what this is all about."

"He's missing, Miss France. His sister hired me to look for him. I'm a private investigator. I talked to a girl in San Francisco who said she got a call from him about the time he dropped out of sight. He was phoning from here on a Monday night, a full day after anybody else I've talked to had seen or heard from him. That led me, eventually, to you."

She folded her arms and rocked slowly from side to side. "You're quite sure that you're not working for Jerry's wife, Mr. Bragg?"

"No, I'm not working for his wife. When I first arrived this evening I didn't even know if Jerry's friend was a man or a woman. But I've talked to Jerry's wife. She's pretty young. A little hardened in some ways, soft in others. His being gone is starting to rattle her. My job is to find him, not to delve into any of his relationships."

"Now whoa, mister. Jerry and I are friends, period. We rap a lot. Like a number of other people I know, he just likes to chat about things. I guess I'm a pretty good listener."

"So I gathered," I told her, looking over to where Joe Dodge was smoking and drinking and gesticulating.

"Yes," she replied without emotion.

"Do you know where Jerry is now?"

"No, I don't. I thought he'd returned home."

"This girl in San Francisco is a nurse who tended him last year when he was in the hospital with a back ailment. She and Jerry struck up a friendship. She said he told her on the phone that this friend in Barracks Cove had advised him to go back to his wife and try a little harder. Was that you?"

She nodded slightly. "Yes, but it's not really the sort of

66

thing I'm comfortable talking about, Mr. Bragg. It was kind of a heavy, personal conversation. Not the sort of thing you pass along to a stranger."

"Please try not to think of me as a stranger. Try to think of me as the best friend Jerry might have right now. He had good reason not to drop out of sight. He was coming into a sizeable inheritance, and he knew it. I've gotten the impression he's the sort of boy who would like that."

She nodded in quick assent.

"So I figure he's gotten himself into some trouble. I'm not bad at my work, Miss France. I could probably help him, if only I could find him."

She thought about it for a minute. "All right. I'm ready to leave here anyway. I don't have a car. You can drive me back to town and we can have a drink somewhere, if you'd like."

"Be happy to."

"But I'll need a little solitude on the drive back, trying to remember."

"That makes sense."

"One other thing," she told me. "Do you have something showing you're who you say you are?"

I showed her the photostat and gave her a business card. She compared the license with the card, then walked over to a group of elderly persons.

"Mr. Hanson?" she addressed one of them, a balding fellow with an alert face. "This is Mr. Bragg, from San Francisco." She gave Hanson my card. "He's giving me a ride back to town, so I won't be needing a lift after all."

"I see," said Hanson, taking a good look at me. "You're the one this fellow was looking for then."

"I guess so. I'll see you all later."

She rejoined me and led me up the back stairs to the Parsons kitchen, where Minnie and Big Mike were tidying up. Allison thanked them for the party, told them the same story she'd told Hanson and asked me for another business card. She gave it to Big Mike, then we went back out and around to the parking area in front. I cleared my throat.

"I have another ten or twenty cards on me if you'd like to spread them around."

She gave me a little smile. "That won't be necessary."

"You're a pretty smart girl, aren't you?"

"You betchum."

She climbed into the car beside me. Moonlight silhouetted her figure.

"Just one thing before you lapse into your trance, Miss France."

"Yes?"

"Who the devil are the Lodi Buckeyes?"

She laughed. "I don't really know. This is just something I picked up for a dime at the Salvage Shop in town." She paused, then added, "Call me Allison, if you'd like."

"Swell. I'm Pete." I put the car in gear and headed back to town.

Chapter 9

Allison directed me to a large, stucco-walled establishment on the opposite side of the Square from the frame and art shop. It was a bar and restaurant called the Ten O'Clock.

"I do a little waitressing here from time to time," she told me. "It's owned by a lovely old gentleman called Frisco."

We sat in a corner booth, across a floor full of tables from the long bar. Several people were still eating and the bar stools were filled with noisy drinkers. The waitress took our order, a Scotch for Allison, a bourbon for me, and I looked around the place.

"It's quaint. Do you like living up here in the boonies?"

"Very much so. I come from right out of West Hollywood. It was okay when I was a kid, but you must know how Los Angeles is these days. And up here, oh, you know, the people are a little more loose and friendly, and God, the scenery. When it's sunny it's gorgeous, all the green hills and crashing waves. And when the fog rolls in it's like something out of 19th Century England. It's a great place to work."

The waitress brought our drinks and we touched glasses. "What is your work?"

"Lots of different things. On the serious side I'm still exploring with techniques, themes, color and design. I'm not sure where that's apt to take me. On the more practical side I design greeting cards, which have sold fairly well to some of the larger companies. I also do some pop art for fairs and festivals. I pretty much live off the greeting cards and art fairs. I only wish it didn't take up so much of my time, keeping me from these other things I'm trying to work out inside of myself."

"Back at the party, Benny said you're a hard worker."

"I guess I am. I have a lot of things to get done. That's one of the reasons—oh, I was thinking about it on the way into town. How maybe I should have spent a little more time with Jerry that night. He wanted to hang around longer and talk some more and things. But after three or four hours I shooed him out. I had to get up early the next morning. I was running late on a greeting card contract."

"He wanted to talk—and things?"

The girl nodded. "Yes, which surprised me a little. I guess only because it had never come up before. He wanted to spend the night, and I don't mean on the front room sofa. I wouldn't let him."

"Where did he spend the night?"

"At a motel, I suppose."

"And you only saw him that one night?"

"Yes."

I took out the photo of Lind with his wife. "Just to make sure we're speaking about the same Jerry Lind."

She looked at the photo. "Yes. Is that his wife?"

"Yeah. Marcie's her name."

"She's very pretty."

"You've never met her?"

"No, I didn't even know he'd gotten married until he mentioned it this last time I saw him. He's funny that way, though. He seems to keep his life compartmentalized. You know, a set of people he works with. A set he raps with. A set he plays with. Although maybe now the lines of demarcation are softening a little."

"Because he wanted to spend the night?"

"Yes."

"It would be hard for a boy not to try."

69

"Most boys, perhaps. But I thought my relationship with Jerry was different from that."

"With you more the mother, or older sister."

"Yes, exactly."

"Jerry seems to bring that out in a lot of the women who know him. But not in his wife. This last time you talked to Jerry, did he talk about his wife much?"

"Not really. It was almost in passing. It made me sit up straight. Here he'd been carrying on about his tenuous relationship with this nurse, then it casually came out they have a tough time making it together because of her schedule and *his* wife."

She shook her head and had some of the Scotch. "So then I started asking about his wife, a little obliquely, which usually is the best way to learn things from Jerry. He was evasive. I asked if they fought. He said no, he just wanted more out of life than her. I had the impression he felt the same way about his job, but he was too lazy to do anything about that either."

"He could afford to be, knowing he was coming into a half million dollars or more."

"That much?"

"That much for him and that much for his sister. That's one of the reasons she hired me. If something terminal should have happened to Jerry before their rich uncle died, the entire estate goes to the sister. Do you know her, by the way?"

"No. I'm aware of course that she's that person on television. She doesn't strike me as anybody I'd want to spend a lot of time around."

"That's the one. So knowing about the money in the offing could leave Jerry impatient with his job, but still willing to bide his time. But his wife seems to think Jerry likes the job."

"Maybe he does, but he isn't happy with what he's accomplished so far. He thought it would be a little more romantic."

"His wife said he tends to pump it up more than it deserves. Apparently he thinks of himself more as some cloak and dagger figure than just a clerk who gets to travel some in his job."

"He at least used to think something more could come from it. May I have another drink, please? I pretty well curbed myself at the party. It's not really fair to you, but . . ."

"Don't worry about it. It goes on the expense account. Jerry's loving sister is paying for it."

Allison beamed. "Then make it a double, please."

I ordered more drinks. Another waitress was clearing food platters off a nearby table.

"I haven't had much to eat today," I told Allison. "The food here any good?"

"Yes, but I don't know if they're still serving. I'll find out."

She left the booth and crossed to the kitchen doorway at one end of the bar. She returned a moment later, prompting all the jolly gang at the bar to spin on their stools to watch her cross the floor. Allison leaned into the booth and took a sip of her fresh drink.

"Sorry, Pete, the cook's finished for the night. And I have to go to the john. Be back in a minute."

She put down the glass and crossed to a back hallway. One of the men standing at the bar was still ogling her. He was heavy-set with a large face full of little veins. He looked like the sort of guy you love to run into in a strange bar when you're with a girl who looks as sensational as Allison. I practiced some even breathing and waited.

When Allison returned she sat and threw back her head, closing her eyes. "I'm beginning to feel relaxed."

"Weren't you relaxed at the party?"

"No. The fellow I took the stroll with, Joe Dodge, is pretty uptight. Intense. He wanted to talk, and in order to carry on a conversation with Joe, your head has to gear up to his level, which is pretty far up. And out."

"I meant to ask what his problem was."

"Please don't," she said, opening her eyes and reaching for her drink. "It's only too bad I couldn't let go out there. Big Mike really puts on a spread."

"So I noticed. What brought Jerry up here?"

"He just likes to come up and visit once or twice a year. Usually we talk about painting. He dabbles at it himself. If I'm using a different technique or something he likes to know all the details. But this last time it was more as if he wanted to talk about his relationship with this girl, the nurse. It was really quite childish. I almost felt as if I were talking to an eighteen-year-old boy, and not a very mature one at that, who was experiencing his first difficult relationship with a woman. And that was before I knew he was married, even. What makes a person do that?"

"In Jerry's case I think it was background more than

71

anything else. He and his sister were orphaned at a young age. They pretty much clung to each other after that. She's older, and obviously the stronger of the two, and since he's grown up I think Jerry still looks for that sort of relationship with his women. This is just guessing, but his wife, though young, doesn't strike me as the sort of person who would accept that. She's a strong person, but I don't think she was looking for anybody to mother just yet. Not her husband, certainly. I think it intimidated Jerry. So he's casting around for ways to experience the earlier relationship. He's in a hospital, he's nursed, and that looks promising, but the girl probably didn't want to go on playing nurse once she was off duty, and Jerry probably was just learning that."

"It sure fits in with the conversation we had, though I had no idea what was behind it."

"Like I said, I'm just guessing."

Allison was looking at something behind me. I turned around and there was redneck Charley from the bar, sort of rocking back and forth with a big grin on his face, staring at Allison as if she were what he found on the table when he came in from a hard day in the woods.

"We don't want any," I told him, turning back to Allison. "Do you know the guy?"

"I've never seen him before."

"That's good news. Maybe he's a newcomer in town himself."

"I'm sure he is."

The stranger went down the hallway leading to the johns.

"Maybe we should leave," Allison said.

"Not yet. I haven't been chased out of a barroom since I was a boy. We can go when we finish our drinks. Did Jerry talk much to you about his job?"

"Not really. He always said he was trying to build it into something more significant."

"What did he mean by that?"

"He said many times he couldn't pursue things to his own satisfaction. Just to the company's."

"What sort of things?"

"He wasn't too specific. He said the company only was interested in keeping its losses to a minimum. Once his investigations showed little possibility of recovering anything more without prohibitive expense, they would take him off what he was doing and put him on something else."

"That makes sense from a business standpoint."

"I suppose it does. But it grates on Jerry."

The beefy faced stranger returned about then and began to grate on me. He pulled up a chair to the booth and waved a five dollar bill in the air.

"Let's all have a drink," he said, looking around for a waitress. "Girl!"

"I guess you didn't hear me earlier," I told him. "We're not looking for any more company right now."

He ignored me. A waitress approached with a worried look.

"Drinks all around," the stranger said.

"No, thanks," I told the waitress. "No more drinks. And we don't care for this gentleman's company."

Over at the bar people were beginning to turn around to watch the fun. The bartender was a skinny little fellow who didn't like the looks of what he saw. I decided he wouldn't be much help.

"My name's Homer," the stranger told Allison. "It's not a pretty name, but it's got a history behind it." He laughed, and reached across to nudge her arm.

Allison shrank from him and I slid out of the booth, stepped around and yanked Homer's chair out from beneath him. He fell heavily. Across the room there was a door with an unlit exit sign over it.

"Where does that lead?"

"An alley," Allison told me. "He's awfully big, Pete."

"I know. That's why I want some room."

After a couple of surprised grunts Homer rolled over so he could get to his feet. As soon as he was up I stepped around and clamped one hand on his shirt collar and with the other jerked up the seat of his trousers so the material pinched his crotch. It makes you want to step out when somebody does that to you. Homer almost ran to the side door. I managed to get us both through it and the door slammed shut behind us. My closing the door gave Homer a chance to bust free and turn and plant himself. I was in a hurry. I didn't want to spend the rest of the night rolling around in the alley, and I didn't want all the fellows from inside to have time to gather around and watch. Homer raised his hands, either to defend or to attack, I didn't know which. I just kicked him in the groin. It brought both his head and hands down. I stepped in and clapped my palms hard against his ears. Homer screamed. I grabbed his collar again to hold him still and pumped a fist into his face several times. It wasn't all that necessary, but the marks and bruises would stay with him for a few days, and maybe he'd think twice next time, if he ever thought at all.

I let go and Homer fell to the ground like a sack of potatoes. I pulled my coat straight and tried to catch up on my breathing before I stepped back into the Ten O'Clock. Half a dozen men from the bar were just crossing to the door. When they saw me come back in they stopped and tried to scuttle back to their drinks in a nonchalant manner. It wasn't easy to do, but they gave it a good try.

I went over to the booth. "Okay, we can go now."

My breathing was still a little ragged. Allison stared at me while she finished her drink. She got up, hesitated, then turned and walked over to the alley door. She opened it and peered outside. Then she closed the door and rejoined me with a little smile. Out on the street she touched my arm.

"What did you hit him with, a telephone pole?"

"Just a secret punch I learned from the comic books when I was a kid." I opened the car door on the passenger side and held it for Allison to get in, then straightened and stared around the Square.

"Come on," she said, reading my thoughts. "There's nothing else open now. Take me home and I'll see what's in the refrigerator."

She lived in a funky old frame home on the edge of town. The front walk ran between a pair of willow trees that shielded the house from the street. Allison had difficulty opening the door.

"I think this woman's been drinking," she told me, rattling her key around the lock.

We went into a cluttered room lit by a lamp in one corner with a red shade. The place wasn't untidy or dirty, it was just very full of furniture on the floor and paintings, portraits, posters and prints on the walls.

"This is where I do my proper entertaining. The kitchen's out this way."

We went through a small dining room to the kitchen. It was large and airy compared to the other two. Allison opened the refrigerator and poked around.

"I can give you a cold roast beef sandwich with leftover potato salad. Or there's some cold chicken. Or I can heat a can of soup." She turned, blowing a whisp of hair from in front of her face. "I'd offer to fix bacon and eggs, only I'm out of bacon and I'm afraid I'd burn the eggs tonight."

74

"The roast beef and potato salad sound great."

"Coming right up," she told me, taking stuff out. "There's some Scotch in that cabinet over your head. Why don't you fix us a couple, if you can drink the stuff."

I took down a bottle of Red Label. "I can drink the stuff, but are you sure you want another?"

"You bet, mister. I don't do this very often."

I found a couple of glasses in another cupboard and got some ice. She had the sandwich made and salad scooped out by the time I had the drinks poured. I sat at a small wooden table and ate.

"This is very good, Allison. Have you ever been married?"

"Yup." She was fiddling with a radio atop the refrigerator. "For a couple of lean years. Were you?"

"How do you know I'm not now?"

"I just do."

"Well, I was once. For about ten years."

She turned her head. "That's too bad. After that long."

"I was a lot dumber than. It took a while to figure out I'd done something wrong."

The radio station she tuned in was an all-night San Francisco station that played old dance band music. She brought her drink to the table and sat across from me.

"I didn't know you could get that station up here."

"I couldn't at first. But I strung some wire and stuff on the roof, so I can get all the big city stations."

"You're handy."

"Sure. I can carpenter, too, mister. Turned an old shed out back into a studio with skylight and everything. It's the fanciest room I have now. But then I spend most of my time there, so why shouldn't it be?"

"I was wondering where you worked. Did you do any of that stuff you have hanging on the walls in the front room?"

"Nothing of note. You can look through the studio in the daylight sometime, if you're around."

"I'll make a point of it. I forgot to ask. Did Jerry say whether his trip up in this area could have had anything to do with his job?"

"No. It never has though, the other times he's been up."

"Had he been up on a weekday before?"

She thought a moment. "No, I guess that's right. It was always a weekend before." She ran one hand through her hair. "Pete, I'm tired of talking about Jerry."

"What do you want to talk about?"

75

"You. Me. Why we're here. Name it. Did you have any children?"

"No, thank God."

"Why the thank God?"

"Because my wife and I were bound eventually to split up. Having kids couldn't have changed that. And it wouldn't have been fair to them, if we'd had any." I finished the food and pushed away the plate. "Outstanding, Miss France. Truly outstanding."

"Thank you very much, Mr. Bragg. I like my gentlemen company to feel at home. The bathroom's through the other doorway, halfway down the hall on your left, if you want to wash up. And there's a new toothbrush on the upper shelf of the medicine cabinet you can use."

"You're pretty thoughtful."

"I'm pretty selfish. If I decide I want you to kiss me goodnight I want you, not roast beef and potato salad."

I went on down the hall and washed up. When I came back out, Allison was standing in a doorway across from me.

"I have one of my pop art pieces in here, if you'd like to see it."

"Sure."

She stood aside. It was her bedroom, with a large bed along the far wall. The room was lighted by some candles. The wall alongside the bed had been paneled with squares of mirrored glass.

"Over here, on the wall opposite the bed," she told me.

I stepped into the room, turned, and very nearly blushed. It was a poster size depiction of a girl's torso. At first I thought it was a blown-up photograph, but closer inspection showed that only the head was a photo, and that was of Allison herself. She had a length of straw in her mouth and was winking. The rest of the piece was a very life-like painting of a girl's body from the hips up. The figure wore an unbuttoned shirt. One hand held back a flap of the shirt revealing a round, golden breast. I tried to whistle but my lips went dry on me.

"Pretty tantalizing," I told her.

"Thanks."

I followed her back out to the kitchen.

"I sell a lot of that sort of thing at art fairs." She refreshed her drink and handed me mine.

"Do they all look like that one?"

"No. I use different poses and scraps of clothing. Maybe

76

show a bare bottom instead of a breast. And I never use my own face, as on that one."

"I'd like to meet your model sometime."

"You already have. I never found anybody's body that was any better for that sort of hush puppy than my own. I do it with mirrors and things." She put down her drink and began moving with the music. "Let's dance, mister."

I put down my own glass and she moved in close, locking her hands behind my neck. I held her lightly. After a while I held her a little closer. I didn't know if she was just particularly susceptible to the drinks, or I reminded her of her father or what. Whatever it was, we both were enjoying it.

"Any special reason for this?" I murmured.

"Nope. Just wanted to, captain. It was my idea and not yours. That's the big difference between now and when Jerry was here. After all, I'm not exactly neuter, you know."

I smiled and just let our bodies go with it. I had put in a couple of long days. I could afford to shut down the business without any guilt feelings. I hadn't expected anything like this to happen, but there it was, and that sometimes was best.

"You're my sort of dame," I told her softly.

"Why's that?"

"You wash your face. You brush your hair. You smell nice."

"Glad you like it. You're my sort of guy, too."

"Why's that?"

"You hold onto me nicely."

"I was brought up that way."

"And you're bold and tenacious."

"Now how can you know a thing like that?"

"I just do. From the way you do things. I'm going to make me a baby boy, someday. When I do, I'll want him to be bold and tenacious too."

We drifted for a few miles, and when I kissed her she responded as if she'd been waiting a while for me to do it.

"I think we should go to bed," she said finally.

I followed her back to her bedroom. She hung up her tan jacket, then turned with a little frown. "Hmmmm. There is something, after all, and I'd better tell you now before we do something to make me forget."

"To do with what?"

"You asked if Jerry's job could have had anything to do with his being up here. I do remember now," she said, lifting

77

the Lodi Buckeyes over her head, "that he said something about being on the trail of a cop."

"A cop?"

"Uh-huh, a detective, he said." She unbuckled the belt of her Levis, unzipped them and stepped quickly out of them. As I had suspected they would, her legs looked grand.

"A local cop?"

"Well now I hardly think so, Mr. Bragg. If it were one of the locals, he would have just gone down to the police station and asked for him, wouldn't he? No, it was somebody from out of town."

"But he didn't say where?"

"Nope."

She was staring me straight in the eye as she reached back to unsnap her bra and shrugged out of it. She threw it to one side and stepped up to me and began sliding the end of my belt through its buckle.

"And don't think for a minute that you're going to do anything more about it tonight, Peter Bragg. What does a girl have to do, flog you?"

Chapter 10

At a little past eight o'clock on the following misty, gray morning, I drove back to the Square in downtown Barracks Cove and turned into the parking area behind the town hall and police headquarters building. I hadn't been sure I would find anybody up and around that early, but the parking lot was crowded with cars, trucks, vans and trail vehicles. Knots of men stood talking, and people were entering and leaving the building. The town hall parking lot appeared to be the place to go on a Sunday morning in Barracks Cove.

I parked my car and went inside. The police offices were at the far end of the building. A small outer office was divided by a counter. Voices came from the room behind the counter off to the right. An elderly woman clerk in khaki uniform sat at a desk doing battle with an old typewriter. She got up and came over. I showed her my photostat and gave her a card.

"The name is Bragg. I'm from San Francisco, on a missing person case. I've traced the individual to this area. I'd like to chat for a minute with the person in charge."

"The chief himself is here this morning, Mr. Bragg, but he's terribly busy right now."

"It won't take long."

She glanced at the doorway. "Well, I'll see."

She went into the inner office. One of the voices from in there said something about telling the men outside. It half-sounded as if they were forming a posse. A minute later a rangy, middle-aged man wearing outdoor clothing came out and passed through a gate at the end of the counter. He frowned at me, as if something weren't quite right.

"You here to help?" he wanted to know.

"Not that I know of."

The man grunted and continued on out of the office. The woman clerk came back out, opened the gate and motioned me in. "The chief's in there, over in the corner," she told me.

The inner office was more spacious. It had a long wooden table with chairs around it, lockers along one wall and a rack of rifles and shotguns along another. The chief sat at a dull metal desk that looked as if it had come from a surplus store. Another woman clerk sat at a radio set across from him. The sign on the chief's desk said his name was William Morgan. He was a large man in his fifties. He looked fit despite a bulge at the belt line. He got out of his chair and came around to shake my hand.

"Bragg? I'm Morgan. Always happy to meet a fellow law officer, even if he's in business for himself. Especially today."

"Why today, especially?"

The chief sat on the corner of his desk and folded his arms. "Because I need help, that's why."

He said it in a voice that indicated I should be falling all over myself to lend a hand. Being a fellow law officer and all.

"We believe that there's a plane down somewhere in the coast range between here and Willits. Apparently it's been there since the storm of Thursday night. An old fellow who lives back up there came into town early this morning to

79

tell us he'd heard it circling around, as if it was trying to make up its mind which way to go. He said it sounded pretty low for back in there. Then he lost track of it. Friday, off and on, he heard what he thought were shouts, but they drifted down from all different directions. Sounds carry weird back in those canyon areas. The important thing is that he heard them, and decided he'd better tell somebody about it. He doesn't have a phone and it took him another day to get his old truck started. Then we had a call early this morning from the sheriff's office, saying an airline pilot headed for San Francisco reported seeing a dropping flare. He circled around some but didn't see anything more. The only problem is he figured it to be quite a distance from where the fellow who heard the plane lives. Come on over here a minute."

The chief had a way of sweeping you up in things. I followed him over to a large wall map.

"Here's where the old man heard the plane, sounding as if it finally went off up a gorge here. Over here is the general vicinity of where the flare was seen. As near as we could make out, the shouts the old man heard could have carried down from here, or over here, or even up there."

Morgan's hand covered quite a portion of the map. "Now Bragg, I try to give my men a break on weekends. I short myself, to tell you the truth, and a lot of the auxiliaries are out of town on one thing or another. The sheriff isn't in much better shape. So all we've got right now is about seventeen volunteers to search an area of several square miles. The Air Force is sending up a couple of helicopters, and I think we'll get some National Guard help, but not until later in the day."

He drew himself up and laid a hand on my shoulder. "Bragg, I need help right now, not this afternoon."

"You're asking a lot, Chief. I'm looking for a missing man. He didn't have any reason to drop out of sight voluntarily. I think he's in trouble."

"That's one man," Morgan replied. "We don't know how many might be back in those mountains, or how badly they might be hurt, or even if there are women and kids up there. After we find them, I'll help you as much as I can on this other matter."

There wasn't any sense arguing about it, if I wanted his cooperation. "Okay. I'll help out for one day. By then you should have enough of your own men back here."

"That's fair enough, and I thank you." He went back around to sit at his desk and reached for the phone. "The fellow who just left here is Bill Fairbanks. He'll be in charge. Go report to him. Maybe he can scout up something for you to wear."

"It won't be necessary."

The chief hesitated. "You're apt to get messed up wearing those duds."

"I've got some casual gear in my car. You never know what you're apt to get into when you leave the big city."

"Smart," grinned the chief. "Damn smart."

I went out and found Fairbanks.

"It turns out I'm coming along," I told him. "I have a change of clothes in my car. When are you leaving?"

"In about fifteen minutes. Do you have any friends you could bring along?"

"I'm afraid not." I went to the car and got out some scruffy pants and a shirt and jacket, along with my hiking boots and some wool socks. I went inside and changed in a men's room. Then I found a phone booth and called Allison. I explained how the chief had drafted me.

"I like that," she said. "It means you'll be around a little while longer."

"It looks that way. I thought while I was gone you might be able to do me a favor, so the day isn't a total waste. How late will you work in your studio?"

"Until this afternoon sometime. What do you need?"

"I'd like you to try to find the motel Jerry might have stayed at after he left you that Monday night."

"That sounds easy enough, we don't have too many here."

"It might be tougher than you think. There isn't any reason I can think of for him to have registered under a phony name, but with his screwy approach to his work, he just might have. I have a photo of him I'll leave here with the woman clerk at the police station. Pick it up when you're ready to start looking. Try to speak with the person at each place who was manning the check-in desk that night."

"Okay. When do you think you'll be back?"

"Tonight, sometime. I told the chief I'd give him one day of my time. I'll take you out to dinner if somebody's still open."

I went back and left the photo of Jerry Lind, then took my street clothes out to the car. Mike Parsons and another older

81

man I'd seen at his party the night before were leaning against the side of a trail vehicle. I went over to them.

"Howdy, Mr. Bragg. Lending a hand, I see."

"I guess so. How are you, Mr. Parsons?"

"Just fine, thanks. This here's Abe Whelan."

Whelan nodded, and we shook hands. He was a tall, hard-looking gent, long-boned and lean with quick-moving eyes, as if he might miss something.

"Was Allison able to help you out any?" Parsons asked.

"Not really. She was the person I was looking for, but she couldn't tell me much."

We were interrupted by a startled cry to one side. I turned. It was Homer from the alley the night before, purple welts on his face and all. He jabbed an accusing finger at me and grabbed the arm of a large, uniformed police officer he was with.

"That's him! The punk who waylaid me."

The cop moved toward me with a mean expression. I got out my wallet, opened it and held it up.

"Before you make a bad move, officer, you'd better hear what I have to say about that gentleman. I work out of San Francisco. I was conducting an investigation into a very important matter last evening over at the Ten O'Clock, questioning a witness. Simply because the witness happened to be an attractive woman, Romeo there behind you, drunk, came over and tried to move in on us. I asked him to leave a couple of times and he didn't. Instead he started annoying the witness. So I took him outside and put him to sleep."

"What did you use on him, knucks?"

"Just my hands."

"What's he saying?" Homer demanded.

I guess his ears were still ringing from the banging I gave them the night before. The cop made a motion for him to stay back, then turned to me again.

"He says you used judo or something on him. He can't hear so well. He thinks you popped an eardrum."

"I just wanted to take the fight out of him."

"Why didn't you have the bartender call us? That's what you're supposed to do in a case like that."

"Bullshit, and you know it, officer. It happens too quickly in a bar. What's the big concern on your part? Homer file a complaint?"

"He doesn't have to. He's my brother, down visiting from Eugene. That makes it my complaint."

"Sorry to hear that," I told him, putting my wallet away. "But the stuff I handle isn't penny ante. There's a man missing. He might be dead. It's that serious. Your brother was impeding my search for him by making a jackass of himself and I can dig up a dozen local witnesses to back me up. Now if you or Homer want to pursue this any further, let's go in and have a talk with Chief Morgan. I've been in to see him once this morning. If I go in again I might have a complaint of my own to make."

The officer was stopped cold and his face reflected that. It was unfortunate it had to happen in front of the people he worked and lived with. That showed on his face as well.

"All right, buddy," the cop said softly. "But it seems to me you could have done it a little differently." He turned and took his brother's arm to lead him away.

"What is it, Stan?" Homer asked. "Why didn't you lock him up?"

The men gathered around didn't have much to say. They briefly studied me with a variety of expressions. I didn't much care for the way the day had started.

"All right, men," called Fairbanks from the bed of a pickup truck. "We'll move out now and assemble at the River Run Campground. For any of you unfamiliar with the area, that's about thirty-five miles east of here on the road to Willits. That'll be our operations base. Let's go."

I got in toward the rear of the string of cars and trucks that rolled out of the lot and streamed out of town. I had to break the speed limit some to keep up. These were a serious bunch of men. I just hoped that Jerry Lind, wherever he was, or if he was, could appreciate that and hang tough a while longer. Thirty miles out of town I was passed by Homer's cop brother, Stan. Stan gave me a lingering look as he went past. I kind of wished they'd kept him behind to guard the town.

The road played tag with the Stannis River on its winding track up a canyon on the west face of Piler's Peak, the highest point for several miles in the coastal ridge formation. It wasn't a tall mountain by the standards of a boy out of the Pacific Northwest, but it was a rugged-looking, timbered area that hadn't been completely worked over by loggers. Even the areas that had were by now covered with a tough second growth. The River Run Campground was north of the highway. It was at a place where the river flattened some, making it a good fishing site. Also, it was the jump off

point for several trails leading up the mountain. The highway cut back away from the river just above and meandered
over to a draw between Piler's Peak and the next high point
down south.

The men left their vehicles and crossed to a picnic area.
Fairbanks was spreading out a large map on one of the
tables. I opened the trunk of my car to get out my day pack.
It was a bag I kept filled with first aid stuff; a flashlight,
matches, rope, Spam and chocolate, small axe and a signal-
ing mirror, a whistle, compass and anything else I figured
might save my tail some day. I decided also to take along
one of the handguns I'd put in my suitcase. It would make a
good communication device back in those canyons. I took
the lighter weapon, a Smith & Wesson .38 caliber revolver.
It was a nice little weapon called a Combat Masterpiece that
I'd picked up one time after I'd been thrown in with a group
of Marines during some very disorganized days in Korea. I
looped my binocular case over a shoulder and carried the
gear to a picnic table near where Fairbanks was going over
the map and organizing things.

By now there were about thirty of us in all. Fairbanks
said we'd all hike up to where a foot bridge crossed the
Stannis River, about a half mile above the campground.
There we'd split into two groups. One bunch would cross the
bridge so we could work up both sides of the river toward
the top of the peak. The assumption was that since it was
the highest formation in the area, it would have been most
apt to have been hit by a low-flying aircraft. I have a pal
who has his own plane, and from things he'd told me about
weather and this sort of country, I knew that Fairbank's
assumption wasn't necessarily valid. But then I wasn't in
charge of things and wouldn't have a better idea anyhow. I
did ask him if somebody had thought to notify the Civil Air
Patrol and see if they could get an air search underway. He
said they were working on it.

Fairbanks had some walkie-talkies. He left one with a
slight fellow he picked to stay at the campground to man a
larger portable radio unit that could reach police communi-
cations in Barracks Cove.

"Something else we should think about," one grizzled old
guy told Fairbanks. "If there are survivors, one of them
might be trying to make their way down from the top. Could
have gotten below us here, even. There's all them old, beat-
up logging roads that used to come out a couple miles back

84

down the highway. Maybe someone should go back in there
and do some honkin' and yellin'."

"A good idea," Fairbanks agreed, looking over the crowd.

I left them to their scratching and planning and found a
water tap where I could fill my plastic canteen. There was
another five minutes or so of discussion before they began to
move out.

"Any of you men who might be out of shape," said Fairbanks, "don't push yourself so hard we have to come and get
you out as well." He smiled briefly in my direction. "From
the looks of your outfit, mister, you might have done a little
tramping through the country."

"A little."

"Fine. Then you go with the Hawkes group across the
river. It's a little rugged. How many of the rest of you feel
up to that side?"

Several men raised their hands. I was cheered to see that
Homer's cop brother wasn't one of them.

"That's enough," said Fairbanks. "The rest will go up this
side with me. Now try to keep in touch with the radios. Any
questions?"

There were none.

"Okay. It's apt to be a long, hard day. Somebody's arrang-
ing to get some grub up here for us by late this afternoon, so
there is at least that to look forward to. Let's get going. Oh,
and Hawkes, let's leave any town troubles back in town,
huh?"

The cop grunted and I sighed. That's why he hadn't raised
his hand to join the cross-river party. He'd be leading it.

Chapter 11

Going up the initial part of the trail there wasn't much
chatter. Everybody was huffing and puffing and trying to
get their bodies into some sort of trail rhythm. When we
reached the foot bridge, Fairbanks and Hawkes conferred
for a minute before we split up. The bridge was a sturdy log
and plank affair about twenty feet long that spanned the
Stannis where it was pinched into a narrow channel by
granite outcroppings. Hawkes was leading the column, so I
hung back toward the rear with a fellow named Kennedy.
He was a man of about thirty who turned out to be the chief
of the volunteer fire department back in Barracks Cove.

"You must be familiar with the country up here," I told
him.

"Should be. My old man began dragging me up here to
hunt when I was twelve years old."

"Does the river narrow in many places like back at the
bridge?"

"Not that I know of. There's some places high up, where a
bunch of springs start to feed her, where you can get across
pretty easy."

"How is it down below?"

"Tough," Kennedy told me. "It drops pretty fast, and the
channel's deep. Water comes up to a man's ass most places. I
wouldn't try fording it myself, 'less there was a goddamn
bear after me or something."

We kept climbing. The sun was starting to break through
the morning mist. I was beginning to appreciate why Fairbanks wanted more experienced climbers on this side. The
trail got steeper. It crossed a rocky slope and led us north of
the river. There was considerable sweating and grunting on
all sides. When we reached a wooded plateau Hawkes called

a break. He tried to raise Fairbanks on one of the walkie-talkies. I took off my jacket and stuffed it into the pack. When Hawkes finished his conversation he came over to where Kennedy and I shared a log.

"Okay, Will, I think we'd better split up some more here. You take half the men and one of the radios and continue up this general route toward the top. I'll take the others further north. Whenever you reach a timber area be sure to send some people through it for a look. But don't spend too long. If there's a plane up here it's probably near the top. No sense thinking we won't have to go all the way up."

"Right," said Kennedy, getting to his feet.

"Take Panter, he's got one of the radios."

I rose and started to follow Kennedy.

"You," said Hawkes. "What's your name?"

"Bragg."

"Yeah, Bragg. You come with me. I forgot to bring binoculars." He turned and began calling out the names of the others who were to follow him. We climbed north, through a stand of redwoods, then climbed some more. The terrain alternated between bare granite shelves and stands of redwood, pine and oak, but it was all of it an upward haul. Radio transmissions were spotty. We couldn't reach Fairbanks, on the south side of the river, and by around 11 o'clock we could barely reach Kennedy.

We continued to climb and slip and mutter. I was beginning to wonder if I'd been smart to haul along all the stuff I had in the pack. It was weight I would have been happy to shed. Each time we came to a wooded area we spread out and thrashed through it. A little before noon Hawkes called another break. He tried to make contact with Kennedy without success, then he borrowed my binoculars and scanned the slopes both below us and to the north. After a couple of minutes he handed them back without a word and led us off again, up another steep stretch. It became grueling.

When we finally reached another more level slope it was more than two-thirds of the way to the top from the campground. Hawkes spread us out some more now. He sent the radio man and another guy on a southerly course to see if they could regain contact with the other parties. He told me and a man named Smith to circle further north, around a wooded stand above us, while he and the others searched through the timber itself. I had to admire him for taking part in the toughest work. There was no trail above us, just

87

tangled scrub oak and fern to slap your face, and poison oak and slippery footing to slow you down.

Smith and I hustled along. We still were on a rudimentary path of sorts, more likely a game trail, but we had a roundabout way to travel before we would join up with the others above the timber. We came to another nearly verticle granite outcropping. There was no way to get across the face of it, so we had to drop down to where we could make our way across, then climb back up beyond it. We finally came to the northernmost shoulder of Piler's Peak, where it dipped down to join with a ridge off a lower mountain to our north. We paused and I searched the nearby slopes through the binoculars. I didn't see anything special and gave the glasses to Smith.

He didn't have any better luck, but said, "I think we should try again. Up a little higher."

We started up again. The ground here was more like grazing land. We were able to climb quickly. Halfway up the flank of the thicket that Hawkes and his men were combing we stopped again. I sat to brace myself and searched the area below and across from us. For the first time I saw something to make me grunt.

"What is it?" Smith asked.

I handed him the binoculars. "Take a look at that little bald spot on the far ridge, about four hundred yards north."

Smith did as I told him. "Those rocks?"

"Yeah."

"Think they mean something?"

"Maybe."

There was a sharp whistle above us. Hawkes stood in the open above the thicket, motioning us up. I pointed north, then gestured for him to join us. He shouted to somebody in his party then came down the slope at a trot.

"What's up?"

I gave him the binoculars. "Take a look at the bald patch on the far ridge."

Hawkes studied it. "I see a couple of rocks."

"Right. They're close enough so somebody might have left them as a marker. If there were a third one stacked on top of one of them we'd know for sure. Was it windy the night of the storm?"

"Sure was," said Smith.

"Maybe another rock was knocked off by a falling branch from one of those nearby pine trees. Or maybe they were disturbed by an animal. I think Smith and I should go on over for a closeup look. If it seems they were put there as a marker we could go on downhill to see if we can find anybody."

Hawkes stared at the far slope with his lips pinched, then turned and looked back up at the top of Piler's Peak. "Can't do it," he said. "Don't have enough men now to cover where we should as soon as we should." He turned back to me. "You go if you want. It's worth that. I'd like for you to leave your binoculars with me, though."

"Sure. What's the land like down below there?"

"I've never been into it," Hawkes said.

"I was down there once," said Smith. "It's not easy country, in places. Pretty thick, and there aren't any roads this side of the river. There's supposed to be another stream on over north somewhere. I tried getting to it once to check out the fishing, but I finally gave it up."

"How did you go in?"

"From the campground, across the footbridge. I think it would be difficult crossing the river anywhere else."

"Okay, I'll see what I can find."

"We'll wait on up above here," Hawkes said. "After you've had a look at those rocks give me some kind of signal to let me know if you're going on down or coming back."

"Right. I have a revolver in my pack. If I do go on down and find anybody and they need help, I'll fire a couple of rounds."

Hawkes nodded and he and Smith started up the slope. I trotted on down the ridge, then climbed up the far one. I got to the patch of ground and looked around. There weren't any fallen branches nearby, but there was a third rock by a nearby tuft of field grass, along with some deep V clefts that had been made by deer. The ground beneath the two stones seemed to have the same texture as surrounding earth. I wasn't enough of an outdoorsman to say for sure that the rocks had been placed that way since the storm of Thursday night, but my instincts told me they had.

I stood and waved across to Hawkes, then turned and gestured west, down the slope. Hawkes gave a brief wave of acknowledgment and turned back to resume his search. I started on down with the assumption that if somebody had indeed put the stones down as a marker, they weren't familiar with the country any more than I was. On that basis I figured they'd always head for the clearest looking areas, assuming it would be easier country to travel through, and hoping to cut a road or trail. It wasn't difficult to pick my own way using those assumptions. The route of least resistance was in a generally northwest direction, unfortunately, leading a person further from Piler's Peak and the main highway.

From open slopes I entered a timbered stretch that ended abruptly at a cliff face dropping a hundred feet or more. It seemed less steep further north. I went that way and scanned the country below. A piece of yellow color on a tree branch below caught my attention. I made my way down to it. It was a strip of nylon material that somebody had tied onto the branch. I continued on in the same general northwesterly direction. Two hundred feet further I found another strip of the yellow nylon. Whoever had tied them was unwittingly traveling in a direction that put another spur of the ridge between himself and the river canyon road. I paused long enough to dig the revolver out of my pack and attach its holster to my belt. I fired off a round and called out. A light breeze fluttered the tall grass on the spur to my left and the birds quit singing, but there was no replying shout. I continued on down at a trot. I could see where the wayward traveler would be going, below and still further to the north. It was the way the land led you to the thinnest part of the next wooded area crossing the entire breadth of the slope below. At the edge of the woods I paused to catch my breath and study the area ahead. The land dipped sharply to my right and climbed on the left. I went into the woods searching for more colored markers, but there were none. It was getting thicker, but now I heard running water, up north. It must have been the stream Smith said he'd searched for one time. The crash survivor, if that was whose trail I was on, probably would have made for the stream, figuring it would lead him down off the mountain.

When I reached the water, the land below, on my side of the stream, appeared nearly impenetrable. It looked to be easier going on the far side, so I rolled up my pants and spashed on across, not bothering to take off my boots. It was cold enough to make your blood back up. On the other side I just kept going down, trotting where the land allowed it. The stream entered a defile and dropped abruptly for thirty feet. I kept on north to where the land was gradual enough so I could scramble down to a clearing below. I stepped and slid my way down, and once I reached level ground I stood to brush off the seat of my pants and the bottom of the knapsack, then started back toward the stream. That's when I saw that the first part of the day's work was done. On the ground near the splashing water was what looked like a huddled midget.

When I called out the figure sat up with a start and turned in my direction. It was a freckle-skinned youngster of about twelve with tufted red hair, bruised face and suspicious eyes. I went over to him and dropped my pack.

"How you doing, pal?"

"Geeez, guy, you scared me."

"Sorry, didn't mean to." He only had one shoe on. He'd removed the one from his right foot, and the foot was tucked at a curious angle. "Something wrong with that ankle?"

"Sure is. I think it's busted. I twisted it pretty bad when my dad's plane came down the other night. Up above. Then when I was coming down that cliff over there I lost my footing and fell wrong on it. Was all I could do to drag myself over to the dumb stream here. Hurt like the dickens. Then last night I tried to move when I thought I heard a bear shuffling around out there. I found out fast I wasn't going to move any."

"What did you do about the bear?"

"I growled at it, what else could I do? After a while it went away."

"How are you otherwise? Do you hurt inside any?"

"Nope. Got a lot of bruises. And I banged my head when we hit down. Other than that I'm okay."

"That's good. What's your name?"

"Roland Xavier Dempsey. But everyone calls me Tuffy."

"Why's that?"

The kid shrugged. "Beats me."

"Okay, Tuffy. My name's Pete. There are other men up above looking for your dad's plane. You crashed three nights ago?"

"Yeah. He told me to stay near the plane all day Friday. He said somebody might fly over and see us. But it didn't work out. So yesterday I just decided I was going to get down off this mountain."

"What sort of shape is your dad in?"

"He's hurtin' some. Pinned in the wreckage. We hit some trees that folded the wings back alongside us. Dad said it was a good thing, that they helped cushion us from the rest of the banging around we did. He keeps passing out. But I found water up there, and the plane's first aid kit had some

91

pain pills. He's doing all right, or he was when I left him. Of course, since I fell and hurt myself yesterday I've spent some time wondering what was going to come of us. Him up there and me down here and both of us out of action. Where'd you come from?"

"I was with a search party looking for the plane. I spotted some rocks I guess you left as a marker way up above."

He nodded. "Dad gave me a couple tips before I left the plane. Did you see the yellow streamers, too?"

"I sure did. Where did you get them?"

"Dad carries some on the plane. He says you never know. He's pretty cautious, my dad is."

"Good thing. And apparently one of you shot off a flare last night that was seen by an airliner."

"That must have been Dad. I guess he's still okay, then."

"You hungry, Tuffy?"

"Yeah, sort of. I had a sandwich I brought along, but I ate that last night. You got something?"

"It just so happens." I got out and opened the tin of Spam and left it with him along with my knife while I took a small, lightweight axe I carry and prowled the area until I found an old branch about four inches in diameter. From that I fashioned a crude pair of paddles to serve as splints to keep the boy's ankle from moving sideways. I trussed him up the best I could. Whenever I hurt him he let me know about it.

"Was anybody on the plane besides you and your dad?"

"Nope."

"Where you from?"

"We were on our way down from Seattle."

"Hey, no kidding? That's where I grew up."

"Yeah? When was that?"

"Oh, I left there before they built the Space Needle."

"Wow. You are an old timer."

"Sometimes I feel it more than others." I got him to his feet and helped him hobble across to a nearby log. In addition to the broken right ankle it turned out he had a bad left knee. I told him to try exercising the knee while I hunted around the area until I found a notched limb I could hack into a crutch for him.

"Where were you headed for, Tuffy?"

"Mendocino, originally, but there was too much weather around there, so we made a dogleg east and planned to land at Willits. We were trying to make our way up a valley but

92

it was a mess. There was rain and fog and all of a sudden this big old ridge loomed up ahead of us. Dad tried to get over it but we stalled out. And the next thing you know we were knocking through the trees."

"Sounds to me as if you were pretty lucky."

"That's what Dad said. When he became conscious."

"Did your dad have the plane's transponder on?"

"Yeah, but he figured we were too low for the signal to be picked up."

"Where is the plane from where you put the rock marker up above?"

"North."

"Are you sure?"

"Yup. Quite a ways. Four or five miles, at least. Dad said to hike south, but to try staying in the open so I could try to signal any planes going over. So I just stayed near the top of the ridge. There wasn't much timber along the crest. But then I finally decided, shoot, there weren't any planes looking for us, and I started on down. I put up the rocks after I'd come quite a ways from the plane."

That meant Hawkes and Fairbanks were far south of the crash site, and the helicopters probably would start their search way off base as well.

"Okay, Tuffy, stick this in your armpit and see how you can manage." I propped the crutch under his arm and tried to steady him as he moved slowly around the clearing. He hobbled a half dozen yards before his left knee buckled and he slipped out of my grasp and fell again.

"Geeez, guy, that isn't going to work," he said, rubbing at his sore knee.

"It looks that way. How much do you weigh, Tuffy?"

"About a hundred pounds when I empty my pockets." He cocked his head and looked up at me. "Why you asking?"

"It's beginning to look as if I'll have to carry you out of here."

"You're kidding."

"I'm afraid not. Besides, I'm the one who'll be doing all the work. What's your bellyache?"

"Nothing personal. You just don't look up to it." He rubbed one hand on his pants and looked away. "I think you should go on ahead. Get somebody up to my dad."

"We'll get somebody up to your dad. And let me worry about whether or not I'm up to it. You want to spend another night here with the bears?"

"No, sir."

"Then don't be so critical."

"I was just trying to help."

"Thanks."

"Which way you planning to go?"

"Well I'm sure not going to try lugging you back up the way we both came down. That would take us a month or two. We'll just have to keep on going until we come to a trail or a house or the Pacific Ocean, if it takes that."

He stared at me a moment then heaved a very adult sigh. I realized I wouldn't be able to carry much more than this hundred pounds of smart talk. I took the coil of rope out of my pack and looped it around my middle. I put the compass and some chocolate bars into one pocket, an extra box of shells for the revolver into another and stuffed everything else back into the bag. I climbed a nearby tree to hang it out of the reach of bears and other curious creatures.

"Thirsty, Tuffy?"

"Nope. I been drinking out of the stream all night and most of the day. It gets boring just lying around."

The kid had spunk bordering on insolence. It took a while to get him up in piggyback position so that his ankle was comfortable, then I started down through the woods beside the stream until I came to a handy place to splash back across it.

"Hey, guy, how come you did that?"

"Did what?"

"Go through the water like that."

"Because the only highway I know about is over in this direction."

"I mean without taking off your boots and socks."

"They'll dry soon enough. It's warmer to keep them on my feet."

"My mom blistered me once for going through puddles on my way home from school. She said I could catch pneumonia that way."

"Mothers have been known to pass along a lot of punk information. Now shut up and let me save my breath."

Chapter 12

We broke through into sweeping grassland that extended down for a half mile or more. Beyond that was more timber. I couldn't tell from above how thick it was and I didn't see anything that looked like a trail or a house or the Pacific Ocean.

"Don't joggle so much," Tuffy said about ten minutes later.

"I'm doing the best I can."

"When you joggle it hurts. I think you almost made me faint back there."

"Might be a good idea if you did."

"Funny."

We kept on going. The woods below the grassland weren't too thick, and the configuration of the land took a reversal of what we'd been through earlier. We dropped down a funnel of partially cleared slope bearing to the southwest, toward the Stannis River and the highway. It heartened me some. About every twenty minutes now I had to take a rest break. The kid was smart enough to leave me alone during the first couple of breaks, letting me catch my breath. But I didn't spend long I was afraid I'd stiffen up so badly somebody else would have to come in and carry out the both of us.

At a later rest stop he started to complain about the ankle. I tried to repack the splints a little more snugly, but he continued to moan. I think he just wanted somebody to talk to. I wasn't in the mood. The day so far had been a hard one, and the rest of it didn't promise to be all that much better. I gave him a chocolate bar and told him to practice being stoic, like an Indian.

We went through another wooded area, this one thicker.

It slowed us down and took more out of me. I was beginning to hurt in several places myself. We finally broke out into the clear again, into a flat meadow that made the going comparatively easy. I tried to put the aches and pains out of my mind and concentrated on covering distance. I hit a stride that grew comfortable and was moving nicely for a few minutes before I heard from my partner.

"You're joggling."

"We're making good time. Think about something else."

We were nearly across the meadow when he began to mark cadence to my steps in a small voice directly behind my right ear.

"Ow, ow, ow, ow, ow, ow . . ."

"Oh, for God's sake." I set him down against a tree stump and arched my back for a couple of minutes before settling down nearby.

"How far you think we've come?"

"I think I've come about a hundred miles since I started out this morning. I don't know how far I've lugged you. Three, four miles maybe."

He grunted and lapsed back into blessed silence. Briefly.

"Pete?"

I opened my eyes and stared across at him. It was the first time he'd called me something besides "guy" or "you." "What?"

He was staring over his shoulder, into the trees and brush bordering the meadow. "Ever had the feeling you were being watched?"

I sat up and took a look around. "I guess I have. There are all sorts of creatures in this kind of country. They're curious and wary when strangers come through."

"That's not what I meant. How much further you figure we got to go?"

"I don't know. Maybe as far as we've come 'til now. Maybe more. Heading toward the coast doesn't seem to be the answer. I think we have to find the Stannis River and a way to cross it, then just keep going until we find the road beyond."

He still was searching the country around us with a frown on his young face. "Let's get out of here. I won't complain any more. I promise."

I hoisted him up and we started off. True to his word he kept his mouth shut. "You really were nervous back there, weren't you?"

"Yes."

"How come?"

"I don't know. I just was. One minute it was okay, and the next—I had this thing *growing* between my shoulder blades."

There were two things I was willing to concede kids were good for. One was their power of observation. They haven't put in enough years to muddle up their memory, so what they do observe and experience is etched pretty sharply on their minds. A deputy sheriff who patrolled an island out in Puget Sound had told me about that years ago, and I'd put it to good use on several occasions since.

The other was what Tuffy had just displayed, or might have. It's something bordering on the extrasensory, a sensitivity beyond what most of us can muster when we get older. I'd had something like it myself when I was a youngster. Maybe as with the power of observation it was just a marshaling of concentration you're capable of before life's distractions and dirty tricks set in. Whatever it was, I'd lost it over the years, but it had been real enough then so that I couldn't bring myself to dismiss it out of hand when somebody Tuffy's age professed to feel something I couldn't. Thinking about it made me pause at the edge of the meadow and take a slow turn and look around the countryside.

"You feel it too?"

"No, pal, the only thing growing between my shoulder blades is you. I'm just trying to get my bearings."

Besides the woods on both sides, there was high country stretching both north and south of us. Somebody could have been watching us, through a scope maybe, far enough away so a shout wouldn't carry. Maybe they wouldn't even realize we needed help. Maybe they saw guys stalking through the meadow lugging young people on their backs every day of the year. I eased Tuffy down and stepped a few paces away, unholstered the revolver and fired three times into the air. I waited until the ringing in my ears subsided and scanned the high country on both sides, but saw nothing, heard nothing. I wished I had my binoculars.

Tuffy didn't say anything. He just watched gravely, then pulled himself back up onto me when I hunched down nearby, and we set off once more. One thing the look around did for me was to find a game trail meandering through the meadow grass about twenty yards off and parallel to our own course. I followed it the rest of the way out of the meadow, through a grove of trees and down a thatchy area bearing to our left. There was a steady throb in the lower part of my back now. It would take a couple of days for that to go away when we were finished with all this. I plodded on, my passenger thankfully mute.

A half hour later I heard what had to be the Stannis River. The game trail led us right to it. I helped Tuffy down near the water's edge, then stretched out flat, wishing the aches would go away. A couple of minutes later I rolled over and splashed my face with river water, then split another chocolate bar with Tuffy. He munched with serious eyes.

"What's the matter? You still spooked about something?"

He avoided my eyes and didn't say anything. If something did still bother him, he wasn't going to admit it.

"I'm going to have to leave you for a while now, sport. I have to find a place where we can cross the river."

The boy stared dubiously at the swift, white water.

"I know, I know. The men I was with earlier said it might be a tough job. But over there is where the highway is. Over there is where we can find somebody to get help to your dad. So over there, damn it, is where we're going. Okay?"

"I guess."

He finished the candy and wiped his hands on his pants. I bet myself he was a little dear to have around the house. I got up and started off down river.

"Pete?" he called. "Couldn't we stick together?"

I went back to where he sat. "I haven't got that much stuff left inside me, Tuffy. You still a little frightened?" He didn't answer. "I mean, it's okay to be spooked, pal. God knows it's happened to me enough times. And you've had a rough couple of days. Rougher, I'll bet, than any of the guys you pal around with back home ever had. Are you still feeling the way you did just before we left the meadow back there?"

He shook his head, more in frustration than denial, I felt. "Something's just funny."

I squatted down beside him and took the revolver out of the holster again. "Ever fired a handgun, Tuffy?"

His eyes grew some and the day took on a whole new dimension for him. "No, sir, I never have."

"Well, you are about to. I'm going to leave it with you. Sometimes it makes you feel a little better when you're in strange territory. But first you've got to learn a couple things."

I gave him a little lecture about how the weapon operated and some dos and don'ts, then helped him get his good knee tucked up to use as a platform. I showed him a sturdy,

98

two-hand grip and told him to cock the hammer so the cylinder would revolve before he fired.

"You could just pull the trigger, and the cylinder would turn during the backstroke of the hammer," I told him. "But if you cock it first and get that mechanical work out of the way it gives you a better chance of hitting what you aim at. Now see if you can put a slug into that tree over there."

He fired. The gun bucked back in his hands, the bullet went singing through overhead branches and he showed his keen disappointment and surprise.

"That wasn't where I was aiming."

"And that's what recoil is all about," I told him, reloading the weapon. "The explosive force moves in both directions, pushing the slug down the barrel and at the same time jamming the gun back into the palm of your hand. So you either hold the gun firmly, keeping your wrists locked, or you compensate by aiming lower than you want to hit, or you do both. Now try it again."

He fired twice more and the second slug went into the tree trunk waist high. "You're a marskman already," I told him. "Now don't play around with it. Just keep it there beside you and don't worry about things. I'll be back here in a half hour or so."

I left him with his thoughts and thrashed on down river. About 200 yards below where I'd left the boy I found a place I figured might work. The river narrowed to rush with a torrent through granite formations on either side. It was about a dozen paces across. Beyond the granite the water plunged eight or ten feet downward then appeared to widen again on its swift flow to the sea. I waded in and managed to get myself across, but it wasn't all that encouraging. Footing wasn't so good, and in places the channel dipped, so that I had water between my knees and my hips. I couldn't have done it if I'd had the boy on my back. I tried to get some idea of what the river looked like beyond the brief falls, but couldn't do it. There were sturdy enough looking elm trees on both banks, behind the granite outcroppings, so I could rig a safety line with the rope coiled around my middle, but it still would be risky. On the other hand, I couldn't spend the rest of the afternoon looking for a better crossing. There was more ground to cover, and there still was the boy's father, injured, on the ridgeline somewhere above us. And also, there was Jerry Lind, someplace.

I uncoiled the rope and looped it around one of the elms

and knotted it snugly. I started back across the river, letting out line as I went, then abruptly stepped into a hole I hadn't encountered on my way across. I went partly down, thrashing to keep my balance. It surprised me badly and the coil of rope got away from me. I struggled back upright and watched as the line went over the falls like the uncoiling of a teamster's whip. I said a few words I used to admit to having uttered as a boy back in the days when I went into the confessional. I made my way back to the southern side of the river where I'd fastened the line and pulled it back up from below the falls. I was soaked through up nearly to my chest, but I was more angry than uncomfortable. When I had the rope recoiled I set out again, this time managing to avoid the treacherous pocket I'd slipped into before. I made the other side and fastened the rest of the line around another tree as best I could. I wasn't able to get it as taut as I would have liked, but felt it would do if I didn't encounter any more surprises. There was thick overhead foliage at that part of the river. It imparted a sense of damp gloom. I didn't like the place at all, and would be happy to be away from it.

I made my way back up to Tuffy. Nothing had come charging out of the woods at him while I was gone, so I reholstered the weapon, told him the game plan and carried him on down to the rope. He noticed my wet clothes but didn't say anything. He did say something when he saw the rope.

"What's that for?"

"That's to help me keep my feet when we go across there."

"Across there?"

"Yes. We can do it. I've already been across there, obviously, to tie the rope. But you've got to help me by keeping still and letting me concentrate. You ever watch football on television?"

"Sure."

"Well, you know how those guys run out and make those impossible catches knowing as soon as they touch the ball some gorilla is going to smack them, but they still manage to catch the ball?"

"I've seen it."

"That's all a matter of concentration. You've got to let me concentrate the two of us across here and catch the ball."

His grip around my chest tightened. I shifted him higher on my back and wormed my hands around until I had a good hold on the line. It would take away from my balance some and I started to have second thoughts, but I made myself plunge on in before I froze up completely. I felt the boy was only good for one attempt at this.

It was much harder going with the extra weight. We sagged heavily on the rope. The swift current pushed us closer to the falls than it had when I crossed by myself. At least it was away from the pocket I'd stumbled into. Near the middle of the channel the water was rushing over Tuffy's ankles. I could feel him tense up. I took another step, sagged onto the rope, then another step. I paused and took a deep breath. Then another step. We didn't seem to be getting anywhere. I figured it would be sometime the next afternoon before we got out of the water. I chugged along, my legs moving in slow motion.

And then we were rising above it. The river bed climbed toward the shore. The water still tugged at my knees. I gripped the rope awkwardly and pulled like a doryman as I slogged toward the high ground. That's when the rope broke.

We pitched backward into deep water, Tuffy with a whoop and his arms flailing, me with a nosefull of river water. We couldn't hang onto each other and went over the falls with a lot of yelling and cursing. I banged a leg sharply against a rock below the falls before being swept on downstream. Tuffy was ahead of me, thrashing with both arms. I tried to get to my feet but couldn't. The water wasn't deep enough here to be over my head but it moved with a strong flow. I hit my head on something and probably would have passed out if the freezing water hadn't already put my nervous system into semi-shock. Thirty yards or so further we came to a narrow sandbar in midstream. Tuffy managed to scuttle with his good leg close enough to it to brake himself. I followed and paused there just long enough to spit water and take a couple of breaths. From the bar to the far shore was a comparatively easy journey. Not too far and not too deep. I wish I'd seen that before I tried the rope trick up above. I didn't bother with the piggyback business, but just scooped the boy up and waded on across. We rested by the bank, squeezing out our clothes and gathering strength. I figured the kid had a dozen or so smart remarks to make, but he kindly kept them to himself.

"What happened back there?" was all he said.

"I honestly don't know. The rope gave out. It shouldn't have."

The boy shuddered. I shared the sentiment, got him up on

101

my back again and started away from the river. A half hour later we broke into a cleared hillside that overlooked the highway. Tuffy grunted when he saw it. I was too close to ending it and too dead tired to respond. I just plunged on down with the boy swaying on my back. A couple of autos came around the lower curve and climbed away from us, but we weren't at an angle where they'd be apt to see us. When we reached the road I let the boy down gently and stood there, hands on my hips, blowing like an old horse. I felt exactly like an old horse.

"I hope somebody stops," said Tuffy.

"The first car will stop," I assured him.

It was another six or seven minutes before another auto came around the curve below us. I stepped out into the middle of the road and flagged it to a stop. Inside were an elderly couple who didn't like the bedraggled looks of us. I told them my story and asked for a lift. They were frightened and didn't want to help.

"How do I know it isn't just a trick to get my car?" asked the old gentleman through a narrow crack above the window. "And I see you got a gun on your hip there, too."

Another auto pulled up and stopped behind us. I turned. It was a county sheriff's car. I stepped back.

"It's okay. The deputy will help."

The first car took off with a lurch and a great belch of exhaust.

"What's going on?" demanded the lanky man climbing out of the patrol car. He wasn't in uniform, but wore trail clothes and boots.

"Hear about the plane crash?" I asked.

"Yeah. Got called in. I'm on my way up to Running River Campground now to join the search."

So we'd dropped below the campground. No wonder I felt like something left behind on the battlefield. "I've got one of the survivors over here," I told him, indicating the boy.

"I'll be God damned," said the deputy. "Where did you come from?"

I sighed and looped a hand toward the mountain. "Way up there."

"I'm Deputy Morris," he told me, reaching inside to turn on the flasher atop his patrol car. "You're not from around here."

"No, but I was helping in the search. The boy has a

102

broken ankle and a wrenched knee. He could use a lift to Barracks Cove."

"We'll get help faster taking him up to the campground. There are 'copters in the area that can pick him up and take him to the hospital in Willits. You mean to say you *carried* him down?"

"I sure did. And he grew some on the way." We went over and lugged Tuffy to the patrol car. "Maybe you could get on the radio. Get word to the search parties. The boy's dad is pinned in the wreckage and needs help. It's about five miles north of where everybody's looking. Maybe one of the helicopters can ferry a party over there."

After we settled Tuffy in the rear of the car, Morris got in and tried to radio, but we were in a pocket where his signal wouldn't carry. I got in on the passenger side and we drove on up the highway to where the deputy could relay a message.

"Don't worry, son," Morris told Tuffy. "They'll find your pa in no time, now."

I stretched back and closed my eyes.

"That must have been some hike, mister."

"It was. The name's Bragg."

We rode in silence for a moment. "If you don't mind my asking, Bragg, how come you're armed?"

"I'm a private cop from San Francisco. I was working on a case when I got drafted into the search party. Figured I could signal with it if I found anything. Only by the time I came on the boy I was too far from the other searchers."

Tuffy sat up in back. "You're a private eye?"

I groaned inwardly. "I guess some people still call it that."

"Huh," said the boy. "Maybe Dad should have hired you and saved us all a lot of trouble."

"How do you mean?"

"The reason my dad and me were flying down here was to look for Uncle Bob. He's a detective down in Southern California. We were going to spend the weekend trying to find him."

My eyes opened and I stared at the roof of the patrol car.

"Uncle Bob disappeared a couple weeks ago. The last we heard from him, he was in a place called Barracks Cove."

I sat up straight and turned in the seat. "Tell me about your Uncle Bob, Tuffy."

Chapter 13

Detective Robert Dempsey, according to Tuffy, had spent more than ten years in the Los Angeles Police Department, winning citations, earning promotions and growing an ulcer. He had left, finally, to take a job as chief of detectives in Rey Platte, a wealthy retirement town inland from Santa Barbara, where the pace was slower and the work was easier on a cop's stomach. Tuffy's dad had celebrated a birthday on the Friday before Jerry Lind dropped out of sight, and his brother the cop had phoned him greetings that evening from Barracks Cove. During the conversation, Bob Dempsey had said that he was in Northern California on a special investigation. They learned later that Dempsey had phoned his wife in Rey Platte that same evening. It was the last anybody had heard from him.

In subsequent queries to the Rey Platte police, Tuffy's father, Steven Dempsey, learned that whatever it was his brother had been doing in Barracks Cove, it apparently wasn't connected with current duties in Rey Platte. He was on leave, and had made arrangements to be gone for as long as a month. The department wasn't worried about him particularly, but his wife was. And by now his brother was worried too. Worried enough to fly down from Seattle to look for him.

I doubted that there would have been an army of out-of-town police marching through Barracks Cove on a given day, so I had to assume that Dempsey was the cop Allison had told me about. The one that Jerry Lind, for whatever cockeyed reason, had been on the trail of. I wondered how Jerry Lind would have known where Dempsey was. I also had to wonder, with an unpleasant feeling, what might have

104

happened to a pussycat like Jerry Lind if a veteran police detective like Dempsey had disappeared in the same area.

By the time we reached the campground I was not only sore and exhausted, but worried as hell. I made some telephone calls from the ranger station there. I learned that Mendocino airport, closer to Barracks Cove, was fogged in again. I also learned an intrastate airline made a daily stop at the field in Willits, but not on Sundays, so I phoned down to San Francisco and made arrangements to be picked up in Willits by an outfit calling itself Golden Gate Sky Charter that would fly you anywhere twenty-four hours a day so long as your credit was good. They were based at San Francisco International and I'd used them before. They knew my credit was good, so by the time I'd driven from the campground over to Willits, there was a charter plane waiting for me. They were a reliable outfit, but I grumped a lot over their prices. When we landed at Rey Platte I told the pilot to wait for me. He gave me a slow, rich smile. They charge a lot more than a waiting taxicab does.

After I explained my business the local police gave me the home telephone number of their chief. I called him and he agreed to meet me back at his office at eight o'clock that evening. It just gave me time to get a sandwich and beer at a downtown lunch counter. It occurred to me that for a man on an expense account I hadn't been eating all that well the past couple of days.

The Rey Platte police chief was named Charles Porter. In his office at a little past eight he gave the appearance of a man captured by his desk. He was slow moving, slow talking and overweight, losing his hair and increasing his chins. He sat in a squeaky chair and didn't rise when I was ushered in, but he did lean across the desk to offer his hand.

"So you're the one who found Bob Dempsey's nephew."

It surprised me. "That's right, Chief, but how did you know?"

"A while after you called, I had a phone call from Chief Morgan in Barracks Cove. He said you might be on your way down and asked me to help you any way I could. He said he hadn't been able to give you much assistance so far, but that you were the hero of the day up there. How's Bob's brother?"

"Still alive, anyhow. The last I heard they'd put him on a helicopter and were flying him to a hospital."

"That's something. Now, what can I do for you?"

"I've been hired to find a young insurance investigator from San Francisco who disappeared a couple of weeks ago. I trailed him to Barracks Cove and spoke to a woman there who knew him and had seen him after he left San Francisco. She said he'd been trying to find an out-of-town police officer in the area. Then, this afternoon while I was up on the mountain, the woman was checking motels in the Barracks Cove area for me, trying to find where the missing insurance investigator, a man named Lind, might have stayed.

"I talked to her again just before catching a plane down here. She didn't learn where Lind had stayed, but she did find out he'd stopped by several of those same motels asking if they had a record of this out-of-town cop. By then I'd learned that Dempsey was missing, so I telephoned some of these motels myself, and the manager of one of them has in-laws named Dempsey, so he remembered the name. And it was the name of the officer Lind had been asking about."

"So you figure that your man's disappearance is linked to Dempsey?"

"That's right. I take it that you and Dempsey's wife still haven't heard from him?"

"That's true. But I've tried to tell Coral, that's his wife, that it's too early yet to start worrying about him. I expect Bob to surface in time."

"What makes you so sure?"

"Because he's the best man at his work I've ever run into, here or anywhere else. He's big and hard and smart. He's an able detective. He's worked on some big cases. Both here and in Los Angeles. But he has his own way of doing things. After events get to a certain stage he likes to operate with a degree of secrecy. I guess it was a hard-won lesson from having to contend with departmental leaks early in his career. And I think another reason is that he's a politically ambitious man."

"Did the two of you ever talk about that?"

"No, but the last time he telephoned Coral, I guess it was the call from Barracks Cove, he told her things were going well enough so's he'd end up the next sheriff of the county."

"What could he have been working on that was that big?"

"I'm just not sure, and I've been giving it some thought, too. Of course it could be something from his days with the LAPD, but if he's got eyes to be sheriff around here, I don't know how something from back then could help him much.

There was one thing of the past to come up recently, but Bob didn't seem all that excited about it at the time."

"I'd like to hear about it."

"Well, about five years ago we had a rather spectacular bank robbery just down the street. At the Rey Platte Union Bank. We never knew if it was planned or if the robbers—there were three of them—just hit it lucky that day. Anyway, they struck around eleven in the morning, just as the Corrigan Security armored car was delivering a big cash shipment from Santa Barbara. Back then we had an electronics firm right here in town that had started out thirty-five years ago as a fix-it shop. Mathews was the man who started it. One of his boys went away to the war in Europe and worked on radar equipment. When he came home he went back to school and the next thing you knew old Mathews and the boy were in the electronics business. They got a lot of government contracts and things.

"Well, sir, they did prosper. Had to move around town two or three times, expanding. Finally, about three years ago, they put up a new plant ten miles south of here. The point of all this is that at the time of the bank robbery, old Mathews, to the consternation of his accounting department, still paid all the folks who worked for him in cash, in pay envelopes. Said it had always given him a thrill to get a pay envelope when he was a boy, and he thought his help deserved the same.

"He finally changed his thinking when the fellows who held up the bank got not only the bank's cash but the Mathews payroll from the armored car as well. Nearly half a million dollars.

"It gave me a fit too," the chief recalled somberly. "The bulk of the payroll money was in hundred dollar bills, the serial numbers in sequence and recorded by the Corrigan Security firm and the bank in Santa Barbara. But except for right after the robbery, we never heard of any of those recorded bills turning up, until just about three weeks ago when one of them surfaced at a bank up north, in Santa Rosa. It was kind of a fluke that anyone there even bothered to check it against the lists. But somebody did and we were notified. Seems it came from some doctor in the town of Willits."

I whistled softly. "It's beginning to sound good."

"Well, granted it's the sort of thing that would make Bob

Dempsey's ears stand up, but I didn't think too much of it myself."

"Why not?"

"I called Santa Rosa. Asked about the condition of the bill. They told me it had been put to some use. But those bills were mint fresh when they left town here."

"It could have been purposely made to look more used than it was."

"Maybe, but all things considered, I doubt it. I also called the doctor in Willits, a man name of Nelson. He said he got the bill from some hippie character as part of what he charged for an abortion he performed. It was a young girl who had something wrong inside her, so's a full-term pregnancy would have killed her. Least that's what the doc said. The only address he got from either the girl or the hippie fellow was a post office box number the girl had in Barracks Cove. I phoned there, too, and learned the girl has given up the box and didn't leave a forwarding address. I figure her hippie boyfriend was one of the rich ones. Plays in a band or deals in dope or something. I've seen 'em around here, looking like they was just run over by a truck, but carrying enough cash to buy the both of us."

"Did Dempsey show any interest in all this when the bill turned up?"

"He did somewhat, sure. He asked if I wanted him to go up to Willits, to see if he could learn anything more from the doctor. I told him no, that I didn't think it would be productive. I had the impression then that he agreed with me."

"How long after that did he ask to take a leave?"

"Almost a week."

"Was anybody hurt in the bank robbery?"

"One of the Corrigan guards was shot, not seriously."

"Could a private insurance company have had an interest in any of this?"

"I don't remember. But the Corrigan people must have had some kind of coverage. Let's look."

He got up and crossed to a file cabinet, searched through it some, then brought out a thick packet. He sat back at his desk and began paging through documents. "Yeah, there it is. The Corrigan outfit recovered some of the loss from Coast West Insurance Co."

"The man I'm looking for works for Coast West."

Chief Porter let me go through the file, jotting information. The three suspects in the case all were from Santa Barbara—Paul Chase, Randolph Hayes and Timothy Rowen. The three had been in their middle twenties at the time of the robbery. They had worn masks, but in the exchange of gunfire and fight with the Corrigan guards, the masks were torn loose from the men later identified as Chase and Hayes. Those two, and Rowen, had lived together in Santa Barbara. They all three disappeared after the robbery.

Paul Chase's brother, Wesley, was the only individual who had served time in connection with the case. They found some of the stolen money in his apartment, but they never proved he took part in the robbery itself. He spent eighteen months at a state prison.

"Have you kept track of this Wesley Chase?"

"We did for a while. He served his time then went back to Santa Barbara until his parole expired, then he dropped out of sight like the others. Can't say's I blame him. A lot of people were interested in him, what with all that money still missing."

"Do you think he knew where his brother and the others had gone to?"

"I couldn't say. Never met the man myself. Dempsey questioned him over in Santa Barbara. Anything else you need?"

I riffled through the rest of the file. "I'd like a copy of the wanted flier on the three missing men. And a photo of the brother who served time, if you have one."

"Don't have it here, but I can get one and mail it to you."

"And I'd appreciate a photo of Dempsey, and maybe a telephone call from you to his wife, to introduce me. I want to stop by and see her this evening if I can."

The chief gave me a copy of the wanted poster on the bank robbers. None of the three had ever been arrested before, so the photos on the poster were informal. They were smiling, good-looking boys. One was in an army uniform. It said all three were Vietnam veterans. The department mug shot of Dempsey that Chief Porter gave me showed a man with a hawk nose and a strong chin. He looked tough.

Porter phoned Mrs. Dempsey for me and chatted for a few minutes. When he hung up he gave me her address.

"Her spirits don't seem to have risen much since the last time I spoke to her. But she'll see you."

"Thanks very much for your help, Chief."

"No trouble. If I'm wrong about things and Bob is in some kind of jam, I hope you can help him out."

I paused at the doorway. "Chief, you wouldn't have the names of any people Coast West Insurance sent around to look into the robbery, would you?"

"Sure," said Porter. He paged through the folder some more. "They sent up a fellow from Los Angeles. Stoval was his name. Emil Stoval." The chief squinted at me. "You look like you might know the name."

"I do. He's been transferred to San Francisco. He's now the boss of the man I'm looking for."

Porter grunted. "In that case, maybe I better let down my hair a little. You never know how one thing leads to another."

I went back and sat on the edge of a chair. "That's right, you don't."

"Well, this is unofficial, and all I can tell you is what Bob Dempsey told me after being over to Santa Barbara to question Wesley Chase, the younger brother who was convicted as an accessory. Apparently this Stoval is the man who found the money in Chase's apartment. There was some other evidence, but the money is the thing that convicted him. And the rumors around the Santa Barbara police department at the time were that the insurance fellow might not have found that evidence in a strictly legal manner, under the rules of search and seizure and all. A lot of people, Bob Dempsey being one of them, had the impression that a good lawyer might have developed that end of things and gotten the boy off. But he couldn't afford a good—I mean a high-priced lawyer. He had a public defender who wanted to plea bargain with the prosecutor's office down the hall. That's what the insurance fellow wanted too, for Wesley to cooperate and tell them where his brother and the rest of the money was. But the Chase boy refused. He denied all knowledge of the crime or his brother's whereabouts."

I took a cab to the Dempsey home. It was a tidy, stucco house in a neighborhood of neatly trimmed lawns. The front porch light was on and Coral Dempsey opened the door soon after I pushed the buzzer. Dempsey was married to a woman several years younger than himself. She was attractive in a dusky way with long, dark hair. She wore black slacks and a white blouse, and after letting me in, crossed the room to turn off a small color television set in the corner. The room lights were dim, but from what I'd seen beneath the front porch light, she hadn't been sleeping well.

"I'm glad you found Tuffy and Steve," she told me.

110

"I only found the boy. He was able to tell us how to find his dad."

Mrs. Dempsey sat at one end of a sofa. I settled in a chair across from her. There was a box of tissues by her side and a wastebasket on the floor. She'd been using both.

"What is it you want, Mr. Bragg?"

I told her about Jerry Lind and his search for her husband. "The main thing I'm trying to find out now is what your husband was doing in Barracks Cove."

"And that's the problem, of course. He never talked about his work to me or the children."

"Did he drive up?"

"No, he flew to San Francisco and rented a car."

"I understand that during a call you had from him, he said something about becoming sheriff."

"Yes. His last phone call." She reached for a tissue. "We did use to talk about his dreams—our dreams."

Her face started to fall apart. She got up and excused herself before going down the hallway and closing a door behind her. I could hear water running. She returned looking about the way she had when she opened the front door.

"I'm sorry, Mr. Bragg, but the evening is when I can let it all out. After the boys are in bed. They're four and six. I don't want them to see. I haven't figured out how I'm going to tell them yet."

"But tell them what, Mrs. Dempsey? Chief Porter says . . ."

She sat erect and spoke firmly. "I don't care what Chief Porter or anybody else says. I don't need to. I know that Bob is dead. I know that he has been for days. I could almost tell you the hour." She rose and crossed to a floor lamp to turn up the light. "Mr. Bragg, I don't mean to be rude, and I don't like people to see me when I'm looking so rotten, but there is something that I want you, or Chief Porter, or somebody to understand. The love that my husband and I had for each other was something quite extraordinary. Something quite different from what you find between a husband and a wife who have been married almost ten years. Perhaps it would be easier if you knew the terrible loneliness of a police officer's work. Do you?"

"I know something of their miseries."

"Miseries. Yes, that's what it was. And for my part, Mr. Bragg, I used to be a singer in a little club on the strip in L.A. More than a singer, I was supposed to be an entertainer, I found out. When I landed the job I told myself, God, how wonderful. My first step to fame and fortune."

She crossed to a small stand, took out a cigarette and lit it. "I soon found out it was more like the first step to being a hooker. Nothing official, you understand, but we were encouraged to mingle with certain special customers. And if one of them asked to take out any of the girls working there, when we were through for the night, we were strongly encouraged to go along. It always meant a nice little bonus in the next paycheck. But I didn't like that. I tried to get work at other clubs. Finally a fellow I met arranged for me to get an interview with an assistant producer of a TV show. Over in Burbank. The assistant producer turned out to be a very nice guy. He had me audition for him. He listened to me sing a couple of numbers, then in a very gentle manner told me that I didn't really have much of a voice. Then he asked if I could dance. He said I had nice looking legs. I had to tell him I'd never danced, so that was the end of the audition.

"But at least it made things finally fall into place in my head about how it was at the club where I worked. The attraction was my body, not my voice. So I stayed on at the club feeling miserable and sordid, but making a lot more money than I could have doing much else. Until the night I met Bob. There was a shooting at the club. A man was killed. It was some sort of minor gang feud. Bob was the detective in charge of the investigation. The shooting had happened during one of my sets. I'd seen the whole thing. Bob interviewed me two, maybe three times. After that he'd stop by the club from time to time. I assumed it was to talk to other people about the shooting, but it turned out he just wanted to watch me. I figured that out after the trial, when there wasn't any official reason for him to be there. So I went over to the bar one night when he was there, after my numbers, and said hello."

She paused, with a little smile. "We were married one month later. And for our married life, no two people ever loved each other more, or better. And we grew so close in some ways. . . . There was this thing that bound us, even when he was away from home, working. Before he phoned home in the evenings, I would know if he was happy or sad.

"The night he phoned from Barracks Cove, he was elated in a manner I'd never heard nor felt before." She crumpled a tissue and stared at her fist. "Two days later I knew that he

112

was dead. I think—I think I knew it later that same night, even, but didn't fully realize it."

"Has he ever missed calling home in the past while he was away?"

"Never. We spoke to each other at least once a day since that night back in the club when I walked over to say hello."

"That could explain the funny feeling you have. Maybe just because he hasn't called . . ."

"No, Mr. Bragg, that's not it. My Bob is either dead, or something so horrible has happened to his head and his heart that I couldn't bear to see him that way." She lapsed into another silence, staring at the floor. She was beginning to make me edgy.

"When he called from Barracks Cove, Mrs. Dempsey, did he say anything—anything at all about what he was doing, or what it was he had found?"

She shook her head. "No. He just said he'd tumbled onto something that would make him sheriff. It was something he wanted. He was getting restless here in Rey Platte, but at the same time, he didn't want to go back to the tensions of a large city."

"What did you talk about during that last call?"

"The kids. Us. What I'd done that day. What we would do if he finished whatever he was working on in time for us to have a few days to ourselves before he would be going back to work here."

She was staring at me with a starkness bordering on the mad. "Oh, God, please leave. I can't help you any more. I just want to be left alone."

I thanked her and left quickly. I walked the half dozen blocks back into downtown Rey Platte before I found a taxi to take me back out to the airport. The night air was warm and gentle, but I felt a chill. Being overly tired could explain some of it, but the meeting with Mrs. Dempsey had taken its own toll. It was like with Tuffy back in the meadow. The sort of conviction she professed in her husband's fate wasn't acknowledged in medical textbooks, but my own hunch was that she knew what she was talking about. I decided I wouldn't call Jerry Lind's sister or his wife that night to tell them of the day's events. There wasn't a chance I'd be able to keep the gloom out of my voice.

Chapter 14

I slept all the way to San Francisco on the plane from Sky Charter with the smiling pilot. I didn't have enough pizazz left to go the rest of the way home, and I wanted to get an early start the next morning. So I got a room in a hotel near the airport and slept seriously. When I rolled out of bed Monday morning my muscles had things to tell me. I wasn't used to that much hiking, hauling and dunking. I sneezed a couple of times and got on the phone to call around until I found the rental car outfit Bob Dempsey had used. It was an economy firm that had leased him a VW bug. Dempsey had shown them his police identification and a credit card and told them he would need the car for an indefinite period. Subsequently, the firm had received a phone call from the police in Willits. The auto had been abandoned at the field there. The rental outfit asked the Willits police to impound the vehicle, but to hold it for another few days in case the client returned.

Next I called the airline that bounced into small towns around the northern part of the state, one of them being Willits, where my own car was. Their rates were a lot more reasonable than Sky Charter's and they had a flight that left in an hour, so I made a reservation and also asked if they had a record of a Robert Dempsey flying out of Willits in the past two weeks. They said they would check and call me back.

Then I phoned Coast West Insurance and spoke with Laurel Benson. She confirmed what I suspected by then. The other case Jerry Lind had been working on, the one Stoval hadn't told me about, concerned the hundred dollar bill that had been taken in the Rey Platte bank and armored car robbery. But she had some other news for me. Stoval had shown up in the office that morning with a suitcase. He'd gone through his mail and made some phone calls and then told Laurel that he would be gone for a couple of days. She said he'd never done that before.

I went in to take a shower and was toweling off when the small airline phoned back. They had no record of Dempsey flying out of Willits. I phoned Ceejay Mackey at the office, introduced myself and tried to stifle a sneeze.

"Are you phoning in sick?"

"No, I'm at the airport. Has Janet Lind called this morning?"

"No."

"If she does, tell her I'll check in with her either tonight or tomorrow."

"A Marcie Lind called. Is that the missing man's wife?"

"Yes. What did she want?"

"She just wanted to know how things were going."

"If she calls again tell her you don't know."

"That's what I told her before. How are things going?"

"You wouldn't want to hear." I sneezed and hung up and went out to catch an airplane.

The acting chief of police in Willits was a lanky young man of twenty-five or thereabouts with sandy hair and a long, droopy mustache. His name was Simms and he had a casual manner that bordered on malfeasance in office, but he knew what he was doing. He said they had checked out the VW license plates with Sacramento after the car had been at the airfield for about ten days. After then calling the rental outfit in San Francisco they'd towed it back into town.

"Did they tell you the name of the man who rented it?"

"They did indeed, and I have it right here on my desk somewhere," he told me, picking through the papers on his desk.

"It was Dempsey," I told him. "He's a detective from Rey Platte. He's been missing for a couple of weeks. For strong reasons of her own, his wife is convinced he's probably dead."

"What do you think?"

"I'm afraid I have to agree with her."

Simms stared at me a moment then got up and took a visored cap from the hatrack behind his desk. "You know, I

115

don't think any of my men ever checked out that car. Want to come along?"

The corporation yard where they'd put the VW was only a couple of blocks away, so we walked. On the way over there I told Simms about Jerry Lind and the connection with Dempsey, the hundred dollar bill and even the father and son crash survivors in the Willits hospital. He'd heard about the last two. I did my explaining in fits and starts, working in a word here and there between all the greetings the chief exchanged with merchants in their doorways and people on the street. Even the young people with long, untamed hair had smiles for him.

"You seem to be a popular man, Chief."

"I should hope so. We keep a good eye on things. The business community appreciates that. And the younger, tangled-looking citizens know I smoke a little dope from time to time. Makes them feel comfortable."

"I'll bet it does."

"Of course the town fathers are a little nervous about me being so popular. They figure something must be wrong somewhere."

"They'll get over that. How long have you been acting chief?"

"Three years now."

We turned into the maintenance yard. There were a couple of trucks and a street cleaner parked to one side, some piles of sand and stacks of scrap lumber. The VW was parked over beside a low wooden building. Simms waved at somebody through the doorway of the building and we went around to the car. The door on the driver's side was unlocked. Simms opened it and leaned his head in. I went around to the other side.

We searched under the seats and in the back. The car was empty and clean. I took out a small pocket knife and popped out the tip onto the release button of the glove compartment and opened it. Inside was an open map of California and a VW key. I lifted out the key by the loop of wire it was on and passed it over to Simms, who stared at it a moment then just took the key between his fingers.

"There's nobody around here I know about who has talent enough to bring out prints on this little thing." Simms climbed into the car, put the key into the ignition and started the motor.

"What's the gas gauge say?"

116

"Half full."

"Mileage?"

Simms read off the numbers and I wrote them down. He turned it off and climbed back out, looking around him for something.

"How about the trunk?" I suggested.

"That's what I was thinking. If I'd known we were going to be so damn professional I'd have brought along some tools." He went around the corner and into the building. A moment later he returned with a length of wire that he twisted around the hood release and pulled. The front panel popped open and the chief went on around to lift it. There was a large suitcase inside. Simms hefted one corner. It was heavy.

"Well now," he said. "I suppose a fellow could fly off somewhere and forget his luggage . . ."

"Seriously, Chief, do you have a man who can look for finger and palm prints?"

"Oh sure, not to worry. We got a man named Corning. Even the sheriff uses him." Simms straightened, staring at the car with his hands on his hips.

"Do you have a photograph of the man who rented this?"

I nodded, getting it out. "The Rey Platte police gave it to me."

Simms squinted at it. "He never stopped by to say hello. Can I have this long enough to get some copies made?"

"I'd like to show it to Doctor Nelson first. I'll bring it by your office after."

We walked back to the center of town and I got directions to the doctor's office. It was in a building across from the hospital. I drove on over and showed a receptionist there my ID. I said I wanted to see Nelson. She said he was busy. I said it was important and involved a hundred dollar bill. She gave me a look, but asked me to be seated and went through a doorway and down a hall. In the waiting room with me was an elderly couple holding hands, a guy who looked as if he worked in the woods, a young, good-looking girl with no bra beneath her T-shirt but a slow smile for everybody and a young mother with a boy of about five who eyed me as if I'd come to collect the rent. I'd just opened a last year's copy of *Newsweek* when some sort of fuss erupted down the hall. Somebody dropped something and a guy with a loud, sharp voice was coming our way. He sounded a little hysterical, raving about people with acute emphysema, some-

117

body crazy in the head who had hemorrhoids, a couple of people he didn't know what was ailing them and other assorted complaints.

The voice came from a fellow about my age or a bit younger wearing a white smock. He stomped into the room, looked around, then stared at me. "Are you the one asking about that hundred dollar bill?"

"We all got problems, Doc," I told him, getting to my feet. "Yours and mine aren't all that different. We want to keep people from dying."

His voice lost some of its edge. "How do you mean?"

"There are two men missing. They both were trying to find where the hundred dollar bill came from, and now they might not be alive. There are two more persons, a man and his son, in the hospital across the street who were in a plane crash a few days ago."

"I'm well aware of that."

"They were on their way down here to look for one of the missing men and nearly got killed themselves. So you see, there's a lot of mischief tied up to that hundred dollar bill."

He gave a gusty sigh. His gaze shifted to the little five-year-old who by now was clinging to his mother.

"Oh, hello, Billy," said the doctor. "Did I scare you? I'm sorry, I didn't mean to." He turned back to me. "All right, I'll give you four minutes. Follow me."

We went down the hall to a small office with a desk in disarray and a diploma from a Midwest medical school on the wall. The doctor sat at his desk, brushed at a lock of hair on his forehead and gestured toward another chair.

"You are Doctor Nelson, I take it."

"God, am I ever. Fifteen years in medical practice back in Chicago. Got so I was coming right off the walls back there. So I decided to move out here where I could take life a little easier. Ha!"

"I know. It's getting so there isn't any place left. I've heard the story of the girl you gave an abortion, and the fellow who paid for it, so you don't have to repeat that, unless something new might have occurred to you."

"It's hardly had time to."

"And you hadn't seen either of them before or since?"

"That is correct."

"Didn't you make the girl give you her name, before performing surgery?"

"Of course I did," he replied tartly, "She said her name
118

was Cherry Sunshine. I told her, 'Young lady, you'll have to do better than that.' She told me to go fuck myself." His eyes rolled ceilingward.

I took out the photo of Dempsey and put it on the desk. "Did this man come by later asking about the couple and the hundred dollar bill?"

Nelson studied it. "Yes, he was one of the men asking about it. A police officer from down south somewhere."

"Rey Platte. Can you remember when he was here?"

Nelson studied a calendar. "I'm quite sure it was the weekend of the seventh and eighth. A colleague and I take turns manning the office on weekends. But I'm not sure whether it was Saturday or Sunday. He had photos for me to look at also. Some of them were on a wanted poster."

I showed him my copy of the wanted notice on the suspected bank robbers. "Like this?"

"Exactly. Then he had photos of another man. They showed both the man's profile and his face straight on, as if he'd been arrested sometime."

"That probably was the brother of one of these men on the poster."

"Yes, that one."

He indicated Paul Chase. Which meant that Dempsey had also carried photos of Wesley Chase, like the ones I'd been promised from Rey Platte. "Did any of them look at all like the man who paid for the girl's operation?"

Nelson slumped back in his chair. "I honestly couldn't say. The fellow had a beard, long hair, dark glasses. He just slouched around the waiting room. And he didn't pay what I ordinarily charge for such things, either. But a hundred dollars is better than nothing."

"How about this man, have you seen him?" I gave him a photo of Jerry Lind.

"Yes, I repeated my little yarn to this young fellow shortly after I saw the police officer. He didn't have any photos to show me. Actually, he seemed rather distracted by it all. More as if he were going through the motions than anything else."

"Could you be more exact about when you saw him?"

"Oh, boy. Well now, wait a minute, yes I can." He paged through an appointment book. "He made me late for a conference across the street. He was a well-mannered young man and I didn't want to be too brusque with him. It was the day we all met to decide what to do about Mr. Dustin.

Yes, here it is. Monday, June Nine. Three p.m. So the young fellow must have arrived at around two-thirty in the afternoon."

I felt a little glow inside. It meant that Jerry Lind had been there a few hours after his uncle's death. Even if something had happened to him since, Marcie would get some of the rich pie.

"There's an estate matter involved in this as well, Doctor. If it comes to it, would you be willing to sign a statement to the effect you'd seen this man on that day, at that time in the afternoon?"

"Absolutely. If his name is . . ." He rummaged around in a desk drawer until he came up with a card. "Jerry Lind, and he works for Coast West Insurance Company."

I glanced at the card. It was one of Jerry's. "That's it. But you can't tell exactly when the detective was here."

"Not really. But it doesn't seem as if it had been just the day before this Lind came by. Probably it was two days. That would make it Saturday, the seventh."

It was the night of the seventh that Dempsey had made his last known phone calls from Barracks Cove. It seemed as if I finally was pointed down the right street. Dempsey would have been able to recognize the man who served time for helping his brother, the bank robber. Even if Wesley Chase had grown long hair and a beard, Dempsey would have known what to look for. One or both of the Chase brothers had probably settled in Barracks Cove, and Dempsey had found them.

"You've been a big help, Doctor."

"Well frankly I'm more concerned about the missing men than I am the fellow who gave me that hundred dollar bill. I guess that's why I blew up when I heard you were here. I thought you had come to ask the same tired questions as the man earlier. I tell you, it's enough to send a person straight back to Chicago."

"What man earlier?"

"Oh, I guess you don't know about him." Nelson groped into his shirt pocket and brought out another card. "I see he works for the same insurance company. Stoval was his name. He was in here today a little before noon asking about the man who paid for the abortion."

I went across the street to the hospital to look in on Tuffy, but I'd missed him. It turned out that with a cast on his ankle and an elastic bandage on his knee, plus a small pair

120

of crutches, he was mobile again and had left the hospital to stay in a nearby motel with his mother, who had arrived that morning. His father was expected to be bedridden another couple of days. I stopped in to say hello. He was a man in his early thirties with a medium build. He seemed to be recovering nicely. We chatted a few minutes. I asked about the phone conversation he'd had with his brother on the night of his birthday, but he wasn't able to tell me anything I didn't already know.

I finished my business with the local police and headed west, but planned to make another stop on my way back to Barracks Cove. I wanted to go back in to where I'd left my pack the day before. The small, nicely balanced axe alone was worth the trip, I figured, aching body and all. I drove to where Tuffy and I had come out the day before. I at least knew the country I'd been through, and without having to carry the boy I figured I could get up to the clearing and back inside a couple of hours or less.

I parked alongside the road, changed into the outdoor clothes that still were a little damp from the day before and started out. I hiked in and crossed the Stannis again where the sandbar split the river into a pair of channels. I had a brief, tough climb back up and around the granite outcropping that formed one side of the falls and finally reached the spot where I originally had intended to cross the river with Tuffy. My rope was still securely tied around the tree at the river's edge. It trailed on down out of sight through the falls below. I pulled it in, shook it off and coiled it, then tried to make out what had happened the day before when I put the strain on it. There were a few uneven strands at one outer segment of it. The rest of the stub was evenly cut off, as if my axe had chafed it one time, cutting through a portion of it. Which puzzled me, since I normally am careful to keep the axe sheathed while lugging it on the trail, just to keep from severing my own spinal column. On the other hand, maybe it was cheap rope. I couldn't recall where I'd bought it.

I got back onto the game trail above and climbed on up the ridge, through wooded pockets, the long meadow and the slopes above. My legs still ached from the day before, but I didn't rest along the way and arrived back at the northern stream and little clearing where I'd found Tuffy in just under an hour. I splashed on over, retrieved the pack, took a drink of water and started back down. My mind was ranging over the events surrounding the missing Jerry Lind and the time went quickly. I made better time than I had on my way up. I intended to circle around the granite shoulder at the falls in order to cross the river at the shallower, broad stretch along the sandbar. But part way down the sharp, inner slope, something peculiar occurred to me. It had to do with the area up above where I'd strung the rope. I wasn't positive, but it nagged me enough so I reversed myself and climbed back up to the granite outcropping. I was right about there being something wrong. The shorter length of rope that should have been tied to the tree across the river was missing. Things had happened in a pell mell, tumbling rush on the day before, but I was certain the rope had parted, and not become untied. I wasn't happy about having to waste any more time, but the missing rope bothered me. I took a deep breath against the chilling shock and plunged back into the river, making my way slowly and most carefully to the far side. Once there, I looked carefully around. The rope wasn't on the tree or anywhere else nearby.

I shifted the pack on my back and started through the underbrush near the river bank. A couple of dozen paces further along I found something I would have seen the day before if I'd scouted around some before going back up to fetch Tuffy. It was one of the old logging roads lacing the area that Fairbanks had been reminded of. It was partially overgrown and rutted, but it still made a handy slash through the surrounding country. It curved in from the direction of today's highway then roughly followed the river's course uphill. I went up it a ways out of curiosity. Then I caught a whiff of something unpleasant. It's the sort of aroma that you never forget once you encounter it. My nerves turned a little raw and it didn't have anything to do with the cold I figured I was coming down with. I hunched my shoulders and picked up the pace. The road made a little bend. Thirty yards beyond, it turned away from the river, and that's where I spotted the dark hulk. It rested in the trees between the road and the river. It was a car, or the remains of one. The partially burned metal body of a Ford Mustang.

I paused to catch my breath. If I still smoked cigarettes I would have had one. But I didn't. So there was nothing to do but finish it. I moved a little closer and stopped again, but this time it was just part of the job. I examined the surrounding ground, then circled the auto body, seeing nothing of value. The license plates had been removed. I finally stepped up to the car and peered inside. There was a man's body in the front seat. I felt just one small consolation. I still had a job. It wasn't the body of Jerry Lind. It was Dempsey, the missing detective. Somebody had held a gun close to his face and pulled the trigger. The exit wound had made a mess. The body hadn't been affected by the fire, so far as I could tell. It looked as if somebody had set fire to the rear of the vehicle. The gas tank had exploded and the area around it was chewed and scorched, but the flames had gone out before gutting the vehicle and Dempsey's body. Somebody had been in a hurry. It was sloppy work.

I put aside my everyday feelings as a human being and went through the dead man's pockets. His wallet had been removed, but he still wore a four-inch Colt revolver, snug in its holster. Somebody had gotten to him without his even suspecting that things were amiss. It was a lesson to us all. I opened the glove compartment. It had been cleaned out. The trunk would probably be the same. But it didn't matter. The people would know where to look, the ones who would have to come in after the body. They'd find identification numbers and eventually establish ownership of the auto. I was confident it would turn out to belong to Jerry Lind. It only puzzled me why it hadn't been his body inside.

Chapter 15

Back in Barracks Cove, I began to parcel out the bad news. Chief William Morgan was upset that an out-of-town police officer had been working in his area without making a courtesy call, the same as it had bothered Simms in Willits. But Morgan did like the fact that the body had been found out of town, so that it would be up to the county sheriff's office and coroner's people to go in and recover car and body. I showed him on his map where to find them, and he gave me the binoculars Hawkes had borrowed.

I went on down the hall to the phone booth and made some credit card calls. I phoned Rey Platte and passed on the unhappy news to Chief Porter. I felt it would be best for him to tell Dempsey's wife. He promised to do it. He said also he had the photo of Wesley Chase that I'd asked for. I asked him to express it up to the Barracks Cove police.

Then I phoned San Francisco and spoke with Janet Lind at the television station. I could almost feel her face fall when I said that I'd established that her brother was still alive after her uncle had died. She told me to keep up the good work. She was busy getting ready for the six o'clock news show and didn't have any more time to talk. I was glad for that. I didn't want to tell her just yet about Jerry's car and the body inside it.

And then I phoned Allison France. There wasn't much else I could do until the photo of Wesley Chase arrived, and I was ready for some relaxation. Allison was working in her studio. I apologized for having to cancel our dinner date the night before when I'd flown down to Rey Platte.

"I'll make it up to you tonight," I told her.

"I should hope so."

"Pick you up at seven?"

"That'll be fine, Pete."

I hung up almost smiling. I was glad she didn't live in San Francisco. I'd find it hard to get any work done.

I went on down to the glass doors leading to the parking lot, then stopped. Somebody was going through my car. I had left it unlocked because I hadn't planned to be away long and it was, after all, just outside City Hall and Police Headquarters, and on top of all that you weren't supposed to have to worry so much about being ripped off in small towns the way you were in big cities. I couldn't get a good enough view to tell who the individual was, but I could guess. He probably spotted me driving in there. He wore a suit and a hat and dark glasses. He was leaning into the car on the passenger side going through things in the glove compartment.

I slipped outside and circled around a couple rows of cars so that I could come up on the prowling figure from behind. I quietly placed the binoculars on the blacktop. The figure in my car was working quickly. He slapped shut the door to the glove compartment, backed out and closed the car door as he turned. It was Stoval, from Coast West Insurance.

"Hello, Emil," I greeted him. Then I poked my fist into his

124

mouth. I didn't hold back anything. I did it like they used to tell me when I fooled around gyms in my youth. I threw the punch as if I were aiming for a point about an inch in back of his head.

It was a good pop. Stoval slid down alongside the car almost elegantly, and leaned sideways. He blinked a time or two and tried to clear his head. His dark glasses dangled from one ear and his hat had landed on the ground beside him. I went over to get my binoculars and put them back into the trunk with my other gear. When I walked back around the car Stoval was starting to come around. He took off his glasses and gingerly touched his face. He was bleeding inside his mouth some. He spat and coughed. I leaned against the side of the car parked next to my own.

"Jesus," Stoval said finally. He squinted up at me and put his dark glasses back on. "What did you have to do that for?"

"To teach you not to go through my car, Emil. What were you looking for?"

"Nothing particular." He started to get up.

"No, Emil, you just sit right there while we talk."

He quit trying.

"Now tell me what it was you were looking for that wasn't anything particular."

"I don't know. I'm playing catch-up on an old case, and not doing so hot. I thought maybe I could get some idea of where you've been."

"You could ask."

The insurance man looked up at me. "Okay, I'm asking."

"Screw you, Emil, do your own leg work. Still, asking is smarter than sneaking. So you decided it was worth looking into what you figured Jerry was looking into, the Rey Platte money that turned up."

"You know about that?"

"I know about a lot of things, now. I also know you called on Jerry's wife the other evening and tried to get a little romance started."

He gave a weak wave. "I'd been drinking."

"I don't care if you'd been shooting smack. That sort of thing only complicates my own work, Emil. Don't do it again."

"What's the matter? You want the little twist to yourself?"

125

He was getting his spunk back. I kicked his forehead and bounced his head off the door of my car. His sunglasses clattered to the ground.

"Jesus!"

"Emil, do you know Mr. Alexander Forrest, a Coast West vice president in Los Angeles?"

"Of course I know him. How come you do?"

"I did a job for him and your company a while back. If you have anything more to do with Mrs. Lind other than strictly business by mail or telephone, I'm going to snitch on you, Emil. I'm going to tell my very grateful ex-client Mr. Alexander Forrest about this restless stud they have up in San Francisco who sends the guys in the office with the best-looking wives on a lot of out-of-town jobs so he can make a play for the lady of the family."

"You can't prove that."

"Emil, you dumbbell, it's common gossip. I'm surprised somebody hasn't called you on it before now. And if you're figuring your staff would be too chicken to tell on you, I'll just track down Harry Sund and see what he has to say."

I watched the blood drain out of his face.

"You seem to be in charge here."

"That is correct."

"What am I supposed to do, just sit here the rest of the night?"

"No, just until you tell me anything else you might know about Jerry Lind, or anything he could have been involved with."

"I don't understand."

"You held out on me about the Rey Platte money. I wasted a lot of time not knowing about that. Jerry has been up here asking about it."

"How do you know?"

"I'm good at my job. I've even been down to Rey Platte, talking to the police there, Emil."

"So you're thorough."

"And a cop from down there came up here trying to get a lead on the money. That's what led me to what Jerry was doing."

"What cop?"

"A man named Robert Dempsey. You might have met him during the investigation down south. At the same time that funny things were going on in Santa Barbara. I understand

126

that was common gossip too, at least around the locker room of the Santa Barbara cops at the time."

Stoval took a deep breath and stared glumly at the asphalt, as if I'd just stolen his last secret.

"I can't tell you anything more about Lind. I didn't tell you he was working on the money because I didn't know for sure myself if that's what he was doing when he left town. And I have a personal interest in the case. You already seem to know that I was in on it from the start. Naturally, the company would like to recover as much of the money as it can. We took a substantial loss."

"Make me weep, Emil. Loss rates are adjusted; premiums are boosted; life goes on."

"Sure, but I'd still like to recover the money."

"Why didn't you follow up on it yourself, instead of putting Lind on it?"

"I called the bank in Santa Rosa. I figured it for a fluke is all. But I told Lind he could come up and nose around some if he wanted to."

"Then why have you come up here now? I can't believe you're looking for Jerry."

"No, I'm not looking for Jerry. The kid can look out for himself, so far as I'm concerned. Maybe he was looking for the source of the money, sure, but Lind did other things that could get him into trouble."

"What other things?"

"He ran around a lot. With other women."

"How do you know that?"

He looked at me, trying to decide something. "Because my wife told me so," he said quietly. "She models in the city. Uses the name Faye Ashton. She never told Jerry she was my wife. And my wife, in one of her usual destructive moods, wouldn't tell me if it was her or one of the other girls in the agency Jerry was seeing. But he was seeing somebody there."

"Okay, so you don't have any great love for Jerry Lind. You still haven't told me why you're up here."

"Another of the bills turned up. In New Mexico. I just heard about it Saturday. The bill was just two serial numbers removed from the one that the doctor in Willits had."

"Why didn't you go to New Mexico?"

"It's not in my territory. The only angle I had to work on was up here. So up here I came. But I haven't had much luck so far."

"Neither has the cop, Dempsey. Did you know him?"

"Sure. What do you mean?"

"I just found his body inside a burned-out car up in the hills. Somebody made a hole between his eyes."

Stoval looked as if he were going to be ill.

"Personally, Emil, I think you're getting a little clumsy for this sort of work. A man could get killed. Now get up and show me where your car is."

"Huh?"

"Don't grunt, just show me your car."

Stoval struggled to his feet. He led me across the lot to a tan, late model Cadillac and unlocked the door.

"Good, Emil. A really subtle car. How long has it been since you did field work?"

"What difference does it make? What did you want to see it for?"

"What do you suppose?" I asked, jotting down the license number. "I know it's supposed to be a free country and all that, Emil, but if I see this automobile again in the course of my current job, I'm going to track down the man driving it and physically abuse him. Think about it some."

I bought a bottle of bourbon and checked into a comfortable motel over near the highway. It had a swimming pool, but I didn't feel as if I needed the exercise. I took a long shower, shaved and dressed, then poured myself a walloping big drink and settled down to watch the six o'clock news show that Janet Lind was on. There were two male newscasters who handled the routine stuff, then they would use Janet Lind for things of a more lighthearted nature. Still, with all her elbow cocking and eyebrow curling she made the things she talked about seem more complicated than they were. I wondered why they let her get away with that stuff and found my mind drifting back to the Jerry Lind thing. It soured me some hearing about Lind and Stoval's wife, or if not her at least one of her co-workers. More and more, any personal concern I felt was shifting from Jerry's circumstances to his young wife. She deserved far better than she was getting. I just hoped she'd be able to handle that okay when she found out about it.

Janet Lind was back on doing one of her field reports. I wondered what sort of person she really was beneath the flutter and makeup. She was interviewing a guy who had walked on the moon. He was in town for something going on at the space facility at Moffett Field. She asked him how he

128

felt about it—the moon walks—these years later. He said he still had dreams about it. I got up and fixed myself another drink. Then I turned off the TV and leaned back and wondered if somebody had meant to kill me and the boy the day before along the Stannis River.

Chapter 16

Allison was waiting for me when I drove up. She came down to the car and got in before I could even make the gesture of going around and opening the door for her. She wasn't wearing her brown Levis and tan jacket over a white T-shirt advertising the Lodi Buckeyes. No, sir. This time she was wearing a taut pair of white hip-hugger pants and a red and white striped jersey top. It fit closely around her neck but had a high waist.

"My God," I murmured.

She leaned across to brush a kiss past my ear. "You like?"

"I like."

"That's why I wore it. I thought you might like. And it doesn't seem we get a chance to spend time together during the day, when these duds would be more appropriate."

"There is that problem," I agreed. "Where can I take you looking like that and not get into a fistfight?"

"I thought of that," she told me. "There's a place down at the cove. A lot of people come in by sea and tie up for dinner. Nautical attire is quite appropriate. I don't suppose you brought along a captain's cap by any chance?"

"No, but I've got some wet hiking boots in the trunk."

"That won't do at all. Anyway, I wanted to show off a bit for you. We can go there and I can do that and nobody will bother us."

"That's nice. You're giving me all the bother I can handle at one time."

Her smile was naughty and she moved over into my arms. We kissed as if we'd just made up our minds about something. Her hand loosened my collar, then moved around to stroke the back of my neck. One of my own hands, the devil, explored her bare midsection. We were kissing deeply. Sometime later on that evening we broke off to catch our breath.

"Wow," said Allison, brushing back a few strands of hair.

"I guess we could always climb into the back seat," I suggested.

"No, we'd better go eat first. I don't want to miss out on that again."

I took a cloth from the glove compartment and wiped the inside of the windshield where it had fogged over. "What will your neighbors think?"

"If any of them are watching, they'll think we're having a grand time."

"I guess they'd be right at that." I started the car and headed for the highway.

"You're quite a celebrity around town."

"How's that?"

"Finding the boy yesterday. Carrying him out all that way."

I grunted. "The town might change its mind when it hears what I found today."

"What's that?"

"No, we'll save that for later, if at all. I'd just like to go off duty for a while."

"You should have told me. I have some nice grass back at the house. We could have smoked a joint."

"I didn't mean that far off duty."

"Do you? Smoke grass I mean?"

"Sure. But it's usually when I take a holiday out at the beach or something. It doesn't happen too often."

She directed me to a road that looped back from the highway and dropped down to the cove. We passed fishing boats and dock facilities and curved around to the far side to a long pier with several pleasure boats tied up. Across from that was a parking lot, three restaurants and a couple of bars. Allison led me into a place called The Bell. It was a low, spacious building partitioned by screens and planters in a way to give each of the tables and booths a cozy feeling of privacy. It was done in a maritime motif, the walls draped with nets and cork floats and red and green lanterns. We were led to a table in the rear, next to a window looking out over the water and marine yards.

"Cute," I told her.

"I like it. But don't let the decor trick you into having seafood, unless there's something you really crave. They don't do it all that well."

"What do they do well?"

"What do you suppose the fellows with bellies and expensive boats who come up here from San Francisco or Sausalito or Alameda order?"

"Steaks?"

"You've got it. Under all the feel of wind-in-hair and salt spray you have here a first class steak and chop house."

She was right. After a couple of drinks we had a pair of tender filets. It was a leisurely meal, and there was nice conversation to go with it. I asked her about her work and she asked me about when I was growing up. It was a switch. And it made me remember a lot of things I hadn't thought about for a long while. After the meal we sipped coffee and Bisquit and continued to gently poke and explore for the things we wanted to find out about each other. We even held hands across the table at one point, and I hadn't done that with anybody for at least a dozen years. It was heady, dangerous stuff. And I loved it.

"You're incredible," I told her. "I feel as if I've known you for a long time."

"You have a funny tug on me too, mister. I'd like to think we could have talks like this thirty years from now."

"You're going to make it tough for me to pick up and drive back to San Francisco when I finish my work."

"Then why not stay around for a while? You could open a little detective shop in a corner of my studio. And answer the phone for me and things."

"In a corner of your studio."

"Sure. And I'll get out my hammer and saw and build you a little cupboard where you can keep your disguises and magnifying glass. And paint you a couple of signs—'The Detective Is In' and 'The Detective Is Out.' "

"Funny."

"Uh-huh. And when I was feeling a little randy and you were between jobs we could put up a sign saying 'The Detective and Artist Are Far Out' and go in to bed."

"You make it sound pretty good."

131

"It could be. Do you ever take a vacation, Pete?"

"Not so's you'd notice. I've been trying to get to London for about ten years now. Something always seems to come up."

"Well, if you stay around here for a couple weeks, maybe I couldn't offer you a tour of Parliament, but I betcha we'd have a pretty good time."

"I'll give it serious consideration, Miss France. That's after I find Jerry. Or learn what happened to him."

"Oh yes, Jerry."

I was sorry I'd said that. It dimmed her glow. She stared at the table top and thought about things for a minute, then lit a cigarette.

"What was it you were going to tell me?" she asked.

"About what?"

"What you've been doing. What it was that you found today."

I took a deep breath. "I suppose if you really want to hear about it . . ."

"Of course I do. I'm worried about Jerry."

"Yes. I'm starting to feel the same way. Don't let it hit you too hard if I find him dead. When I find him."

I gave her a terse summary about Tuffy's uncle, my visit to Rey Platte, the long ago bank robbery and the hundred dollar bill. I told her about today's trip to Willits and my talk with Dr. Nelson. And finally I told her about going back onto the mountain for my pack, and about finding the car and the dead cop. Sketchily, I told her about finding the cop. But even before I had gotten that far, the story had started to bother her. I had been afraid that it might. That's why I hadn't been keen on telling her in the first place.

"What are your plans now?" she asked.

"I just have to wait, until at least tomorrow. The Rey Platte police are sending me mug shots of this Wesley Chase, the brother of one of the suspected robbers."

"You think he had something to do with all this?"

"It's a good possibility. The dead cop, Dempsey, was looking for him. But Dempsey told his brother and wife there was more to it than that. Something bigger. Maybe Wesley's brother showed up, or one of the other gang members, or all three of them. If Dempsey had a hunch he could recover some of the money and bag the three people who took it, that would be something bigger."

"What will you do when you get the photographs?"

"More leg work. Show them to people around town. See if

somebody recognizes him. The doctor in Willits said the guy who passed him the bill was wearing a beard and long hair. But maybe somebody local saw him before he grew a beard. Or maybe the beard was fake. It's just something I'll have to work on. It might take several days. If so, I'll have a chance to buy you a few more dinners, even if the vacation later doesn't work out."

Allison half-turned in her seat and stared out over the cove. She was clearly upset.

"What is it?"

She shook her head. "Nothing."

"Nothing my foot. You've got bells going off inside . . ." And just then somebody kicked me low in the stomach. "Hey, wait a minute. Santa Barbara . . ."

Allison crushed out her cigarette. "Please, Pete. Don't pursue this."

"What do you mean, don't pursue it? It's all I've got. The guys who pulled off the robbery, and the brother who did time. They all were from Santa Barbara. And so are you, the same as Jerry Lind. You do know something, or you remember something, don't you, Allison?"

She stared tight-lipped out over the water, the color rising in her face.

"Look, kitten," I said gently. "Your telling me isn't going to change anything except save me a little time and maybe get me to Jerry Lind quicker. I've got a wanted poster with pictures of the three suspects. And tomorrow probably I'll have photos of the brother. If any of them are around this part of the country I'm going to find them."

She turned toward me then. "No, Pete. Don't. Take my word, please. There's nothing in it. Your theory is all wrong. Those three men aren't anywhere around here."

"But the brother is?"

She didn't reply.

"What is it, Allison? Is an ex-con more important to you than the missing Jerry Lind? You said you felt motherly toward Jerry. This isn't being very motherly. And the dead cop upriver. Think about him for a minute, then tell me there's nothing in it."

"That wasn't nice, Pete."

"Neither was the way that cop looked. He had the back of his head blown away. I'm trying to keep that from happening to Jerry, if it's not already too late."

Allison raised one hand to her mouth. "Excuse me," she said. She got up and left quickly.

I got up too, and took a few steps past partitions and around bursting Boston ferns to see her go into the restroom. When I felt this close to a break in my job I hardly trusted myself, let alone anybody else. I went back to the table. The waitress came around and I told her to take away the rest of my drink but to bring another cognac for Allison and fresh coffee for myself. When the coffee and brandy came I asked her for the check. I got that and paid it and waited some more until I knew I'd waited too long, even for a distraught woman. I got up and went out to ask the bartender at the front of the house where the nearest public phone was. The guy told me there was a booth out at one side of the parking lot. I could see it through the front window. Allison was inside it speaking to somebody, gesturing with one hand balled into a fist as she talked.

I went back to our table and sipped coffee. Allison took a few minutes longer. She had regained her composure. She sat and sipped some of the Bisquit.

"Sorry I was so long," she told me.

"That's okay. Want to talk about it now?"

"No."

I stared at her until she raised her eyes.

"I can't, Pete. I just can't."

I put my coffee aside and leaned forward to clasp my hands on the table. "Allison I'm going to tell you one more story about when I was growing up in Seattle. It's not one I'm particularly proud of, but it's a part of me and a part of the way I feel and act today, these many years after.

"Along about the time I was in the seventh grade I got both my first bicycle and my first girlfriend of sorts. She had moved in two doors up the street from where I lived. About a block further up the hill lived another kid our age named David Young. We all three of us attended the same parochial grade school, about a mile and a half from where we lived. Sometimes we all three rode our bikes to school together. It was a hilly, up and down route. One day we all were riding together when David stopped for some reason. Probably to fix something on his bike or to adjust the schoolbooks in his carrying rack, or whatever. Anyhow, the girl and I didn't realize he'd fallen back until we were several blocks further on. We were talking, you know, and though I didn't really know what a girlfriend really was in those days, I was old enough to be showing off and making smart remarks. And I remember I was carrying on this pretty good routine that morning and I didn't want to interrupt it.

"When we finally noticed that David wasn't with us, we stopped to look back, but didn't see him. So we just continued on to school, figuring he'd stopped off at a friend's house or decided to go another way. Hell, I don't know what we figured. We were having too much fun to worry about it. David was a year ahead of us in school, so we didn't share the same classroom, and I didn't realize he'd never made it to school that morning. Turns out a car had hit him when he stopped. It was hit and run. The driver apparently panicked. They never did learn who hit him or how it happened.

"David suffered a severe concussion. He must have laid out on the pavement for twenty or thirty minutes before somebody found him and called an ambulance. For two weeks nobody knew if the kid would live or die. It finally turned out that he lived, but he was never right in the head again after that. I've carried that guilt on my back ever since. I should have gone back to look for him.

"Anyhow, it taught me quite a lesson, Allison. That's why I had to carry that youngster down off the mountain yesterday. I just couldn't leave him, even for a few more hours, the way I left David that time. And it's the same right now, with Jerry Lind. And whatever you know, I would like you to tell me. Even a few hours might make a difference. People can die fast."

"You don't understand, Pete. Believe me. Whatever I know doesn't pose any threat to Jerry Lind."

"Maybe not. But if there's somebody you know who's at all connected to any of this, they might be able to light up another dim corner and give me something that will lead to Jerry. Please, Allison."

Her mouth twisted. "Oh God, Pete, I want to but I just can't!"

I leaned back and stared at her. "Okay. I guess then I'll have to manage on my own. Do you want me to drop you off or should I call you a cab?"

"What do you mean? What are you going to do?"

"I'm going to start hunting for the mystery person. Whoever it was you called a few minutes ago from the phone booth outside."

"You are low, aren't you?" she asked quietly.

"I'm working, Allison. I'd butt heads with anybody to find out what I have to know. I guess probably I'll be looking for the brother who did time. I imagine you feel sorry for him, especially since there was some doubt about whether he really deserved to go to prison. Once his parole was lifted he took off. Left Santa Barbara. He could well have come up here. He could well have been a painter himself, even. I never had a chance to find out, but it makes sense you might have known him in school. Jerry Lind could have known him as well. You could all have been friends. That's why you would believe he didn't have anything to do with Jerry's disappearance. They were friends. One wouldn't harm the other."

I watched her closely. She tried to keep her face a blank, staring out over the cove. But she was too passionate. Her senses were alive; her emotions too near the surface. She wasn't tough in that way, and I kept picking away.

"He would have changed his name, of course. Nobody would know him around here as Wesley Chase."

She continued to stare out over the cove, her chin high and her eyes unblinking. And then I remembered something.

"I'll bet I know," I said softly.

Allison looked quickly at me.

"I am getting a little slow. I should have thought of it sooner."

"What?"

"The fellow you were off wandering and talking with the night I met you out at the Parsons place. He seemed agitated, and you were calming him."

The panic was rising in her eyes. There was no mistaking it.

"What was his name? Joe something. Lodge? Dodge? That was it, Joe Dodge. I'll bet he's Wesley Chase. It's even a nice play on words, Chase into Dodge. That's it, isn't it, Allison?"

She sat glaring at me. "God damn you," she said softly. "You're going to kill him if he has to go back into prison. You wait. You're just going to kill him."

She got up and gathered her bag. There were tears brimming in her eyes. She made a plaintive gesture. "How could I be so utterly wrong about somebody?"

And then she was gone. I got up after a minute, after I'd gathered up all the memories and stuff I'd let out over dinner

136

and stuffed them all into a dark trunk inside my head and snapped shut the lid.

The waitress was up at the bar, staring at me with something short of exuberance. When I asked, she told me Allison was back in the restroom. I left five dollars and said to give it to her for cab fare when she came out. The bartender, rubbing the life out of a glass behind the bar, stared at me as if he didn't like me much. I couldn't blame him a bit.

Chapter 17

Wiley Huggins, who ran the art supply shop, had said that the area's serious artists could be found at most any bar in town. I drove back to the town square, parked, and began the circuit. At the second place I visited the bartender was able to tell me where Joe Dodge lived. It was an old place northeast of downtown, in the general direction of Big Mike Parsons' place, at the end of Cupper's Road. I thanked the man and left.

I drove out and parked a hundred yards from the end of Cupper's Road. I could see lights through some trees where the road ended. I was opposite an orchard. In behind it were lights from another house. I got out and listened. A breeze stole through the trees across the road. The sky was patchy with clouds drifting across the face of the moon. My .38 caliber revolver was in the glove compartment. I put it on my belt and started up the road. At road's end I concealed myself behind a tall eucalyptus tree that creaked in the wind. I stifled a sneeze and took a peek at the house.

It looked as if I'd arrived just in time. Joe Dodge, or whatever his name was, was preparing to leave, tossing a sleeping bag and things into an old sedan. When he turned and went up a short flight of stairs to the house, I followed, stepping softly. I climbed to the porch and peered inside, making out a dimly lighted living room. More lights came from a hallway off to the right. I went in quietly and crossed to the hall. Off it was a single long room that looked as if somebody had removed the partitioning wall from between two bedrooms. Joe Dodge, it turned out, was indeed a painter, and the room was his cluttered studio. He was at the deep end of the room, his back at an angle to me and a cigarette dangling from his lips. He was paging through a carton of sketches.

"Mr. Dodge?"

I tried to say it casually, but it startled him badly. He turned with cigarette ash spilling down his shirtfront.

"Sorry to disturb you, Mr. Dodge. You might remember seeing me out at the Parsons' place the other evening. My name is Peter Bragg. I'm a private investigator from San Francisco, working on a missing person case. I think Allison France called you a short time ago to tell you about me."

He ground out his cigarette in a nearby coffee can filled with sand, but he didn't speak.

"Mr. Dodge, I don't like to inconvenience you, but I have to ask you to do something for me. I have to ask you to go over to the wall and assume the position. You know, legs spread, leaning into it so I can pat you down."

"You're an intruder," Dodge said harshly. "This is my home."

"I know. But the thing I'm working on, it's that serious. You can make a beef about it later. I could just as well have gone to the local police with the information I have, and had some of them accompany me out here. Then we'd go down to the station and they'd lock you up until they had an opportunity to check out a few things. I thought if I came out here by myself, maybe we could avoid all that. We could just have a talk. Only first, I don't want to be worried about you."

I nodded toward the wall. Joe Dodge caught his breath and crossed the room. I stepped up behind him to run my hands along his arms and sides. I stooped low to pat down his legs, and that's when he made his break. He didn't make any threatening move in my direction, he just shoved off from the wall and ran across the room and out the door. I stumbled and pursued him. Dodge went out the front door, slamming it behind him, but he didn't really have much of a chance. At the bottom of the stairs he hesitated, staring at the raised trunk lid on his old car. I lunged from the porch and dragged him to the ground. We rolled in the dirt for a while.

I was a larger man than Dodge, but it wasn't any taffy pull I found myself in. We rolled and twisted and he turned out to be surprisingly strong. I tried to subdue him with wrestling holds, but he wouldn't let up. I finally managed to stun him with an open-handed blow to the side of his head. I picked him up and half carried him back up the stairs, through the front of the house and back into his workshop. I gave a shove and Dodge stumbled into the middle of the room. I turned and closed the door to the hallway and leaned back against it, holding open a flap to my jacket so he could see that I was armed. In the middle of trying to catch my breath I had to sneeze again. It nearly brought tears to my eyes.

"Feel like talking?" I managed finally.

Dodge turned with a glare in his eyes. "How did you get Allison to talk? Beat it out of her?"

"Not really. She didn't tell me, but I finally started putting things together. She tried to stall me, but I was afraid something like this might be going on." I glanced around at the half-packed cartons. "Your real name is Wesley Chase, isn't it?"

He didn't reply.

"I have photos coming up from Rey Platte. They'll be here tomorrow. Then I'll know for sure that you're Wesley Chase. But Allison tried to protect you. She thinks you're in the clear about everything."

"Like what?"

"Passing stolen money, killing a cop from down south, things like that."

Dodge looked at me sharply. "What cop?"

"A man named Dempsey, from Rey Platte. If you're who I think you are, he questioned you in the Santa Barbara jail."

"Everybody questioned me in the Santa Barbara jail. So I'm Wesley Chase. So what are you going to do about it, put me up against a wall someplace and execute me? I don't know anything about any dead cop."

"Then why did you try to run just now? Why were you planning to leave at all?"

"Why not? I don't know you from a birdbath. So you say your name is Bragg and you're a private cop from San Francisco."

"I am. And Allison has seen my ID. I'll show it to you."

"Forget it. I don't care if you're the Pope. I don't want to talk to you."

"Too much is going on for you not to talk to somebody, Chase."

"Not to do with me, there isn't, and don't call me Chase." He patted his shirt pockets then looked around. "What will you do if I move around some, shoot me?"

"Not likely."

He went over to a chest of drawers and opened the top one. I brought out my gun. Dodge looked at me nervously and brought out a pack of cigarettes.

"Cigarettes, see?" He tore open the pack and lit up.

I leaned back against the door and put away my revolver.

"Jeez," said Dodge, puffing nervously. "How come you're so jumpy?"

"I'm the guy who found the dead cop. You'd be jumpy too."

"I was born jumpy. What's the cop got to do with me?"

"That's what I'm here to find out."

Dodge shook his head. "Don't know any cops. Alive or dead."

"Maybe not. Why did you try to run?"

Dodge blew a cloud through his nostrils. "Have you ever done time?"

"No."

Dodge nodded. "You should try it sometime. Quite an experience." He took a deep drag on the cigarette then stabbed it out in the sand. "It fucking near killed me."

He half-turned in the middle of the room and looked around at his paintings. "Some guys," he said, "were always being hassled over sex." He crossed to an easel that was turned away from me. He had a drawing pad on it and turned to a new sheet, picked up a piece of charcoal and began to sketch.

"Some guys had trouble with the concept of being imprisoned. The regulation, the routine, the crushing boredom. A lot of guys managed to cope with that, but some couldn't. But the biggest thing—the worst—was the way you had to just suck your life down to the shakiest little space you could get it into, then walk quietly. Oh, so quietly, man, and hope to dear God you would not die before it was your time to leave that place. We had twenty-three stabbings while I was there. Some guys had nightmares every night."

He worked quickly at the pad, then put down the charcoal

and lit another cigarette. His hands were steadier now, and his voice had calmed.

"I went through all those things. The hassles, the fear and the dread, wondering if some guy would stick a shiv in me for some fancied slight. I was out on parole from there for a little more than a year before I got my first unbroken night's sleep." He opened a flat little box of colored chalks and continued his work at the pad.

"That still doesn't explain why you tried to run just now, unless you've done something that'll send you back in there."

"That's how things look to you. I know different. I know that you don't really have to do anything to get sent in there."

"But maybe this time you did something."

"Like what?"

"Pass some of the stolen money from the Rey Platte bank job."

Dodge worked silently at the pad. "Are you working for the insurance company?"

"No, I thought Allison would have told you that. I'm looking for a man named Jerry Lind."

He nodded. "She told me. But you seem pretty interested in the bank money."

"I am. It's one of the things Jerry was interested in when he dropped out of sight. He was working for the insurance company that covered the Corrigan Security losses."

Dodge shook his head with a wry smile, ground out his cigarette and lit another. "That's very funny, man." He did some more work on the pad. "Okay, I'll tell you about the money. What I know about it. The evening of the day the bank was robbed, my brother came by my apartment in Santa Barbara. He didn't stay too long. I was working. I do a lot of work at night like this. There didn't really seem to be much point to his visit. Whenever Paul and I saw each other, it usually was for a definite reason. We'd never hung out much together. And we saw even less of each other since he got back from Vietnam. Only this time there wasn't any reason. We talked some. He drifted on back to the front of my apartment. In fact, I thought he'd left. But he came back a few minutes later and said good-bye. Probably for good.

"While he was wandering around the place he was stashing some of the stolen money. He probably figured he was doing me a good turn. He left some in a fairly obvious place.

Under the front room rug. That's what the cops found. Or rather, a guy from the insurance company did."

"How did he find it?"

"I don't know. He must have gotten into the apartment sometime when I was out. He came by and we talked once. Sort of in the doorway. I didn't invite him in. Just told him I'd seen my brother that night, but I didn't know anything about the robbery. And I didn't. But that hadn't surprised me, the robbery. Paul and the two guys he roomed with— they were all in 'Nam together. They saw some hard times there. I guess you could say they were a little bitter. And the things they'd talk about—they were like animals, man. I mean a guy like me, I've always been a little jumpy. Prison made that worse. But in my head, I'm not all that soft. But those three guys . . ."

He shook his head and stepped back to look at his work. "Those three guys didn't belong in society any more. Not when you heard what was going down inside their heads."

"Could those three have killed a cop like Dempsey?"

"In a minute, smiling all the while. But I'm sure that they didn't. My guess is that after the robbery they split for Mexico or Spain or somewhere."

He fiddled with some chalk pieces and went to work again. "Anyhow, that one talk was all I had with the insurance guy, before I was arrested. The next day he showed up again with a couple of cops. They had a search warrant and the insurance guy went directly to where the money was. He kicked back the rug and there it was. Five big ones. And I was the only surprised guy in the room."

"What was the testimony in court? To do with finding the money?"

"The insurance guy lied in his teeth. He said I'd let him into the apartment during his first visit, and he spotted a corner of a bill sticking out from under the rug. Which was all bullshit, of course. Before it got that far even, he came to see me in jail. He told me maybe we could work out a deal if I told him where my brother and the others were. And the rest of the money. I couldn't have told him that even if I'd wanted to. So I went to prison."

"But they must not have found all the money your brother left."

"That's right. I had a friend sublease the apartment while I was in prison. I didn't tell anyone, but I figured there might be some more hidden around. When we were kids, my brother and I used to devise elaborate hiding places around home. We spent a lot of time there together back then. When I was paroled my friend moved out, I moved back in and began looking for more money."

"Didn't the police search the place?"

"Yeah, but only in the obvious places. They didn't know about this game my brother and I had about hiding things. He stuck a couple of bills under the backing of a small print I had hanging on a wall. He put a couple down inside a can of green oil I'd bought that day, and had just left on the kitchen table. He rolled up a couple to about the size of a thin cigarette and taped them to the top of a window casing. Things like that. Only one or two in any one place. Not in a bundle like the cops were looking for."

"How much did you find?"

"About two thousand, in all. I had another friend who was going to Europe not long after I got out. I gave most of it to him. Asked him to unload the bills on his trip. Gave him a third of the proceeds. He brought me back the change."

"From most of it."

"Yeah. The rest was dumb, admittedly. I hung onto a couple of the bills just for the hell of it. Then last month I met this girl. She was the nicest little thing. Only about seventeen. In trouble. Pregnant. She had some sort of female infection. We didn't have any romance or anything. I felt like her older brother more. So I took her to Willits. Put on a false beard, shades, the whole thing."

He shrugged. "She didn't want to stick around after the surgery. Don't know why. But then she was just a kid. Guess she didn't know what she wanted."

"Do you have any more of the money?"

"After I paid the doctor in Willits I had one bill left. I gave that to the kid. Told her to go far away before she spent it."

"She went as far as New Mexico."

Dodge looked up. "Yeah? That's something." His eyes went back to the drawing pad. "There is one thing you've done for me, Bragg. You got me to verbalize on some things I've been trying to hold down. Maybe it'll help my head some."

He swung around the easel so I could see what he'd been working on. It was a strange and bleak combination. The lower part of the sheet had a charcoal sketch of a man's arms reaching into the drawing from below, fingers gripping a window sill. Beyond the window he'd drawn, beyond a pale wall, a bursting world of color. Blue sky and brilliant green knoll in the distance. Atop the knoll was a single cow, looking back toward the window, as if wondering about it.

"For eighteen months," Dodge said quietly, "this was the only thing I saw of the outside. You could see this from the prison library. Barely. That's why, you talk about stolen money, I don't think of it that way. Least not the money I had. Who does it really belong to? The insurance company, since they had to make good on it? What did the insurance company do for me? It sent me to prison for a year and a half on a bum rap. That figures out to be a little more than a hundred dollars a month. I don't call that stolen. I call it hard-earned."

He wiped his hands on a rag and stared at the drawing.

"How about Jerry Lind?" I asked.

"What about him?"

"Did you know him?"

"Sure. From Santa Barbara, same as Allison."

"Were you good friends?"

"More like acquaintances. He couldn't paint very well. But he liked to hang around people who could. As if he'd pick up something that way."

"You didn't keep in touch, since Santa Barbara?"

"No. I hadn't seen him in years until a couple weeks ago."

"You saw him here in Barracks Cove?"

"Yeah. Bumped into him on the street one afternoon. We were both surprised. Went in and had a beer together."

"Did you tell him about the Corrigan money?"

"No. He didn't ask."

"That's hard to believe. He was looking for the source of the bill you gave the doctor."

Dodge shrugged. "I would have told him the same thing I told you, if he'd asked."

"What day was this?"

"It was the day after he saw Allison. We talked about it on the phone just a bit ago. Neither of us had thought to tell the other about seeing Jerry."

"That's interesting. That puts him around here a day later than I'd heard of before. I wish Allison had told me about it back at the restaurant."

"Allison's playing guardian angel for me. I'm not putting her down for it, God knows. She's been good to me. She tries to soothe the hassles oho knows I've been through. She was

144

still down south when I went to prison. She used to write. We've always respected each other's work."

"Did you tell Lind you'd been to prison?"

"No. I don't tell anybody I've been to prison."

"And he didn't mention the stolen money to you?"

"No."

"What did you talk about?"

"Santa Barbara days. Painting. . . ." The expression on his face changed. "Hey, that's something."

"What is?"

"You keep talking about the money, but Jerry wasn't looking for that. At least it wasn't all he was looking for. He was trying to find a cop. Maybe it was this—what did you say his name was, Dempsey?"

"That's right, and Dempsey was looking for the source of the money."

"But that's not what Jerry said. He said the cop was looking for a painting that had been stolen in San Francisco. The museum people told him about it, and about the cop. Jerry was trying to find that same stolen painting." Dodge shook his head and lit another cigarette. "I couldn't see it myself. It was a bizarre little piece, but it didn't have much else going for it."

The chemical works I carry around inside was beginning to make a fuss. "How did you see the painting?"

"Jerry had a transparency of it. He said the company photographs all the pieces they write a policy on. Jerry wanted to find out why the cop was so interested in it."

By now the chemical works was making a major assault on the lining of my stomach and everything else in reach. If Dodge was telling the truth, I'd just spent the past twenty-four hours running in the wrong direction.

Chapter 18

At 10:30 the next morning I was back in the office of Dean
Bancroft at the Legion Palace Museum in San Francisco. I
told the wiry, tense man behind the cluttered desk and
overflowing ashtray about what I'd been told in Barracks
Cove. That Jerry Lind had expressed interest in a cop who'd
been looking into the theft of a painting. That Jerry had
found out about the cop from somebody at the museum.

"You didn't mention that, Mr. Bancroft."

"Because it never happened," Bancroft replied.

"Think about it some. Maybe it slipped your mind."

"I did think about it, after you were here before. Trying to
be the good citizen and all that jazz. You left me your card
and asked me to give a call if I remembered anything more.
Well, I just plain haven't."

Sometimes when I don't get enough sleep, my face or eyes
or something tends to betray my feelings. My disappointment must have shown. Disappointment not only in Dodge,
but in Allison's trust of him as well. The whole thing just
kept getting worse.

"What's wrong?" Bancroft asked.

I dismissed it with a tired wave. "Just job problems. If
what you say is right, it means somebody else lied to me. I
didn't want that to be the case."

"I can see that," Bancroft said quietly. "Let me think
about this some more." He got up from his desk and wandered over to a window facing north. His mind might have
been groping all the way to Barracks Cove, getting a sense
of the good and the bad up there.

"There could be one thing," Bancroft said, turning to push
a button on a call box. "Mary, find Artie for me, will you?"

146

A woman's voice said that she would, and Bancroft stared at me with pursed lips.

"Who's Artie?"

"My chief operational aide. He's the one who actually took that Lind fellow down the hall and showed him where the stolen painting had hung. I was, as usual, up to my nervous ass in several other things."

The door opened and in came a young fellow with long, braided hair wearing an Indian headband and puka shell necklace and staring out at the world through thick eyeglasses.

"Artie, this is Mr. Bragg, a private investigator. He's interested in that Pavel work that was stolen."

"Oh yeah. That was a piece of bad stuff."

"What Artie means, Mr. Bragg, is that he liked the Pavel piece."

"That's what I said," said Artie.

"Okay, Artie, I'm also interested in an insurance investigator named Jerry Lind who was looking into the theft. Mr. Bancroft here says you showed him where the painting had hung."

"Right, I remember him. And he in turn was interested in the cop."

"And that," put in Bancroft, "is what I want to know about, Artie. What cop?"

"The cop who came through a day or so before then and asked all the questions about the Pavel piece."

"That sounds like somebody I didn't see," Bancroft told him.

"That's right," Artie agreed. "It was the day Mrs. Munser came popping through asking for the twentieth time when you were going to find room on the walls for that ratty stuff her late husband left us."

Bancroft sat down with a little moan. "I remember that day."

"Right," said Artie. "Your ulcer turned over."

"And I went home early," said Bancroft.

"That's why you didn't see the cop and I did," said Artie.

"Was it a local officer?" I asked.

"No, man, he was from down south. That's why it knocked me out that he should show such interest in the Pavel piece. He showed more interest in it than anyone. Which made me feel he might have been a little weird himself."

"Why is that?"

147

"You sit in a room staring at it all day and you'd know what I mean." He half shuddered. "Man, I loved it."

"You don't remember the cop's name, do you?"

"No, but I have his card here," said Artie, reaching for his wallet. "Here it is. Robert Dempsey. Rey Platte, California."

I got out the photo of Dempsey. "This man?"

"Right. Mean-looking mother. I mean, he was pleasant enough and all, but he sort of impressed you that you'd better not give him any shit or he'd break all your fingers."

"Tell me what you can remember about what he said. What he asked. What you told him."

Artie weaved his head and grimaced. "He asked maybe three thousand different questions. My mind was reeling. I answered as best I could. First he wanted to know everything about the theft. What day, time of day, what hours we were open, how our lighting setup works, the foot traffic we had going through, how the frame was hung, where the guard station and routes were. You'd think he was going to shoot a movie or something. He was very interested also in what the stolen painting depicted, and whether we had a copy of it. We didn't, but I described it as best I could."

"Which would be pretty good," said Bancroft. "Artie has a good eye."

"The painting showed a woman looking off a porch with a shock on her face?"

"Shock?" repeated Artie. "More like two seconds from a cardiac arrest. Then he wanted to know where the exhibit had come from and if we knew who owned the painting and all. I told him the owner was this guy Bo somebody in Santa Barbara."

"Did Dempsey make a note of that?"

"No. He seemed to already know about him."

"Did he give any idea of why he was so interested?"

"Oh no, he was very good at dummying up himself, while pumping me like a girl's arm at the Grange dance. He only said he'd been a fan of the guy who did the work for a long time. And that he'd read about the theft in the papers down south."

"How long did he spend here?"

"An hour or more. And he looked at the other Pavel works we had in the exhibit. Seems he'd seen two of them before, but the third one captured his interest. He took notes on it."

"What did it show?"

"A guy looking out at you as if he'd just seen his mother run over. Whew!"

"Did Lind question you about the cop's interest?"

"Quite a bit, yeah. I don't know if he asked about the technique, though, or whether I even thought to tell him."

"What about technique?"

"The cop asked if there was anything peculiar about the Pavel works, other than the subject matter. So that if he did some other subject matter, there would maybe be something recurrent to identify it."

"And you saw something?"

"There was one quirky thing on both the painting that was stolen and on one of the others. They were outdoor scenes. This guy, whoever he was, had a peculiar way of doing grass. Not that there was a lot of it, but when he depicted individual blades they appeared thin where they sprouted from the ground and thick at the top. And he had a mathematical sequence of painting broken blades. I don't remember exactly, but from one broken blade, the next one would be four blades over and three up, or something like that. But it was consistently that way. In both of the paintings that had grass in them."

Artie chuckled. "You know how it is. Some guys get a little goofy in their work. Of course that guy Pavel, whoever he was, the people he painted—he must really have been a wacko."

I made a phone call to Mr. Bo Smythe in Santa Barbara. Mr. Smythe was in. I said I was looking into the disappearance of his painting and asked if he'd be home the rest of the afternoon. Smythe sounded a bit eccentric and he spoke with an irritating rasp, but he said he'd be at home and he told me how to get there. I didn't tell him I was phoning from San Francisco International. I just told him I'd be there in a couple hours. Then I phoned the office. Ceejay told me there hadn't been any calls relating to the Lind case, and they were the only sort I wanted to hear about just then.

At the Santa Barbara airport I rented a car and followed Bo Smythe's directions, driving out east of town and into the fancy hills that caught on fire every couple of years. Smythe didn't live too far into them. He was high enough so you could see the Pacific Ocean from the road out front. The grounds and driveway leading to a parking area were guarded by high hedges. Smythe came out from his yard to greet me as I was getting out of the car. He was a hard-looking little guy from sixty to seventy years of age with skin the color and texture of old saddlebags. He wore a Mexican sombrero, bright plaid walking shorts, leather sandals and a withered goatee.

"Bragg? I'm Smythe."

He had a calloused hand capable of imparting a firm grip and impish crinkles at the corners of his eyes.

"What do you think of her?" he asked, gesturing toward the big, pink stucco house overhead. The roof was red tile and there was a large green and yellow Yin and Yang painted on the wall facing the drive.

"It catches a fellow off guard," I told him.

"You bet. Where you from, Bragg?"

"I work out of San Francisco."

"Good. I don't worry about folks passing through. It's the idiot locals I can't abide to have hanging around. Boy, the things you have to do for a little privacy, if you can't afford electrified fences and your own corps of bodyguards. C'mon into the garden."

It was a pleasantly bewildering place. A white pebble path meandered around bird baths and fountains and statuary sprinkled among beds of roses, palm trees and big, shiny green-leafed things I didn't know the name of. The area was a pastiche of Luther Burbank sincerity and Southern California luck.

Smythe led me to some wrought iron furniture painted white and motioned for me to sit down. He watched my looking around.

"Something, isn't it?" he asked. "Worked forty-two years so I could find a place like this and do it up the way I wanted. Don't really care what others think. I like it."

"It's all that should matter."

"That's how I feel about it."

"Are you married, Mr. Smythe?"

"Sure. Why, you want to talk to Thelma? You didn't say so on the phone. She's in town having her hair done."

"No, I just wondered if she likes the way you've done things."

"She doesn't have to. She has her own garden over on the other side of the house. What was it you wanted to talk about?"

150

I reeled my mind back in. "The Pavel paintings you loaned out. I was wondering how you acquired them."

"I bought them, at various places. First one I saw was at an art fair down at Laguna Beach. Picked up another at a little gallery in Long Beach. Different places like that."

"How about Santa Barbara here?"

"No. Never saw any in this area."

"I'm curious why you're so fond of them."

"Fond? You think I'm crazy, young man? No, not fond. Fascinated, perhaps. I'm a doctor of psychiatry, Bragg. When I was active at it, I spent very little time in private practice. I couldn't find the stimulation there. I did a lot of work in prisons, with disturbed children, things like that. I didn't make as much money that way, but I left it all with a feeling of satisfaction at my life's work. And these paintings you ask about, or at least the man who did them, fascinate me the way some dark and twisted mind would fascinate me. I take 'em out and look at them from time to time, but good heavens, it isn't the sort of thing you hang over your bed now, is it?"

"No, it isn't, Doctor."

"Call me Bo. What's your name?"

"Pete."

"Okay, Pete. I'm thirsty. Want a beer?"

"Sure, I'd love one."

"I have five more of those Pavel things. Want to see them?"

"I'd appreciate it."

He led me across a patch of lawn to a basement door. He went over to a refrigerator. It was filled with beer and white wine and fruit juices.

"The paintings are under that tarp over there," he told me, indicating a bench along one wall. "Bring 'em on outside."

The paintings were all about two-by-two-and-a-half feet. I lifted them in a stack and carried them outdoors.

"Gotten so I don't even like to look at them inside anymore," Smythe told me. "They give me the willies. Just stand them up against the serving cart over there."

I did as he asked. It was a dark undertaking even among the bright greenery and chirping birds overhead. They were the way the other paintings had been described. They showed men of various ages and means in different settings. Only the terror on their faces was the same. One of them depicted a man in front of a cabin. There was a patch of grass beside

151

it, and it had the telltale details that Artie, back at the museum, had described. Individual blades grew from a thin, reedy base to a thick, outer blade. Even the broken blade pattern was there. Artie had it just backward. From the lowest broken blade, the others were three blades over and four up. I went back to my chair and took the beer Smythe handed me.

"Beauties all, hey?"

"What do you make of them?"

"Oh, God, who knows? Obviously something haywire about the man who did those. I could see a fellow trying one or two of those things, to get something dark out of his soul, but not a whole string of them. I tried to run down the man who did them, unsuccessfully."

"Did you learn his name?"

Smythe took a tug at his beer, then lowered it with a nod. "John Roper, it was. At least that's what somebody at one of the galleries told me."

"What else did they tell you about him?"

"Very little. Nobody I talked to had ever met him. There was always a third party of some sort, either peddling the work at art fairs, or approaching the galleries about displaying them."

"Did you find out where he lived?"

"Nope. Found a lot of places where he used to live. He seemed to be one of those fellows who moved around a lot."

I took out my picture of Dempsey and handed it to Smythe. "Do you recognize this man?"

Smythe stared at it with a frown. "I ought to. It's a hard face to forget. I can't place it, but I'm sure I have seen him somewhere."

"He was a police detective."

"Oh sure, he came by here a couple years ago. He was interested in my collection of Pavel stuff, too."

"How so?"

"He was a little more blunt about it than you are, young man. He wanted to know why any man would want to collect this sort of stuff. I told him about the same thing I told you. Introduced him to Thelma and she charmed him some. Showed him my old medical degree, stuff like that. He finally accepted my story."

"Did you ask why he was curious?"

"Sure, but he was here to ask questions, not to answer any. He just told me he'd heard I had a little collection of

152

the stuff, and that he'd always had an abiding interest in the man's work himself."

I caught a flight to the small Rey Platte airport, and from there took a cab out to Coral Dempsey's home and asked the driver to wait. I didn't want to spend long with the widow. Just long enough to find out what she might know about her late husband's interest in art.

It was the middle of the afternoon. Sounds of children came from behind a house across the street. At the Dempsey house the blinds were closed and there was no response to my ringing and knocking. I went around to the driveway beside the house. The carport was empty. I went back to the street in front. I was about to go across to the house where I heard the kids playing when the screendoor on the house next door opened and an overweight woman of thirty or so in a white halter and pink shorts came out.

"Were you looking for somebody?"

"I wanted to see Mrs. Dempsey."

The neighbor shook her head. "She left this morning. There was—a terrible accident in the family."

"You mean Mr. Dempsey?"

"Yes."

"I know about that. When will Mrs. Dempsey be back?"

"She didn't say. She packed up the kids and left first thing this morning. Wasn't it awful?"

"Yes it was. Did she say when she'd be back?"

"She didn't know for sure. They went to Barstow. She has folks there. I'm sort of keeping an eye on the house for her. Would you like to come in?"

She was the concerned neighbor, with the morbid curiosity that concerned neighbors have. She figured she would find out more about what happened to Dempsey than Mrs. Dempsey would have told her. On that score she was right, but I didn't want to ruin the rest of her day by telling her about it.

"No, that's all right. Do you know the name of her folks in Barstow?"

She shook her head. "But she'll phone later in the week."

I nodded. "Thanks, anyhow."

I took the cab back downtown to the police station. Chief Porter was deep-bottomed into his chair as if he hadn't moved since I was there Sunday night. But he showed some strain, as if he hadn't been getting enough sleep, and he indicated what had been bothering him when he asked me to describe in detail the condition of Dempsey's body when I'd found him. I did it as clinically as I could, but I'm not a coroner's deputy, and the telling of it bothered us both.

"His revolver was still in his holster?" the chief asked.

"That's right. He didn't realize he'd found whoever, or whatever, he was looking for."

"And what do you think that was?"

"Until last night, I figured the insurance man I'm looking for, and Dempsey, had both been looking for the source of the stolen money. But somewhere along the line Dempsey changed directions. I've learned he had great curiosity about a painting that was stolen last month from the Legion Palace Museum in San Francisco. Dempsey visited the museum and asked a lot of questions about it. Then he continued north and eventually ended up in Barracks Cove. My boy was a couple of steps behind him all the way. I think he disappeared while looking for Dempsey. I think he wanted to ask Dempsey why the painting was so important to him."

"What kind of painting?" the chief asked.

"It was a wacky portrait. In fact, one of a whole series of weird figure studies I've learned Dempsey was interested in over the years. All of them done by somebody calling himself Pavel."

Porter just stared at me a minute, then scraped back his chair and went over to a file cabinet.

"Gone," he said finally, banging shut the drawer. "Guess Bob took it with him."

"A file?"

"Yes, but hell, it was more his than the department's, with all his own time he put in on it."

"Tell me about it."

"It started with a terrible story we heard from a local woman, Mary Madigan. It was about a painting that turned up at the art festival we have here in the fall. We got a lot of rich old boys living hereabouts, retired, you know, so this art fair attracts a lot of people from all over the state, both artists and dealers. Anyhow, one of the displays put up by a gallery from Los Angeles included one of those Pavel things. Mary Madigan saw it and nearly fainted. She said it was a painting of her brother, even down to the tip of his left middle finger that she said was lopped off in an accident when he was a youngster, and the necktie she said he wore the day he was murdered. Decapitated, to be exact. His body had been found a couple years earlier in a vacant lot back east, in Pittsburgh. The brother had been running a food specialty business that was a growing concern, supposedly making inroads on a competitor that had racket money in the operation. The Pittsburgh police told us later they believed it was a hired kill.

"Well, sir, Bob and I both went over and looked at the painting. It was a grisly thing, right enough, but a lot of what Mary thought she saw in it wasn't all that apparent to me. It wasn't as sharp as any photograph, after all. What she saw as a lopped-off finger could have been a smudge of something else. And the tie—hell, I could have found a couple resembling it in any men's store. I figured it to be more a piece of Mary's imagination, still upset over her brother's death and all."

"And Dempsey?"

"Well, Bob was fascinated at what it could mean if she did turn out to be right, so like I said, he started putting a lot of his own time in on it trying to find out who this Pavel was. He even learned the man's true name, or at least the name he was using then, but it was a whisker too late."

"What was the name?"

"John Roper."

"That's the same information I have."

The creases deepened on the chief's forehead. "Anyway, Bob had some extensive phone conversations with the Pittsburgh police. They never caught the person who murdered Mary's brother, but they told Bob they thought it was a fellow with a terrible background who called himself Hobo. I'd heard stories about that name myself."

My mouth went dry on me. "So have I."

"Anyway, Bob nosed around a lot of art galleries along the coast, found and took photos of a number of those Pavel works. Sent copies around to a lot of major police departments, asking if they resembled victims who might have been killed in their area. He did get back a few tentative IDs, but it was all pretty iffy stuff.

"But there was one strange thing Bob found. This Pavel fellow wasn't looking for any publicity. He always worked through intermediaries to get his work displayed. Then like I said, Bob got lucky. I think it was through some dealer in L.A. he knew. Found out the fellow who painted under the name Pavel was the Roper fellow. And we were practically neighbors. He lived just southeast of here, but it took another week for Bob Dempsey to learn that, and by the time he went there this Roper had moved, just days before. Didn't leave a trace, either. Was like the earth had swallowed him. That's the last I knew of Bob doing anything about it. I didn't know he was still pursuing that theory."

"Theory?"

"Yes, that Roper and Pavel and the Hobo were all the same fellow. That he was some sort of madman who painted from memory what his victims had looked like just before he killed them."

"You personally didn't buy it?"

"No, Bragg, I didn't. Like I said, it was all so iffy. Of course now, after what's happened, I'd hate like hell to think Bob was right and I was wrong all this time."

Chapter 19

I couldn't blame Chief Porter for his doubts, but the aggravating thing was it did make sense in light of everything that had happened in the Jerry Lind case. I had heard enough, from enough sober cops, about this individual who called himself Hobo to know he existed, that he was ruthless and that he was responsible for a lot of carnage. That he could be a painter as well was not outside the realm of possibility. And if he were a painter, that he might be driven to portray his victims made a lot of sense. Dempsey, who seemed to have been nobody's fool, had pursued that theory with vigor to the moment of his own death.

I made my way back north, by scheduled and charter flights. We were able to get back into Mendocino airport by late afternoon, just ahead of a thick, wet fog booming in from the sea.

The first thing I did was put in another call to the San

Francisco homicide detail to ask John Foley the staus of the guy who called himself Hobo.

"Our best information," said Foley with an edge to his voice, "is that he went into retirement a few years back. That is the word that came down in various state prisons and other places. Why do you ask?"

"There is a possibility that to avoid exposure, he has come back out of retirement."

"Jesus, pal, I hope you're wrong about that one."

I made a note of the date and time in a pocket pad I carried. By now I was pretty grimly sure that Jerry Lind was dead. If that were true, I wouldn't charge his sister for any more time I might spend poking around in Barracks Cove. And I fully intended to spend some more time poking around in Barracks Cove.

The one person locally who'd given me the biggest break was the man calling himself Joe Dodge. Maybe he could tell me more, now that he'd had a day to think about it. I looked up his phone number and dialed it. The line was busy, which told me he was home, so I got my car out of the airport parking area and drove up to Barracks Cove and out Cupper's Road. What I found at its end displeased me. Joe Dodge's old car was gone, but parked just up the road from the house was a tan late model Cadillac with the license number I'd jotted down the day before during my encounter with Emil Stoval.

It was a further complication I could have done without. I went up to the front door of the Dodge home and rapped on it loudly enough to stir apples in the orchard down the road. Nobody answered. I couldn't hear anybody moving around inside. I went around and tried the back door. It was unlocked. It opened into a kitchen with dirty dishes in the sink and the musty, old, kick-around aroma of bachelor quarters.

I shouted Dodge's name a couple of times, getting no response. Then I noticed a small, reddish stain on the kitchen linoleum near the doorway leading into the rest of the house. It could have been painter's oil, burgundy wine or a dab of catsup. Or it could have been blood. I bent down for a closer inspection. It was still tacky and it wasn't one of the innocent substances.

I went on through the doorway and stepped into a room that looked as if a couple of bears had done battle there. Shattered glass covered the floor, chairs were overturned and a wooden table with a couple of busted legs knelt to the floor with lost dignity. Something or somebody had gone through a side window that had a torn roller curtain ripped half off of its wooden staff. The room breathed violence. I went on through to the studio where Dodge worked. Things seemed innocent enough there. I went back to the living room and searched for more of the telltale reddish stains, but couldn't find any. In one corner was a telephone with its cracked plastic receiver off the hook. So much for the busy signal I'd heard. I went on back through the kitchen and outside. I found another splotch of blood on a lower step of the back porch. The land behind the house sloped up toward a grove of trees. There appeared to be a recently made track through the wild grass, where something might have been dragged.

I went back around to the front of the house and over to my car. I opened the trunk and got out the shoulder holster and the .45 caliber automatic it held. I don't like having to wear it, but it wasn't just a missing person case any longer. It hadn't been since I found Dempsey's body. I took off my jacket and wrapped and tied myself in the leather gear. I vividly remembered the way Dempsey had looked, up by the Stannis River, with his gun snug in its holster. I thought about that for a moment then got out my revolver also and clipped its holster to my belt before putting my coat back on. If I'd had an old cavalry saber I would have hung that on me as well.

I closed up the car and went over to Stoval's Cadillac. It was unlocked and the window on the driver's side was rolled down. Inside, the car was clean and empty. I went around to the side of the house with the broken window. In the weeds nearby was a smashed table lamp that had been pitched through the glass. I continued on around to the back and started up the slope with .45 in hand. At the tree line the grass gave way to a ground cover of pine needles and earth. I took a good look and listen around the area, assuring myself nobody was lurking nearby, then continued on into the grove of trees where the drag marks led me. I knew how it had to turn out, as if I were taking part in an old familiar play. I rounded a tree and stopped. Emil Stoval wouldn't be bothering anybody's wife again, not even his own.

He was wearing the same jacket and slacks he'd had on the day before. He was lying face up with his unbuttoned jacket scrunched up under his shoulders from being dragged feet first up the slope. His dead eyes were staring into the

158

trees overhead. His mouth was slightly ajar and a big soggy patch of drying blood caked his shirt front. I put away my pistol and got down on my hands and knees to try seeing the shape of his back. The scrunched jacket propped him up from the ground so I could pretty well see he hadn't sustained much damage there. I got back up and brushed off my clothes. There was a mark over his left eye that could have been made by a blow to the head, but it wasn't anything sensational. I leaned over to study his hands. There was matter beneath several fingernails. One of the nails was even torn. It appeared he'd come to grips with his foe, and probably put up a fair scrap before somebody shot him in the back. At least that's how it looked from the mess on his shirt front—shot with a heavy caliber weapon that made a nasty exit wound, just as in Dempsey's case.

I searched the ground surrounding the body without seeing anything important. I studied the body some more and wondered if a rough idea of the time of death would be important enough to me to justify fooling with it. Rigidity, or coagulation in the muscles, generally is first noticeable in the neck and jaw, but I didn't feel like messing with his face or head. I bent over and touched one of his hands. It had cooled off some. I tried moving a couple of his limbs. There was some stiffness in his leg, but the arms still moved freely. Which meant it was early in the stiffening process. Emil probably had been killed five to six hours earlier, around noon.

I left the body and went back to the Joe Dodge house. It probably wouldn't matter, but I used a handkerchief to hold the phone receiver and dialed Chief Morgan to tell him what I'd found. He wasn't at all happy about it. I agreed to hang around until he and his men got there, then made a couple more phone calls. I dialed Allison's number to ask her if she'd seen Joe Dodge that day. There was no answer. I made a collect call to check in with my answering service in San Francisco. They said Allison had called, trying to get a message to me, soon after I'd spoken to Ceejay that morning. Allison had wanted me to phone her at another Barracks Cove number. It was the number of the phone I was using right then, in Dodge's smashed-up living room. My stomach felt as if it wanted to go to pieces on me again.

They hadn't had a case of known murder in Barracks Cove for several years. It brought out just about everybody in the department. They all were tramping up to the grove of trees behind the house to get a look at the body. They were giving fits to an area physician who served as county coroner. For that capacity he dealt mainly with the victims of auto collisions and hunting accidents. While it didn't take a medical genius to determine Stoval's primary cause of death, the doc wanted to employ correct preliminary investigative procedures he'd read about over the years, and he wasn't being helped any by the gawking local cops.

Morgan listened in grim silence to what I had to tell him about the Hobo and the curious theories to do with him that the slain Dempsey had been following. Morgan had never heard of the Hobo, but that didn't surprise me. He'd had no reason to in order to do a decent job of policing Barracks Cove. And while he found it hard to swallow the possibility that a man who had slain a vast number of people could be living in Barracks Cove without anyone becoming the wiser, he at least was professional enough to concede the possibility and not just laugh in my face over it.

"Of course," said the chief, "the killer you're talking about could be living here, right enough, but still not have had anything to do with this man Stoval's death."

"It's possible, but I doubt it. I think it's a simple case of a man killing to protect his real identity. I think the Hobo killed Dempsey. I think he probably killed the man I was hired to look for, Jerry Lind, and I think probably he killed Emil Stoval earlier today."

"This Stoval was by my office yesterday. But he told me he was trying to trace some stolen money that turned up recently."

"I know, but so was Dempsey, early on. Then he stumbled across something that put him on the Hobo's trail. The same thing could have happened to Jerry Lind, and now to Stoval."

The chief rubbed one ear, then fixed me with a gaze that told me he was about to say or ask something that he didn't like to think about. "Could Joe Dodge be this Hobo fellow?"

"Not unless he started killing people when he was about eight years old."

Morgan grunted. "Still and all," he said, looking back down the slope toward the Dodge house, "I am going to have a number of questions to ask that man when we find him."

When they let me go I drove across town to Allison's house. She'd left her back door unlocked and I went through her bedroom closet and bathroom. So far as I could tell she hadn't packed anything. I went out to her studio. If she'd

160

left town with Joe Dodge, it appeared to have been a spur of the moment decision. Maybe the two of them had found Stoval's body and fled out of fear. Maybe they'd been killed and hauled off somewhere. I stood amidst the dichotomy of her work. Along one wall was the pop art stuff she made her living from; ships and planes and people in wacky juxtaposition. Many of the people were bare-breasted beauties. Allison herself. Elsewhere in the studio was the serious stuff. Deftly balanced, almost mathematical radiation and structure of lines that made you feel as if you might fall into the painting and become a part of its ethereal universe.

I glanced over a shoulder at one of the buxom creatures. It was Allison's body but somebody else's saucy face winking at me. A far-out hope dawned. It was something I'd almost forgotten about in the roar of events. I winked back at the saucy face and thanked Allison for triggering the bright idea. I went into the house and made another call down to San Francisco, to Janet Lind at the television station. They were putting together the six o'clock news show. She was very busy and made that plain to me.

"I'm busy, too, still trying to find your brother. Or his remains."

"Is it that bad?"

"I haven't been running into many comic moments. There are some ugly murders involved in all this, but I don't have time to tell you about them right now."

"What is it you want?"

"You told me that the last time you talked with your brother you discussed a feature story you'd done about a collection of modern stuff being exhibited at the Legion Palace Museum."

"That's right. It was very trendy."

"I think that very exhibit included some scary paintings by a guy named Pavel. In fact one of them was stolen later. It showed a woman looking off a porch at something awful. She had a terrified look on her face. Is it possible your report included that piece? And if it did, would you still have it recorded on film or tape?"

"Oh, wow. I don't know. We did have a shot of that one all right, but there was some discussion about whether or not it would be in good taste to air it. It was pretty gruesome looking. If we did use it we'll still have it on tape. If not, I'm afraid we won't. How soon do you need to know?"

161

"If seeing it will tell me anything, I need to know immediately."

"Can you come over to the station?"

"No, I'm up in Barracks Cove."

"I don't see how . . ."

"You could show it on your six o'clock news."

"But there would be no justification . . ."

"Sure there would. Tell the viewers it was stolen June Fourth from the museum and that police suspect it to be tied up with a couple of murders in the Barracks Cove area. If anyone has seen that painting they should contact police. One of the victims was an insurance investigator from San Francisco named Eric Stoval. He was your brother's boss. I found his body about an hour ago. He'd been shot. But if you want to use his name you'd better try reaching his wife first, in case the police haven't gotten around to it. She models in San Francisco under the name Faye Ashton."

"All right," she said in a hushed voice. "I'll have to get the producer's okay, provided we have the picture on tape. Who was the other person killed?"

"A police detective named Robert Dempsey from Rey Platte. He'd been shot also. I found his body in a car near the Stannis River, east of here. That was yesterday."

"I'll do what I can. Where can I call you?"

"I'm moving around. I'll phone back in thirty minutes."

I left Allison's and drove back into town.

Chapter 20

There was something else I hadn't gotten around to doing since learning that Dempsey had been on the trail of the stolen painting. I'd never checked back with Wiley Huggins at the town frame shop to ask if the big detective had stopped by there. It seemed reasonable that he would have. I found a parking space across from the shop and went on over. Minnie Parsons was up on a ladder in one corner with a feather duster.

"Hello there, young man," she called. "You're still in town, are you?"

"Not still, Mrs. Parsons, once again. Is Mr. Huggins around?"

"He's next door at the bakery. Should be back in a minute. Can I help you with anything?"

"No, thanks. I don't suppose you've seen Allison today. Or Joe Dodge?"

"No, not today. Here, help me down from this thing, will you?"

I held the ladder with one hand and braced one of her arms with the other as she made her way down, but she still fell slightly into me as she reached the floor.

"What in heaven's name is that?" she asked, thumping the bulge of my shoulder holster.

"Nothing to worry about, Mrs. Parsons. Sometimes it's necessary for me to carry a gun."

She gave an indignant sniff. "Didn't think you'd need it in here, did you?"

"Not really."

"Don't like guns, myself."

The bell tinkled over the front door and Wiley Huggins entered with a bag of things that smelled good. He squinted at me, not quite remembering where he'd seen me before.

"Peter Bragg," I told him. "I stopped by Saturday evening asking about a man named Jerry Lind."

"Oh sure, I remember now," he told me, putting his goods on the counter. He turned to Minnie. "Anybody come in offering to buy the place while I was out?"

"Quit your joking, Wiley. You couldn't sell this place, the town wouldn't let you."

"Oh it wouldn't, huh? Well, just let a body come in here offering the right price and you'd see soon enough what I'd do. And the town could go hang its hat on a willow tree for all I care. What about that bird you said was here this morning? Did he come back?"

"I haven't seen him."

"What about you, young fellow? Wanna buy the joint? Or a painting or something?"

"Not today. But I have another photo to show you. I'd like

163

you to try to remember if you've seen him before. Recently, probably."

I showed him the photo of Dempsey. He adjusted his glasses and squinted at it."

"Oh, yeah. He's that mean-looking one. Asked a lot of questions. Didn't care to answer many in return."

"That sounds like him. His name was Dempsey."

"That I don't recall. I just remember the abiding interest he had in the Cove Pan-o-Ram in the front window there."

Huggins nodded toward the big splashy mural depicting area people and places that I'd noticed my first night in town. It was beginning to fall into place. My pulse picked up some as I went back outside and took another long look at it. And now I knew what made Dempsey change direction. I knew what he'd thought was going to get him elected sheriff. In a portion of the painting representing the state park north of town, there was a patch of grass, with the stems thin at the bottom, thick on top, and with broken blades, three over and four up from one another. I went back inside and tried to sound calm.

"Who painted it?"

"That's the first thing the other fellow asked," Huggins told me. "He was a bit disappointed when I told him half the town had a hand in it. Leastways most anybody who could hold onto a paint brush for the time it took to make a stroke or two."

"I don't get it."

"It was a real community effort," Minnie explained.

"We made it to be the centerpiece of the art fair we had over in the Square last spring," Huggins said. "Made a big hit, too. When the show closed I decided to put her in the window here for a while so everyone in it could come by and admire themselves."

"But how many people actually worked on it?"

"I'd guess forty or fifty of us, wouldn't you, Minnie?"

"At least that many. Not just the painters in town, but everyone who had anything to do with organizing or staging the fair."

"I only spent about five minutes on the thing myself," Huggins said. "I got a business to run."

"What did Dempsey say when you told him that?"

"He wanted to know who'd worked on certain segments of it, but I couldn't tell him that, either. But I gave him tho

164

names of several people who were the major movers and shakers of the project."

"Who were they?"

"Oh, Abe Whelan and Charlie Baldwin, who owns one of the restaurants down at the cove. Big Mike and that policeman fellow, Hawkes."

"Hawkes?"

"Yes, he's quite a good painter. And I believe Joe Dodge was involved. And the Morrisey brothers, some local contractors. They built the stand we put her on, too."

"Who oversaw the actual painting?"

"No one person all the time," said Huggins. "The crazy thing sort of had a life of its own. But I guess the people I mentioned did most of the bossing."

"Allison put in a lot of work, too," said Minnie.

"That's right, she did," said the shop owner. "It's funny, thinking back on it. That Dempsey fellow made a rather lengthy list of the people I told him about. As if he was going to talk to every one of them. But he never did."

"How do you know?"

"Well, I was interested in why he was so all-fired curious about it. So later, I asked the people whose names I'd given him, thinking he might have told them more than he told me. But none of them had ever seen him. How about you? Feel like telling me what this is all about?"

"It involves some missing people. Dempsey was a detective from Southern California. He was subsequently murdered."

"Oh, my goodness," gasped Minnie.

"How'd that happen?" Huggins asked.

"He got careless. And one of the people who worked on that painting in the window killed him. And that same person, I'm convinced, killed another man today out at the Joe Dodge house."

"Oh, no!" cried Minnie.

"Who got it today?" asked Huggins, his eyes gleaming with interest.

"An insurance man named Stoval."

"Stoval," Huggins repeated faintly. He went around behind the counter and hunted around until he came up with a business card and turned to Minnie. "That's the fellow you said was in here this morning while I was up at the nursery."

Minnie raised one hand to her throat. I looked at the card. It was Emil's.

"What did he want, Mrs. Parsons?"

"He showed me a photograph," she said weakly. "Asked if I recognized the person in it. I told him it looked like Joe Dodge. He asked where Joe lived. I didn't like the way he was asking things so I hedged. Told him I didn't know for sure. So he left, and I saw him going around into the other places here on the Square. He must have been asking the same questions. I . . ."

She looked about her, as if searching for a place to sit, then stared blankly at me.

"What is it, Mrs. Parsons?"

"Well, I told you I hadn't seen Allison or Joe Dodge today. And it's true, I didn't. But I did call Allison, right after the insurance fellow left. I don't know Joe Dodge all that well, but I knew Allison was friendly toward him and I thought somebody else should know there was a stranger in town asking about him."

"What did Allison say?"

"Not very much. Her voice took a serious turn, but she just thanked me and hung up. I hope I didn't do anything wrong."

"I'm sure you didn't." And that probably explained why Allison and Joe Dodge were missing. But running had been a mistake. Especially in view of what followed. And it was puzzling that Stoval still had been searching for the money. He hadn't made the painting connection. So why had he been killed?"

"Oh, Wiley, I forgot," said Minnie, her voice still shaken. "Abe called again asking when he could pick up the Pan-o-Ram. Said he wants to get it done and over with so he can forget about it."

"I know, he's been pestering me all week. I told him I hadn't figured out yet what I'm going to replace it with."

"The painting in the window?"

"That's right," Huggins told me. "We're going to put her out of circulation until the fair next spring. Abe Whelan volunteered to stick it in a loft out at his place."

A distant, roundabout curve of an idea came soaring into my head. "Where does he live?"

"He's got a three or four acre spread a ways out of town where he keeps a couple cows and some chickens, like a lot of folks hereabouts. And a horse or two."

"What does he do for a living?"

"He's retired. Same as I'd be if I had any sense."

"Is he a native of the area?"

"Nope. He must have moved here—what, Minnie? Four or five years ago?"

"That's about right."

"Do you know what he did before he retired?"

"I don't know," said Huggins. "Do you, Minnie?"

"No, but Father might know. He and Abe play chess together and go off fishing from time to time."

"Is your husband at home now, Mrs. Parsons?"

"Yes. I was about to call and have him come to pick me up."

"Maybe I could give you a lift. I'd like to speak to him, if it won't spoil your dinner plans."

"Of course not. And it's nice of you to save him the trip down. I'll just give a call and tell him I have a ride."

"Fine. I have an errand to run. I'll be back in a few minutes. Oh, I assume you have a television set at home, Mrs. Parsons."

"Yes. Why do you ask?"

"There's something I might want to watch on the evening news."

I left the little shop and trotted down to the corner where there was a phone booth. At this stage of the game there were things I didn't want other people to overhear. I tried calling Allison again, but there was no answer. I phoned Janet Lind.

"We have what you want," she told me. "They're letting me do a brief item on it early in the program. We couldn't get in touch with Mrs. Stoval, so we won't use the name. We'll do it right after the first commercial break into the show. At about three minutes past six."

I thanked her and started back toward the frame shop, then hesitated. I was afraid of missing something. I figured I was at the stage Dempsey was at just before he was killed. My nerves were getting jumpy and I was afraid there were some things I should have been paying more attention to as they went past. I went back to the phone booth and called the local police number. Chief Morgan was still out at the Dodge house, but the desk man was able to tell me the phone number of Fairbanks, the man who had led the search for the downed plane. I managed to reach him and told him who I was.

"One thing I'm curious about," I told him. "Before we left the campground to start up the mountain, I think you sent somebody back down river to look for any survivors who might have gotten down that far. Can you remember who it was you sent?"

"Oh God, not hardly. I had so many things to do that morning . . ."

"I know, Mr. Fairbanks. But it could be very important. It has to do with the job that brought me up here in the first place. The job I had to postpone in order to help out in the search."

It was no time to be quietly noble or self-effacing about having saved his marbles by finding the boy and getting the searchers over to the right part of the county to find the downed plane. He owed me.

"Let me think," said Fairbanks. "I was figuring one of the men with four-wheel drive would have the best chance of getting back among those old roads. Damn! I remember what the fellow looks like now but can't recall his name."

"Was it Abe Whelan?"

"That's it, sure."

I thanked the man and hung up. It was tenuous, but it was a possibility. Whelan hadn't been up on the mountain with the rest of the men. He was on the lower Stannis River. He could have spotted me bringing down the boy. He could have been nervous about my finding the car with Dempsey's body in it. He could have seen me put my rope across the river very near to where the car was, and when I went to get Tuffy he could have cut the rope enough for it to part when a strain was put on it. And now he wanted to store the painting with the telltale grass strokes on it.

I left the phone booth reluctantly. I still felt I was missing something, as if somebody were doing feats of magic and I'd been watching their hands when I should have been keeping an eye on their footwork.

I went back and got Minnie Parsons and headed out of town. I wanted to think but she wanted to talk. I heard about the variety of jams she had canned the previous fall, the odd gradations in local weather and a rather long-winded tale that involved a local somebody named Mrs. Longworthy who had fallen and broken her hip the year before and now corresponded with missionaries in Africa. She still was on that one when I pulled up out front of her place and went around to open the door for her.

"And you can just leave your gun out here," she announced firmly, stepping out of the car. "Nobody's going to be carrying a gun into this house, thank you."

She went on ahead while I dutifully took off my jacket and unstrapped myself from the carrying rig. I stuck the .45 in the trunk and started after her, then remembered the revolver on my hip. I hesitated, then decided to leave it behind. If I carried it in and she spotted it, she might chuck me out of the place before I learned what I needed to know. I reached in to jam the gun and holster down behind the front seat cushion then trotted around the house after her. She was standing in the middle of the backyard talking to Big Mike, who was telling her some sort of story that necessitated a great windmilling of arms and a guffaw or two. He broke it off when he saw me and strode over to shake hands.

"An honor to see you again, Mr. Bragg. It was a fine and courageous thing you did up on that mountain the other day."

"It didn't take courage, Mr. Parsons. Just a lot of huffing and puffing."

"Come on in," he told me, leading me up the back stairs. "Would you like a beer?"

"Sure. Along with anything you can tell me about Abe Whelan, and the kindness to let me look at the six o'clock news on TV."

"Of course. Minnie mentioned it on the phone. What is it you want to see?"

"They're going to put on something that could be vital to the case I'm working on."

"Is that so?" He brought a couple of beers from the refrigerator and handed me one, waving me on into the living room as Minnie started to fuss at the kitchen stove. "Are you still looking for the young fellow who's coming into the money?"

"You remember that, do you? Well, I don't really hold out too much hope of finding him any longer. Now I'm a little more interested in learning the identity of somebody hereabouts who's done some bad things in his lifetime. He's living here under a different name."

"My gosh. What sort of bad things?"

"A little of this and a little of that. If I find him it'll make quite a stir."

It was almost six. Big Mike tuned in a color television set to the station I asked for, then called in Minnie from the kitchen.

"Big doings, Minnie," he told her, giving her a brief squeeze of the shoulders. "Mr. Bragg is looking for somebody living around here under false pretenses. Isn't that what you call her?"

"That covers it," I agreed, hunching forward to stare at the screen. Big Mike settled heavily in an overstuffed chair to my left while Minnie stood behind me tsk-tsking and murmuring something about the things that go on in the world today.

The show's anchorman came on and began talking about the day's events. I only half listened, and complimented Minnie on a vase of camellias atop a sideboard across the room.

"Shhhh," said Big Mike abruptly, then clapped one hand to his mouth. "That was rude of me. But I thought you wanted to hear the news."

"What I'm interested in doesn't come on for another minute or so. It'll be right after the commercial break."

Big Mike turned to me with interest. "My golly, how do you know something as precise as all that?"

"I rigged it up with a girl on the show. She's the missing man's sister. They're going to show me something that might lead me to the man I'm after."

Big Mike shook his head in wonder and took a great gulp of beer. "If that ain't a sensation."

And then Janet Lind's face was on the screen, staring at me with a fleeting, startled expression, as if the camera had caught her before she was quite ready. She started talking about the killings. It tickled the thing that had been eluding me. And finally it dawned on me like a thunderclap just as somebody in the control booth at the television station punched up the taped image of the stolen museum painting. My heart beat started to run away with itself and I tried hard not to show it, because there on the screen, in the painting of the woman gazing horror-stricken from the front porch of a house, with her hair a different color and styled a bit longer, was the woman standing directly behind me who called herself Minnie Parsons, Big Mike's wife.

The blood was rushing through my head and I couldn't even hear what Janet Lind was saying. I could feel the emotions sparking through the room, and then Big Mike got to his feet and crossed to turn off the television set.

"Well," I said as flatly as I could manage, "I'm afraid that didn't tell us much."

"On the contrary, Mr. Bragg, on the contrary," said Big Mike Parsons in a firmly toned voice that had lost all of its gosh and gee and big howdy lummox ways. "I'm afraid it told us everything we all needed to know."

He raised his eyes to Minnie. "And I'm afraid also, old girl, we'll have to make another of our lightning quick disappearances. They've just gotten too close."

"Damn you," Minnie said bitterly, and I knew she wasn't addressing her husband.

I glanced over my shoulder. She was standing there glaring at me with menace on her face and a small automatic pistol pointed at the middle of my back. She gripped it as if she'd had practice. "We'll have to tear up roots once again."

"Easy, Minnie," soothed Big Mike. "It's not all his fault. He's just the best of them we've seen so far. But there will be others in his wake. We just can't beat them back any more. Not here." He opened a drawer in the sideboard beneath the camellias and brought out a .45 like the one out in the trunk of my car.

"On your feet, Mr. Bragg."

"Where are we going?"

"At the risk of sounding trite," he said sadly, "we are taking you for a ride."

Chapter 21

Jerry Lind, I learned soon enough, was dead. My own situation, as I thought about it a few minutes later, sitting with my arms trussed behind me on the passenger side of my own car with Big Mike driving, was not too hopeful. It was true I had a revolver he didn't know about jammed down in the cushions beneath me, but I didn't see how it would do me much good even if I could dig it out. He'd done a good job of tying me up. I tried to wriggle my arms some and decided it would be some time the following winter before I got free that way. Even if I did reach the hidden weapon, I didn't know what I'd be able to shoot with it outside of my own calf.

Following us along an old dirt road up into the hills was Minnie, driving the Parsons' trail vehicle. He'd pointed out to me that while her main purpose was to provide him with a lift once my car and I were disposed of, she also would be johnny-on-the-spot in case I did something cute with my feet and caused Big Mike to crash.

"You must know," he reminded me gently, "she would just love to empty that pistol of hers into your body, Mr. Bragg. She is really quite angry that we have to move once more."

On the other hand I did have one very large thing in my favor. He hadn't already raised his gun and drilled me between the eyes the way he admitted he'd done to Dempsey. He'd been forthright about it. Dempsey had scared him.

So I slouched down in the seat in dejected fashion and went fishing with my fingers for the .38 revolver. You do whatever there is left to do.

"I used to get headaches, you know," Big Mike told me. He'd been garrulous since we left his place, as if we were going camping together or something.

"It doesn't surprise me."

"The painting thing, it all started from that. It helped make the pain go away. But it was dangerous, you know. Forewarning somebody that way to bring out that meaty expression on their face. So the painting of Minnie was an experiment. She's a good little actress. She pretended terror; I painted. There was no risk that way."

"Did it work?"

"For a time."

"You would have been smart to have destroyed the painting. All of them, for that matter."

"Have you ever created a work of art, Mr. Bragg?"

"I don't have the eye for it."

"Then you wouldn't understand."

"So the Minnie painting turned up in San Francisco and you were afraid somebody from this area would go down to look at the show and recognize her. You already knew Dempsey, in Rey Platte, had made the Pavel–Hobo connection."

"Exactly. I read a review of the show that mentioned the Pavel works and that one of them was of a woman. She was the only woman I ever painted. I couldn't dare take a chance that the painting would somehow be tied to us in our present identity. So I went down there and stole the painting, without any bother whatsoever. It should have been the end to it."

"Yeah, it's tough how things go sometimes."

By arching the right side of my back in an unnatural way and straining my right arm until I wanted to yelp with pain, I managed to nudge a part of the holster with one fingertip. I didn't know what part of the holster it was and I wasn't near getting a decent grip on it. If I stretched myself any more Parsons would think I was attempting to commit suicide by breaking my back. I sat up and tried to think of something different.

"The next thing I knew," Big Mike continued, "that detective was in town. And somehow, incredibly, he discovered I lived in the area."

"He was in town working on another matter," I told him. "What tipped him to your being here was the cute trick you pulled in the town mural in Wiley Huggins' window."

It visibly startled him, a reaction that encouraged me. "You know, the funny grass, thick on the top, with the blades broken in progressive placement."

"That's impossible! I never told anybody about that little signature. Not even Minnie."

"Maybe you didn't, but a lot of people know about it now. And it shows up on paintings that have been tied to your murder victims. Frankly, Parsons, or whatever you want to call yourself these days, I think you and Minnie can forget about putting down roots anywhere. It's my guess the two of you are just in for one prolonged run."

"Now you're bluffing, Mr. Bragg."

I was, but he had no way of knowing it. I had another desperate thought and dipped a couple fingers into the rear pocket where I carried a comb. I had a small knife in a front pocket, but I couldn't get my hands within half a foot of it. I had trouble enough getting my comb out and down into the crease of the seat.

"No, I'm not bluffing, Parsons. I don't see much future for myself. Why bluff? It's just a plain fact. Your cover is becoming all unraveled. I suspect that within a couple more days there'll be several hundred law enforcement people looking for you. You'll see soon enough that I'm not bluffing."

"It won't matter by then. We will be far away. With new identities. We have had vast practice. But tell me, Bragg. Barring the incredible misfortune of Minnie's painting being recorded on tape at the television station, do you think you would have found me out?"

"I had already found you out."

He glanced quickly at me. I had to quit fiddling with the comb down in the seat.

"Not quite soon enough," I admitted. "About a half a second before the painting was shown on the screen. Something that had been bothering me locked into place. By the time Jerry Lind got to Barracks Cove he was curious about Dempsey's moves, and Dempsey's great curiosity about the stolen painting. Lind wasn't the world's foremost investigator by any means, but he knew the rudiments. The Frame Up was the logical place for him to visit to see if he could get a line on Dempsey. But Wiley Huggins hadn't seen Lind. The reason, of course, is the same as why he didn't see Emil Stoval earlier today. He was away from the shop both times. Minnie was minding the store. She was a great early warning system for you throughout the whole thing."

"Yes," he agreed, glancing in the rear view mirror. "She was indeed."

"But Wiley was at the shop when Dempsey got there. How did you learn about him?"

"Minnie was there as well. And we knew about that Dempsey fellow. He was the one who nearly caught up with us down south. We took measures to learn his identity, and obtain a photograph of him. It cost us some money, that. But, as it turned out, it was well worth it. Dempsey asked a great many questions about the town mural. He wanted to learn more about the people who had worked on it. So Minnie stepped forward and suggested he drive out and query me. When he left the shop she phoned to alert me."

"And you must have shot him soon after he arrived."

"The moment he stepped from his car. I could take no risk there."

"But he wasn't in his car when I found his body, he was in Lind's. How come?"

Big Mike snorted. "The cars! Always the cars. They were very nearly more trouble than the people who drove them."

He took a deep breath and thought about it. I probed around with my comb some more.

"It was growing dark when the detective came to the house," he resumed. "I concealed his body and auto on our property for the night, planning to decide the next day what best to do with them. But before I could make that decision,

Lind showed up at the Frame Up. Minnie sent him along to our place. I didn't plan to kill him. I simply told him I had never seen Dempsey. It seemed to satisfy him, and he could have turned and left at that point and have been alive today. But then he made the profound error of disclosing that he had a small transparency of the stolen painting. Once he had seen Minnie, if he ever studied it in a projector, he might well have recognized her.

"And so, I shot him. I now had two bodies and two automobiles on my hands. I had searched through the Dempsey vehicle and learned it was a rental. That made it less incriminating. So later that day, with Minnie's help, I drove Lind's car with Dempsey's body in it to where you found them. They should have remained undiscovered there for years. And then we drove the rental car to Willits and abandoned it, as if the man who rented it had flown out from there."

"So it must have been you who saw me and the boy at the Stannis River the over day, near where you'd concealed the auto. You cut my rope so it would break when we tried to cross, sweeping us downriver from the car."

"Of course. The plane crash, all those men thrashing around on the mountain—it could have ruined everything."

"But Fairbanks told me this evening it was Whelan who searched the lower river."

"It was Whelan he sent. Two minutes later, without a word to Fairbanks or anybody else, I followed Abe in my own vehicle. I passed him on the highway and signaled for him to stop. I told him that Fairbanks had sent me as well, and we were to explore a more extensive area. I suggested how we could divide the territory. Abe agreed, and of course he searched a section of the river miles from the auto. Meanwhile, I myself made straight for a high point where I could keep an eye out for anybody approaching the crucial terrain. Yes, I cut the rope. I only wish now the two of you had drowned."

"Cute. I can understand your wanting me out of the way. But that little kid? That takes stomach."

Big Mike smiled grimly, concentrating on the road ahead. My comb was feathering across something I hoped to be the holster and gun. I settled deeper and fished away.

"Where my own welfare is concerned, Mr. Bragg, I can hardly let age enter into it, now can I? And believe me, one does not toil in the vineyard where I have toiled, for as long as I have, without proper mental toughness."

"What did you do with Lind's body?"

"I brought it out this very road. To an old cabin a few of us in town share ownership in. There are streams nearby. One can fish and do a bit of hunting in season. It is remote enough. I dug a shallow grave in the woods nearby. Unfortunately, I have been pushed for time recently."

"That's where you're taking me?"

"No, not quite. Only another mile or so for you."

I wriggled the comb around like crazy, got a slight hold on the leather holster and gave a tug. I managed to drag it up about an inch before it snagged on something. I jammed the comb down for a better bite. My back was getting damp. I had the worried sweats.

"What about Emil Stoval earlier today? I take it you killed him too?"

"Certainly. He was another investigator, from the same company as the other one, Lind. Unfortunately, I was late getting on top of this latest development. I was out running errands this morning. When I arrived back home I found a rather desperate message from Allison pinned to the door. She said Joe Dodge wanted to avoid some man in town looking for him. So she was taking him up into the hills, to the cabin. I had shown it to her once, and where we kept a spare key hidden, thinking she could go there to work when she felt like a change of pace. The note apologized for her presumption, but said it was very important and begged me to keep it a secret.

"I was trying to absorb this jolting message when I received a call from Minnie telling me about this Stoval. There could be little mystery as to what he was up to. He was trying to find Joe Dodge, but it must have been as a step toward finding Lind. I couldn't think what that connection might be, but I hardly had time to dwell on it. Things were moving too fast. I stewed about it, then decided to run over to Joe's place to see if I could intercept Stoval. And I did. He was inside, snooping. I went in through the back and confronted him. I didn't want to shoot him there in the house. I ordered him outside, but the crazy man attacked me. He fought savagely for a moment, then broke off and tried to escape through the kitchen. I could no longer afford the niceties. I put a bullet through his back, dragged him up behind the house and left him."

"But you also left his Cadillac parked out front."

"Yes. I wanted his body found as soon as possible."

176

"I don't get it."

"It doesn't matter, Mr. Bragg," Big Mike said with a sigh. "It really doesn't matter."

"Maybe not. But you're a real curiosity. How many people do you figure you've killed?"

"I don't know. Tried to sort it out once. Four hundred, anyway."

"Jesus Christ." I got another bite on the holster with my comb and tugged, but nothing gave. My fingers were getting numb. I rested a moment, then tried to rotate the holster to get it around whatever had snagged it.

"But time is now short for you as well, Mr. Bragg. Because of the great threat you pose. It is my respect for your prowess as a hunter that condemns you. I am not, after all, quite the monster you might suppose. I have mellowed with age. Take Joe Dodge, and Allison, for instance."

"What about them?"

"It is one of the reasons I wanted Stoval's body found as soon as possible. To make it safe for them to return home. I don't want to have to kill them. I like them. But young Lind's body was hastily concealed. Curious animals could have unearthed it by now. I only hope we shall be in time. That they haven't found the body yet. Otherwise, much as I like them both . . ."

I made one last, herculean effort to dig up the holster. It was too herculean. The thing slid around and fell deeper into the crease between the cushions, and my near-paralyzed fingers lost the comb as well.

"It is why I must dispose of you before we get to the cabin, Mr. Bragg. So that if they haven't discovered the body, I can allow the two of them to live."

I kept flexing my fingers to bring them back to life. There wasn't any more to be done around there, I decided. I only had one move left. It was foolhardy and a longshot, but so was the whole rest of my life right then. The car I drive has both lock and latch mechanism embedded one over the other on the door panel. I sat abruptly, tugged lock and latch levers and was tumbling backward down out of the car before you could shout four hundred and one.

I slammed hard onto the dirt roadway, rolling as best I could with my arms trussed behind me. Dirt and pebbles scraped skin off one ear and the side of my face, and inflicted varying injuries to my knees, leg and elbow. My head took a painful whack and my body made one last jarring flip, but I

177

came to rest still conscious and heard the skidding of braked tires, both on my car and on the one Minnie was in just before she rear-ended her husband. I gave blessings for the moment of confusion down the road, dragged myself up and pitched headlong down a brushy gully, banging into this and tripping over that, but scrambling as hard as I could, across the bottom of the gully and up the far side until my wind gave out and I had to sink to one knee and gasp for breath.

Chapter 22

My lungs felt raw. Not even hauling Tuffy down off the mountain had cut into my wind the way scrambling up and down with my arms roped behind me did. But as soon as I could get a half breath, I was up on my feet and climbing and slipping and pumping my legs toward the high ground. Over my raspy breath and the conga beat of my heart I could hear Big Mike and Minnie across the way. They were talking loudly. I know the sound of domestic argument when I hear it. Minnie let out a little cry. Parsons countered with a barely suppressed bellow. It was fine with me. The longer they stayed there spatting the further away I'd be. I made the top of the far rise and crashed on through the wooded brow of the hill, then was surprised to stumble out onto a dirt road. We weren't in the sort of country apt to support a grid of highways. I reasoned it was the same road Big Mike was on, and that it circled the far end of the gully I'd just crossed. That put me closer to the cabin and Jerry Lind's body and Allison and Joe Dodge. I was ready for some different company. I started trotting up the road. A few moments later, just before rounding a bend, I heard the spin and whir of tires on dirt back across the gully. They were coming. I kept on running, studying the roadside areas ahead of me to pick out likely spots for me to roll into when I heard them approach.

It took two or three minutes before I heard them again. The gully loop must have been a lengthy one. Down at the end of it must have been where they intended to plant me and my car. I trotted around another bend and saw a column of smoke rising above the trees about a quarter mile ahead. It had to be the cabin. The distance was too far for me to get there before the people behind me. I was pressing my luck and I knew it. I lumbered heavily off the road into the brush and trees, only to have a shadowy root catch one foot and send me spilling onto my belly.

I got up and shook my brains back into place in time to see the Parson trail vehicle roar past. They'd abandoned my own car. Big Mike was driving, staring grimly ahead with his hands clenching the wheel, and Minnie sitting upright beside him chattering a streak, as if she were continuing the argument. Probably it was over whether to continue on to the cabin or just to make a run for it. I figured Big Mike wanted to see if Lind's body had been found. Minnie wanted to cut their losses and get out. She was the smarter of the two, I decided.

I worked my way back out onto the road and started trotting again. The road made a couple more loops then ran straight for about a hundred yards before ending in a clearing that surrounded the cabin. I got a glimpse of the four of them—Mike and Minnie, Joe and Allison, standing in the clearing with Parsons going through one of his windmilling arms and gosh and by golly routines. I left the road and tried to make my quiet way through the woods toward the cabin. I felt a brief wash of relief. Parsons wouldn't have gone into one of his routines if they'd found Jerry Lind's body. Allison and Dodge would have been dead already, I was sure of it.

I circled around until I was behind the cabin, near the edge of the woods about thirty feet from the structure. I could hear just some of the conversation in the clearing. Big Mike was talking about Stoval's body being found. Allison sounded disappointed. She said something about looking forward to spending a night in the woods with dinner already on the stove and some other things that made me wish I could clamp a hand over her mouth.

I didn't dare cross the open space to the cabin. I kept tugging and hauling on the ropes that bound me. There was

179

more indecisive chatter from the clearing. Then Allison turned toward the cabin and said something about water boiling. Big Mike had one arm around Dodge's shoulders and was gesturing and carrying on his hayseed act. Minnie stood there with a tight little smile.

I knew that with my tumbling out of the car and the ensuing scraping along the road, then the clambering through the brush with my arms tied, I couldn't have presented too good an appearance just then. I didn't want to startle Allison into a yelp, but I had to get her attention, so I stayed back out of sight. Minnie had turned back to their wagon. I hissed at Allison just before she entered the cabin, then nearly strangled in an attempt to suppress a sneeze.

Allison hesitated and looked toward me. I whispered as loudly as I dared. "Allison, it's Peter Bragg. Don't make a sound, but come around in back. I need help, and you're in danger."

She stepped around the side of the cabin appropriately astonished. "Whatever on earth . . ."

"Shhhhh! Please keep it quiet. Come back here. I'm not a pretty sight. The going's been tough. And my arms are tied behind me."

When she got back to where she could see me I thought she was going to cry out or laugh nervously or turn and bolt, in about that order.

"My God," she exclaimed. "What happened to you?"

"Keep it down or I'm a dead man. I've been running for my life. From them," I told her, jerking my head toward the clearing in front of the cabin.

"Mike and Minnie? Come one . . ."

"Allison, it's true, I swear to God. I don't have time to go into it. But Mike is a killer. He has been for years. He admitted to me that he killed Jerry Lind and buried his body around here somewhere. That's why they drove out here, to see if you and Joe found it. If you had, he was going to kill the both of you too."

"You are insane," she said slowly.

"Okay, I'm insane. But at least I didn't tie myself up like this. There's a knife in my right front pocket. How about getting it out and cutting me loose?"

"I think you're safer tied up."

"Come on, Allison. I can prove it. And they want to kill me because I'm on to them. They were bringing me out planning to kill and leave me back down the road a ways. I

180

jumped out of the car and ran like hell. That's why I look the way I do. Please, the knife."

She was skeptical, confused and maybe still angry. But she finally roused herself and got the knife out of my pocket to begin working on the ropes. "I still don't believe you."

"You had better start to believe me if you want any of us to get out of here alive. Parsons isn't their real name. For years Big Mike made his living by killing people. He almost was caught about five years ago down south, and the two of them changed their identity and dropped out of sight. Now don't tell me Big Mike and Minnie are an old, established family around here."

"No," she admitted, looking up at me. "But they came here from the Midwest."

"So they told everybody, and for God's sake keep working on the ropes." She continued to saw away. "Big Mike started killing people again just recently to protect his gory past. He killed the cop I found up on the Stannis River, he killed Jerry and today he killed the man Joe Dodge was running from."

She cut the last piece binding me and I shook myself free like a dog just out of the washtub. I now had another dimension of pain to enjoy as the blood flowed back through restricted artery and vein. "Does Joe Dodge have any sort of weapon with him?"

"Of course not."

"How about—did he bring an axe?"

Allison took a step backward. "You are really out of your ever-loving skull crazy."

But at least she was keeping her voice low. Perhaps it was the beginning of belief, but I was one running-scared man and I couldn't stand around any longer trying to interpret the day's events.

"Allison, before I ruined the evening for both of us the other day, I felt something very strong and very special for you. And you've just got to believe I still do. And the only reason I'm telling you is because I sincerely don't want any harm to come to any of us—but especially I don't want it to come to you. I could die tonight and it wouldn't matter much to anybody. It's not the same with you. I'm a hard old rock. You, lady, are a piece of the sky."

She glanced away.

"Go back there, now. Don't tell them you've seen me, and get cracking to do what they want. Get your stuff together

181

in a hurry and you and Joe get out of here as soon as you can. And don't take any last looks around."

She turned back with a little shrug. "There's no harm in that, I suppose. But what about you?"

"I'll get by."

She nodded and turned back to the cabin. I started my great circle route back around through the woods. They were the same old woods I'd staggered through on my way in, but I felt as if I were floating. I had two arms swinging as I went, a little the worse for wear, but they were free, and their movement made everything a lot easier.

It didn't take me long to get up to where I could get on the road again. I looked back and saw thankfully that Allison was doing as I'd asked. She was carrying a couple of sleeping bags from the cabin to Joe Dodge's car. She hadn't bothered to roll them, even. I hustled on up the road. I was improvising every step of the way now, but then so was Big Mike.

When I got back to the gully I'd crossed earlier, I decided to just plunge down and back up the way I'd come. The road was easier going, but several minutes longer, judging by the time it took Parsons to catch up with me on the way in. I had to pause once, climbing the far side, to catch my breath, but a couple moments later I was up to where they'd left my car. It was parked to one side of the road. Minnie had creamed into the rear trunk nicely, buckling it so I couldn't get in to get my heavy automatic. I opened the front door and reached around until I found the holstered revolver. It gave me a keen sense of having done something right for a change. And to think years ago I used to wonder why so many cops carried a second, personal handgun with them when they were on duty.

The Parsons either had my car keys or had pitched them away. But I'd gone off and locked my car with the keys in the ignition enough times to finally wise up and tape a spare key to the back of my AAA card. I got in and started it up and with only a half-formed idea in my head, maneuvered the car around to straddle as much of the road as I could. I got back out, removed the .38 from its holster and planted myself behind the busted-up rear end of the car on the gully side of the road. It was a couple minutes before I heard the Parsons' trail vehicle across the gully, rolling back out from the cabin. There still was a tinge of daylight, but shadows had deepened in the timbered area and Big

Mike had his headlights on. I heard them slow to make the bend at the end of the gully and a few moments later he came over the rise in front of me. He slowed at the sight of my improvised roadblock, probably startled that I'd been able to move the car around. I braced myself, took careful aim and blasted away his left headlight, just to show him I was back ready to play hard ball with him.

I'm not sure what I was expecting. Certainly not what Parsons did, which was to step on the gas and try to ram his way around my car on the gully side where I was standing. I fired once more then started to packpeddle as he banged into the crumpled rear of the car and then me along with it. I went sailing and lost my grip on the .38, but the Parsons wagon came to a precarious stop with its right front wheel over the roadbank. I got up, couldn't see my weapon and decided my only chance now was to crowd them. Minnie apparently had banged her head in the collision, and Mike was momentarily shaken himself. I wrenched open the door, poked him once in the eye and got a tight grip on the collar of his shirt.

He wasn't thinking too fast and put his hands out toward me instead of keeping a grip on the steering wheel. I braced myself and pulled him out of the car like a wine cork. But these things never go as you expect them too. He landed on top of me and we rolled around in the dust for a minute. Having moved first I still was more or less in charge and got to my feet before he did. More headlights were approaching. Big Mike was on one knee, getting up, when I kicked him as hard as I could in the chest, about where I figured his heart to be. It was a tactic that was supposed to slow down a person. I'd read that one time, only I didn't know if it was supposed to take a matter of seconds or until sometime the following week. At least it dumped him back on the road again and I started toward him when there was a sharp bang somewhere just behind my left ear and something singed my cheek. It was Minnie, now leaning out of the car with her little pistol pointing in my direction.

Joe Dodge's car had ground to a halt nearby and Allison was stupidly clambering out and screaming something. Minnie fired again, and missed me again, but I knew she wouldn't miss for the rest of the evening. I feinted once toward Big Mike on the road then hurled myself back around my own car. The scene was approaching general pandemonium by now, and for about the first time since some very scary days in Korea I wondered what in the hell I was doing where I was. Both Minnie and Allison were screaming. Joe Dodge was half out of his car shouting when he snagged his arm on something and started his car horn blaring.

I made a quick move toward the gully, thinking maybe I could get around to Minnie's side of their car. It was too quick, in light of all the work I'd given my legs to do recently. I twisted an ankle and fell to the ground, wincing with pain and feeling absolutely silly. But then I saw my .38 about ten feet away, scrambled over to it and hauled myself painfully around to the front of my car where I could get a bead on Big Mike, who was back on his feet and staggering toward his wagon.

I took careful aim, and just then from out of the night came this big, healthy blonde lady with her arms raised and outstretched as if she were trying to block the punt of a football, only I was the ball. She foolishly and literally threw herself at me and my gun and sent me sprawling backward onto my can for what seemed like the fortieth time that evening, all the while bawling into my face.

"No Pete! For God's sake! You can't shoot him. Don't do that!"

"What the hell," was all I could manage while gargling dust and trying to squirm out from under her. I don't know if it was all the excitement I'd been through the past hour, my throbbing ankle or the work Allison had done with hammer and saw, but she managed to keep me pinned and spinning around like that for the few seconds necessary for Big Mike to struggle back into his vehicle, swing it back onto the road and ram my car the foot or two more necessary so he could roar past in a cloud of dirt and gravel. I heard it more than saw it, because Allison could really play hard ball herself, and was using every device she could think of to keep me down, including butting my head with her own, which both hurt and put an effective screen of blonde hair all over my face and eyes.

She kept it up until the Parsons wagon had roared off, then went limp. I shook her off and staggered to my feet and jammed the .38 into my belt.

"Thanks a lot everybody," was all I could manage.

Joe Dodge was standing nearby with his semi-permanent stricken expression on his lined face. "You people are all crazier than hell."

Allison was crying, sitting with her face buried in her

184

tucked-up legs. When she tried to speak her voice was very tiny and childlike.

"I'm sorry . . . . I'm sorry."

Maybe I was going crazy. Maybe there'd been too much gin and too much knocking around over the years, but at that moment I felt a great, sudden, inexplicable surge of love for her, and I didn't know what the hell anything was all about any longer.

"It's okay," I told her, spitting out some of the dirt and trying to wipe my face. "I guess you were doing what you had to. But now I gotta go do what I have to."

I hobbled over to my car, hoping the damn thing was still functional. It was, and I seesawed around as Allison called my name once. Then I was roaring on down the road in pursuit of Big Mike and Minnie. I came over the brow of a hill that opened onto a fairly long, straight stretch and saw Big Mike's tail lights in the distance. I snapped off my own headlights and stood on the accelerator. It was a futile exercise in concealment. A couple minutes later Parsons turned off onto another road, one different from the way we'd come up. I had to turn on my lights. A couple more miles we were back in the lowlands and the road intersected with a paved road that was well traveled, with traffic in both directions.

I was about three hundred yards behind him and gaining. Between the lights of oncoming traffic Big Mike passed a couple of cars. I passed one of them but then had to lay back a minute in frustration as he sped on down the road. I finally got around the second car. It was an auto full of teenagers, and the driver shot me a look of *macho* indignation as I swooped past. He started to ride my tail, or tried to. We were all doing about eighty miles an hour, and it had been a long time since I'd driven that fast. It bothered me.

A blue and red winking in the rearview mirror gave me a little surge of hope. It had to be a sheriff's or highway patrol car, about a quarter mile behind me. I murmured a small prayer for him to hurry and continued to burn along the highway in pursuit of a man who had murdered four hundred human beings, including a foolish young man I'd been paid to find and bring back. And I hadn't done it.

I was slowly gaining on Big Mike again until he wasn't more than a couple hundred yards ahead of me. There was a station wagon ahead of him now, and beyond that a curve. It would be a very tight judgment to make, especially traveling at speeds you weren't used to. I don't know what I would have done in his place, but Parsons decided to go for it and swung out around the wagon, flashing his highbeams and spurting forward, and that's when forty tons of fully loaded lumber rig trying to beat the federal park deadline roared around the curve ahead of us, and despite an heroic attempt by Parsons to get back into his own lane, the load of logs slammed into the trail vehicle and blew it away in an explosion of metal.

Chapter 23

The station wagon Big Mike had tried to pass missed being involved by a matter of inches. The driver of the lumber rig, other than having his dinner shocked out of him, escaped injury and managed to stop a ways up the road. I hadn't realized it at the time, but Joe Dodge and Allison had been following along behind us as best they could. The car with flashing red and blue lights had been a sheriff's deputy. It made my chores a bit easier, because he'd been involved in the plane search on Sunday and recognized my name as being the one who found Tuffy. And from my busted-up, dirty appearance, he knew I hadn't just been out for a joyride. This was some time after the collision. He had his hands full the first twenty minutes or so just trying to keep traffic snaking around the wreckage that was strewn along the highway until he was joined by other law officers.

Then he listened to my story, but just briefly. I tried to keep it concise, but finally he just rolled his eyes and said I should just answer the questions on his accident report form and make a fuller statement somewhere else some other time.

Allison stood nearby. She didn't approach the larger piece of wreckage where the bodies were. She just leaned against the side of Joe Dodge's car, which Dodge had parked behind my own, with her arms folded across her chest.

Dodge said there was nothing more to be done, and suggested they leave. Allison shook her head and told him to go on back to town. She walked the few paces to lean against the side of my own car and resumed an unblinking vigil into the night.

Dodge approached me with a troubled expression, started to say something, then shrugged and went back to his car and drove off.

Allison didn't say anything to me the whole time. When the deputy finally told me I could leave, she just went around to the other side of my car and wordlessly got in.

"I guess you want a ride back to town," I told her.

"I guess."

"Why did you stick around?"

"I don't know. Maybe to back up your story with the sheriff, if you needed it. Maybe to see if something would fall into place for me. I'm all cockeyed inside. I'm not used to this sort of thing."

We rode back into Barracks Cove. I told her I had some phone calls to make. She just nodded.

"You look as if you could use a drink," I told her.

"I could. Brandy. But I don't want to be around other people."

She directed me to a store that sold a variety of things and stayed open late. She went in with some money I gave her while my sore ankle and I stayed in the car. She came back out with a bag of stuff and I drove over to my motel and limped in while she poured us a couple of glasses of brandy. I began making my calls. Chief Morgan was the first. I got him at home. He'd heard about the accident and listened quietly while I recapped things for him. Allison was listening closely.

"Not that it hardly matters now, Bragg," Morgan told me, "but can you prove any of this?"

"You're bound to turn up something at the Parsons' house. The stolen painting, if nothing else. And if they can recover Big Mike's .45 from the wreckage—I told the deputy to look for it—you can make test firings and maybe compare them with any slugs you might have found in Stoval or around the Dodge house. Or maybe there's one lodged in Lind's body up by the cabin."

187

"That again is out of my territory, thank the Lord. But I don't think you ought to plan on leaving just yet."

"You figure I should go back up there while they dig up the body?"

"Yes. Probably first thing in the morning. I know the sheriff would feel that way."

"I'll stick around," I told him.

I called Lind's sister and gave her the bad news. She'd been ready for it, which helped, but not all that much. Then I started to call Marcie Lind, but half-way through dialing I replaced the receiver. "I'm just not up to that."

Allison was sitting quietly in a chair in the corner with her legs tucked up beneath her. "To what?"

"Telling Jerry's wife. She still thinks he's out there somewhere and I'm the big hero who's going to find him. Only not quite the way we're about to find him."

Allison shook her head and got up to pour us both more brandy. "God, you look awful."

I thought maybe she was going to dampen a washrag and wipe me off or something, but she just went back over and sat down again.

Finally I called Zoom, down in Larkspur. I determined that she wasn't drunk or spaced-out, then told her quietly some of what had happened. Primarily that I was certain Jerry was dead and that Marcie was going to come into a lot of money as a result of it. I asked her to go up and spend the night with Marcie and to try to break both bits of news as gently as she could, mixing it up however she felt best, and to tell Marcie I would call her the next day, after I'd been back up to the cabin with the sheriff's people and coroner's people who by now probably were getting a little tired of me.

"Why can't you phone and tell her, Pete?" Zoom asked softly. "She can take it, baby."

"I know, Zoom, but I couldn't, I don't think. I've gone through a little too much myself today. Tomorrow, huh?"

And then I drank some brandy and hobbled into the bathroom and winced at the scraped and battered face in the mirror. It hurt plenty when I tried to clean it up. Allison came to stand in the doorway and to watch, but she didn't offer to lend a hand. I was beginning to feel resentful.

When I was through she went back to the shopping bag and wordlessly tossed me a rolled elastic bandage she had bought. I took off my shoe and sock and wrapped it around the sore ankle and put stuff back on, then Allison got up once more, poured a lot of brandy into her glass and carried it over to the door.

"Now you can drop me off home."

I limped out into the night air behind her and got in the car and drove across town. She sipped her drink but didn't say anything, but when I pulled up in front of her house she didn't move to get out. She just stared blankly through the windshield. I shut off the engine and waited.

"You know why I did that back there, don't you?" she asked finally, shaking her hair and turning toward me.

"Up where I was fighting with Big Mike?" I raised one shoulder and dropped it. "I guess you felt you had to. It bothered me then. It doesn't now. Let's forget it."

"No, you don't understand at all. It's my very shaky posture right now. Tonight. I've always been so goddamn dead certain about everything I've ever done or set out to do. I've always felt it was one of my strengths. But after last night at the restaurant down at the cove—I've never been hurt that way. And I never wanted to see you again. Or to speak to you. Not ever. But then this morning, when poor dear Joe was terrified at the thought of this man Stoval being in town asking questions and showing Joe's picture, you were the one I wanted to get in touch with. Not out of any liking, but because you were the only son of a bitch I figured to be smart enough and mean enough to be able to help us. God, what a joke."

She held one hand to her face for a moment. I kept my mouth shut and nibbled lightly at an inner cheek where it didn't hurt so much. She looked up again.

"And then tonight, as soon as Mike and Minnie had left the cabin, I told Joe what you had said was going on. His mouth just fell, and a whole different expression came over his face, and he looked back behind the cabin, where he'd been prowling earlier in the day, and he said—he said that you had to be right, of course. That it explained a lot of funny things."

"He must have found where Jerry was buried, not knowing it then."

"He said there were other things about Big Mike, funny things that happened in the past. By then we were in the car, leaving there. And because I have such faith in Joe's intuition—the totality of it finally hit home, and churned up feelings about you all over again."

189

She sat biting one knuckle for a moment. "And then we came on you and Big Mike, fighting in the road. And I saw Minnie try to shoot you, and then you jumped back, and picked up a gun . . ."

She looked away again and I waited. "I don't know what it is with me any more. But I was certain of one thing. I knew that if we were ever going to try to explore things together again, despite how hurt I felt because of you, if it ever was to work, I couldn't watch you shoot Big Mike. You could do it somewhere else and I might understand. But in front of these two eyes?"

She turned back and those two eyes effectively paralyzed me. "It was to keep that one little flicker of possibility to do with the two of us, maybe some other time, maybe in some other place, that made me throw myself on you and risk having all of us killed. And things haven't improved much since," she told me, taking a sip of brandy. "I don't think I belong any more."

"In Barracks Cove?"

"Not anywhere. Everything just lost its underpinnings."

I took a deep breath and exhaled slowly. "I have one small observation to make," I told her. "And I'm a little afraid to try even that."

"Go ahead. I don't suppose this has been a million laughs for you, either."

"You're right enough there. A lot of my work isn't. But what you just said made me think of something Parsons asked me this evening, after I'd learned who he was. He asked me if I'd ever created a work of art. I told him no. But in a way, maybe that's what I'm trying to do every time I take on a job. I've heard it said that the job of an artist is to bring order out of chaos, or make the connections the rest of us can't see right away, or something like that. I don't know if that holds for everybody, but it sure holds for most of the things I take on. Sometimes I do a pretty fair job of it. Sometimes I fail miserably, and other times, like with Jerry Lind, I work my tail off trying, but it all gets taken out of my hands and things just happen. But I do try. To bring some order out of the chaos. So I guess in a way that does make me an artist, not all that different from yourself or Joe Dodge."

"Okay," she said with a wan smile. "And now you're going to tell me we can't give up because of the brutal setbacks."

190

"Something like that. You have to expect to have your face shoved in it some, to do your best work."

"Those are tough terms. What if I'm not up to them?"

"You're up to them. You'll find that out when you go out into your studio tomorrow. You'll find a way to live with it. To get it under control, and one day to use it."

She thought about it some, then sighed and handed me the rest of the brandy. "Thank God for one thing. There are artists and there are artists." She got out a little unsteadily, slammed the door, then leaned back down to the open window.

"What do you mean by that?" I asked her.

"At least I don't have to get up early in the morning and help the sheriff dig up a body."

She straightened and started up the walk. I stuck my head out the window. "I guess you think that's pretty funny, Allison."

She tossed her head and nodded in the affirmative, without looking back.

"Well look, how about tomorrow evening? I don't have to race right back to San Francisco. Will you be here? Can I call you when I get back into town?"

She paused near the top of the stairs and stood with her back to me. She either was having a tough time trying to make up her mind, or she was paying me back some. My neck was getting sore from craning out the window. And then she slowly turned.

"Yes," she said simply.

And then she went on inside and I started the engine and tried to whistle something through swollen lips as I gripped the glass of brandy between my legs and tried not to spill any on my lap as my car and I limped on back to the motel.

JOHN D. MacDONALD

The Travis McGee Series

Follow the quests of Travis McGee, amiable and incurable tilter at conformity, boat-bum Quixote, hopeless sucker for starving kittens, women in distress, and large, loose sums of money.

☐ THE DEEP BLUE GOOD-BY	14176	$2.50
☐ NIGHTMARE IN PINK	14259	$2.25
☐ A PURPLE PLACE FOR DYING	14219	$2.25
☐ THE QUICK RED FOX	14264	$2.50
☐ A DEADLY SHADE OF GOLD	14221	$2.50
☐ BRIGHT ORANGE FOR THE SHROUD	14243	$2.50
☐ DARKER THAN AMBER	14162	$2.50
☐ ONE FEARFUL YELLOW EYE	14146	$2.50
☐ PALE GRAY FOR GUILT	14148	$2.50
☐ THE GIRL IN THE PLAIN BROWN WRAPPER	14256	$2.50
☐ DRESS HER IN INDIGO	14170	$2.50
☐ THE LONG LAVENDER LOOK	13834	$2.50
☐ A TAN AND SANDY SILENCE	14220	$2.50
☐ THE SCARLET RUSE	13952	$2.50
☐ THE TURQUOISE LAMENT	14200	$2.50
☐ THE DREADFUL LEMON SKY	14148	$2.25
☐ THE EMPTY COPPER SEA	14149	$2.25
☐ THE GREEN RIPPER	14345	$2.95
☐ FREE FALL IN CRIMSON	14441	$2.95

Buy them at your local bookstore or use this handy coupon for ordering.

COLUMBIA BOOK SERVICE, CBS Inc.
32275 Mally Road, P.O. Box FB, Madison Heights, MI 48071

Please send me the books I have checked above. Orders for less than 5 books must include 75¢ for the first book and 25¢ for each additional book to cover postage and handling. Orders for 5 books or more postage is FREE. Send check or money order only. Allow 3-4 weeks for delivery.

Cost $_____   Name_____

Sales tax*_____   Address_____

Postage _____   City_____

Total $_____   State_____   Zip_____

*The government requires us to collect sales tax in all states except AK, DE, MT, NH and OR.

Prices and availability subject to change without notice.   8235